The Girl in the Mirror

Book 6

P. COSTA

iUniverse

THE GIRL IN THE MIRROR BOOK 6

iUniverse books may be ordered through booksellers or by contacting:

iUniverse
1663 Liberty Drive
Bloomington, IN 47403
www.iuniverse.com
844-349-9409

ISBN: 978-1-6632-6212-7 (sc)
ISBN: 978-1-6632-6211-0 (e)

Library of Congress Control Number: 2024907969

Print information available on the last page.

iUniverse rev. date: 06/06/2024

Dedication

THIS IS THE LAST IN A SERIES OF SIX FROM WHICH I HOPE READERS can learn from.

I want to thank my neighbor for suffering with me throughout this adventure, as well as my husband who I love dearly.

I hope these books helps you find a relationship with God.

She Has Been Taken

APRIL'S SUPERVISOR WAS ON HIS CELL PHONE WITH THE POLICE. HE gave them the address and told them what he saw.

The police arrived within five minutes.

Yellow tape was strung half way up and down along the street. That brought in many curious onlookers who wanted to know what happened.

No one more so than Eddie. She was heartbroken. Her neighbor and friend was gone. Eddie was so upset that she called her son, who lived in Oho, and asked if she could come and stay with them for a while. She cleaned her house, covered everything, and she left.

April had left behind her backpack which held her cell phone and all her identifying information. She thought that might be a good thing in case they wanted a ransom. This way they would not know she was April Di Angelo. For now she had to wait until they either stopped or she had a chance to get away. But why would a policeman do this to her?

They must be police. The car was legit. It looked like Dad's cruiser, but older. The dash had a computer, a walkie talkie and a full window with wire between the front and back seat.

What in the world did she do that warranted treating her like this? She asked them repeatedly, "What did I do? Are you arresting me? Why didn't you read me my rights?" Over and over she asked questions, and they did not answer her. Instead, the one police officer on the passenger side came into the back seat, pushed her over to tie her legs and taped her mouth, shoving her onto the floor.

April lay on the floor of the backseat of the car. Her legs were tied, her arms were tied behind her back, and her mouth was taped shut. She could barely breathe with her torso over the drive shaft hump. April wanted to cry but would not give them the satisfaction. Why? Why did they take her? Was it about money? Did they want a ransom? She did not know. All she could do was breathe, grunt and not move.

This was insane April thought. I have rights! Even with her mouth taped the two officers in the front of the car could hear her say, "Take me to the police station. I am innocent. I have done nothing wrong." She repeated this over and over and over. Then the car stopped. She was aware that the passenger door was open, and she felt a sting in her buttock. That is all she remembered. She was out.

That is when she realized Edie was right. This was not an arrest. She had been abducted. She had been a target all along. How stupid she was to have not listened to her Dad and Edie. She should have stayed in, but no, she thought she was safe. Nothing would happen to her that she could not get out of! Here she was bound, gagged, and drugged lying on the floor of an old police car.

April did what was second nature to her, she sought God through prayer. "Father in Heaven, please, I beg of you, hear my prayer. Father, in Jesus Christ's holy name, I am afraid, and I am a prisoner because I was ignorant. I ignored all the warning signs and gut feelings I had. I am here because I rationalized this would not, could not happen to me. Father, if thou can help me. I need to be freed of these bonds and escape. I need to get away. Please Father, I beg for mercy. Help me. I need thee Father, please."

Then she recalled in her mind the Father's blessing she had received at home. Over and over that blessing told her to be careful, mindful. She also remembered that God would give her the ability to endure whatever she would be called on to endure and that angels would attend her. How she prayed she would be worthy of that. She could not give up hope.

April was groggy, in and out of a sleep like in a fog. She tried to hear what the officers were saying or to be aware of the sounds around her. It was all confusing, all jumbled up. She saw monsters and felt like she was falling down a deep cliff into a chamber of rocks that was pitch dark. When she tried to get out, the rocks cut her hands. They were slippery and wet. She could not get out and that unnerved her, then she awoke with clarity.

April could clearly hear the officers when they spoke although she lay still as if the drug still had a grip on her. "We should stop before too long. I need to take a leak," the one said. "Yeah, I know. I do too, but we need to go a little farther before we stop. And we need to prepare. You know what I mean," the other said.

There was a distinct difference between the officers. They were both very heavy, but one seemed like he was simple-minded. His head was huge, one eye was much bigger than the other, his teeth were widely gapped, and he drooled. He was not as mean sounding as the other one.

The other officer had a mean bark to his voice. It was obvious he was in charge. He was obese with thick black hair, bushy eyebrows, bulging eyes, and had tattoos on both of his upper arms of naked women.

It seemed like forever, but finally they stopped. The officer in charge opened the passenger door and pulled April out. He cut the rope on her legs so she could stand. He pulled her by her hair to a picnic table and forced her to sit down. He left her arms cuffed behind her back, and she begged him to release them allowing feeling back into her arms. Then he said something quietly to the other man who drooled and put his fingers in April's mouth pulling on each side which caused great pain.

Then April realized the cuffs were off as the bushy man pulled her arms forward. She felt like her arms had been cut off. Tears rolled down April's cheeks as they cuffed her wrists in front of her, and the two officers laughed at her.

The bushy one went to the cruiser returning with a small box. As he stood behind April, she heard a click, then a motor sound, and she realized he was running something on her head. He was shaving her hair off.

She pulled away, and he hit her with his fist very hard, while yelling at her to sit still. April thought if her legs were a bit stronger she could run, There was a highway one hundred or so yards away, but she needed two feet distance from them to get started. She doubted they could catch her since they were too obese.

As they stood her up from the picnic table while looking at their barber job, April took that opportunity to run. She ran straight to the highway and down the center of the road, hoping for a car to come by. They started to chase her but gave up. She hoped and hoped for a car and kept running. Her legs did not fail her. They felt strong and she pushed with all she had. A car came towards her, it slowed down, but kept going. She was shocked.

She had hand cuffs on, and her mouth taped with duct tape, and they did not stop.

That is when she felt a car behind her. It hit her and she went down. It was the two officers, Twiddle Dee and Twiddle Dum. One of them pulled on her arms to get her up as he pulled her backwards towards the car.

April fought him. She hit him in the face with her cuffed wrists and stomping on his foot.

The man cried out in pain and stood there protecting his face, giving April another chance to run.

This time she ran in the other direction. She thought she saw a building and hoped it was a roadside diner. As she neared it, she saw the diner had long ago been abandoned. April kept on running, pulling at the duct tape over her mouth. She knew the two would chase her in the car, but she would not give in. The road then went into a steep down slope. April looked to the right and saw a steep cliff with a raging river far below. She wanted to throw herself over that side, but there was a sizable guard rail along the front of it. As she ran to jump it, the officers' car came fast along the rail blocking her.

April turned slightly left and kept running. The road had a bank beside it, from dirt piled up long ago. It had trees and roped wire on posts all along that top side. She could not use her hands to pull herself up or to steady herself, so she kept running. April could hear the car behind her. The engine revved to scare her, but she was not scared so long as she was running. Then a large truck came towards her, and April stopped right on the road blocking him.

The trucks brakes screeched, and April ran to the driver side window. "Help me, please. I have been abducted. I was taken from Pittsburgh PA, and I am afraid they are going to kill me," she said.

The man could not believe what he was seeing. Beside his truck stood a woman, completely bald with open cuts on her head. He saw she was wearing handcuffs, blue jeans, a white shirt with a sweater, and a blue jacket. The woman was visibly frightened, crying and begging for help. He also saw a police cruiser heading towards him.

One officer got out of the cruiser with the lights flashing and a pistol aimed at the woman. "Don't touch her!" the officer hollered. "We are transporting her to Wisconsin jail. She was convicted of murder," he yelled as he kept the pistol aimed at April.

"It's not true!" April screamed. "I am a student at Pittsburgh, and these two abducted me early this morning. Please, I beg you, help me!" she screamed.

The officers were approaching the man's truck and the man did not know what to do. He did not know who was telling the truth. It all looked right, a prisoner escaping. What student would cut her hair like that. Nope, he sided with the officers. He did nothing but roll up his window.

April saw the men coming towards her with their pistols aimed at her. She didn't care. She was not going to let them take her again. Then she noticed a number of cars were behind the truck, and, as she ran through them, one driver opened the car door knocking her to the ground.

The officers were suddenly there picking April up roughly. They slapped her and kicked her. Then the driver who had knocked April down realized this was wrong. No officer ever treated a prisoner like this.

He got out and asked for their badge numbers. Then the bushy officer hit him on the head with his pistol knocking him out cold and leaving him lying on the road beside his car.

Other drivers saw this and were appalled, but they did nothing. They sat in their cars too afraid to get involved.

April was taken to the police car where the Twiddle Dum put his hand with a cloth over April's mouth. It was chloroform. She knew that smell. She fought as much as she could and then she was out.

They shoved her in the back of the cruiser and sped off.

Many drivers were on their cell phones to report the incident when the officers left. Several got out of their cars to attend to the man that had been hit. Others maneuvered their cars to get out and went on their way. The trucker saw what had happened in his rear view mirror. He knew right away he had made a mistake. He made the wrong choice. He got on his CB immediately and radioed the police and all truckers within minutes. He told them the road and route numbers. Then he started his truck and within minutes everyone had cleared out.

The driver that was hit had been stunned, but he was okay. Everyone had left within minutes. You would never have known anything had happened.

The two officers were angry. They talked about how they would punish April. She needed to know who was boss and listen to them.

April heard it all. She was NOT going to be a statistic. She was determined to rely on her cunning and the promptings of the Holy Ghost. She could do this. She would not give in or lose hope.

They drove for about four hours or so, then pulled over to a diner. April sat in the back seat with the bars in front of her and the doors locked. The simple one motioned for her to come out. April inched over to get out of the back seat. The officer was becoming angry with her. "Can't you move any faster than that?" he asked her.

"No, I can't. If I didn't have these handcuffs on I'd do better. I can't use my hands," she said.

The simple man saw it was difficult for her, so he looked at April with his crossed eyes and said, "I will let you out of those if you promise not to run. We are going in to eat. You are hungry, no?" He asked her with his head bobbing up and down.

"I am starving and promise not to run. You are very kind to me," she said, and the simple man smiled at her. April knew to chip away at the weakest link. The phrase, "keep your friends close, but keep your enemies closer," was her plan, divide and conquer.

They walked inside the diner. The bushy man was not happy April was free of her cuffs. They were now dangling at the side of the simple man's pockets. They chose a table far in the corner, it was darker there. April was seated with her back to the other patrons in the diner. Her head was covered with a dirty beanie. They ordered a huge breakfast meal. Nothing for April, she would eat their scraps.

Figuring this might be another opportunity, April said she had to use the bathroom. The bushy man told the simple man to go with her.

"I am eating," the simple man said.

"I don't care, go with her and stand by her door so she can't escape."

April got up slowly waiting for the simple man and they went to the back where the bathroom sign pointed. This was a dilemma. April went into the women's bathroom. All the officer could do was wait out in the hall. Inside the bathroom there was one window. But it was too small and had wire and bars inserted to prevent breaking into the diner.

She put her hands on her back pocket and realized she had slipped in an indelible marker. She was in the stall of the bathroom writing as fast as she could on the stall door. MY NAME IS APRIL DI ANGELO. I WAS KIDNAPPED ON NOVEMBER 11TH AT 7:00 A.M. I WAS TO BE PICKED UP BY THE SUPERVISOR OF THE PITTSBURGH ZOO. PLEASE LET MY PARENTS, GORDON AND MIRANDA DI ANGELO IN FRESNO CA KNOW THAT I AM ALIVE BUT STILL A CAPTIVE. PRAY FOR ME.

"What are you doing in there?" the simple man said to the unopened door.

"I'm Pooping," April lied.

"Well, hurry up! My food is getting cold," the simple man said.

"I can't hurry. Go and eat. I will come out when I am done," she said, and he did. April wrote the entire length of the door and the right wall full of things she had to say. She described the men, gave their badge numbers, the license plate number of their car, and its state. She described the scenery since she was not sure where she was and not sure where she was going. When finished she tucked her marker back in her back pocket, flushed the toilet, and went out to join her captors.

There was no one waiting on her, but she obediently walked to the table and sat down. The two looked surprised and pleased, "Are you hungry, Joe?"

April looked at them and asked for something to eat, please. They laughed at her and threw her some bread and bacon. April knew if she was uncooperative they would beat her, so she was "being good." Still they treated her very meanly. She said nothing and took the meager bits of food and ate them, praying silently.

From time to time they threw bits of their food on her napkin when the waitress noticed what they were doing and came over. "Would she like something to eat, too?" she asked.

"No. No, Joe has been a bad boy," the bushy officer said puffing on his cigarette, blowing the smoke into the waitress' face.

She waved her hand to clear the smoke and looked at Joe. She would have sworn this was no boy. If it was, he sure had a lot of female attributes such as breasts, lovely light skin, and polished nails. And well, she would swear this was a woman, not a boy. The waitress turned away and brought back a sticky bun with icing for the boy and the boy only, because the waitress' instincts kicked in.

April did not dare to look up and thank her. She kept her head down and ate the bun hungrily. The two officers watched her when April tore off the center of the sticky bun and pushed it towards the dummy, who smiled.

"She gave it to me, see? She likes me," he said excitedly drooling. His partner nudged his arm roughly to shut up.

April wanted more than anything for the weakest mind and strongest body to favor her, to protect her, to take her part, and to keep her alive. She fell back upon her military training, divide and conquer. When they were finished eating, April sat still. Only when they told her to get up, that they were leaving, did she stand and walk in front of them.

She got into the car willingly and as she got in the back seat, she looked at her dummy captor and thanked him. He gave her a huge smile and touched her cheek.

They drove for miles and miles. April tried to pay attention to where they were going. But often she closed her eyes to pretend she was sleeping and would listen to her captors' talking. They always talked more when she slept. They joked about going hunting it was something they did every year for the last thirty-eight years.

"And we always get our bag limit. Don't we, Dale?" he joked. So April learned Dale was the name of the simple man. Just then Dale, the simple man, said, "You da man, Dan. You da man." So bushy was Dan and simple was Dale.

They drove most of the day and into the night until Dan said to Dale, "We better turn in for the night so we can be fresh in the morning." He drove until he saw an old motel along the side of the road. Dan drove in a lane to the back. The opposite way of the road they came in on. He parked the car and as usual it was Dale that reached for April's arm to get out. She got out cooperatively and followed Dale reaching for his hand. Dale was surprised and glad. He had nothing against the girl. He just followed what his brother-in-law told him to do. April did not know they were related, but in due time she would.

Inside the motel the men were pleased there was a diner and lodgings. They asked if they could be seated as it was late. The waiter assured them they were not too late, the kitchen was still open. They pulled at April and had "him" sit down at a table. Then Dan went to relieve himself in the bathroom.

Dale was not happy, "He always does this to me. I have to go too, but he always goes first."

"He's not being nice to you," April said, trying to inject some friction between the two men.

"Oh, Dan, is all right. He is real good to me most of the time," Dale replied.

Just then a waitress brought over the menus placing them on the table. April picked one up to study it and leaned over to Dale and said, "Look Dale, they have those cheese sticks you love."

"They do?" he asked excitedly, and he took the menu to decide what he wanted. April made some suggestions and he laughed with her. The two of them seemed to be having a gay old time, which made Dan angry.

He could hear them as he walked up the hallway to where they were sitting. "Having Fun?" he asked them.

"Oh no, Dan, we were just looking at the menu, when she found the cheese sticks that I like so much" Dale said.

"Well goodie for you, go to the bathroom now," with that Dan sat down and looked at the girl. "Are you hungry?" he asked her.

"Yes sir, I am, a little," April answered.

"A little," he laughed at her. "Then you shall have a little." The waitress came around and took Dan's order, she looked at April and said, "Anything for you young man?"

"Give him some French fries and a burger. That's it," Dan said.

The truth was, April felt like she was starving.

Soon Dale was seated and asked if the waitress had been out yet, "Yes, she was, Dale. And because you were not here, you get nothing," Dan said.

"You're kidding, aren't you, Dan?"

Dale's face was all screwed into a big smile to appease Dan. "She will be back out, but don't get a lot. We need to sleep and not hear you in the bathroom all night. You hear me?" Dan said.

They ate. April was very careful to tear off bits of the burger and eat small amounts at a time. She became aware that televisions were playing in several areas of the dining room. April asked if she would be allowed to go to the bathroom. It was only number one and she would not be long.

Dan looked at her waving his finger in her face, "You run, and I will cut you real good," he said.

"I won't," April answered.

As she walked to the bathroom the evening news was on and her face appeared on the TV. It was her face before she was abducted she was smiling in the photo, there were the police and the FBI.

Someone had reported her writing in the bathroom at their last stop and the law stepped in. The police asked people to report if they saw an older blue police car. The report said that April Di Angelo had been abducted, and not been seen in twelve hours.

April went into the bathroom and quickly wrote. "I saw the report of my first writing, I am still alive. We are on Route North I believe. Please don't give up on me. Let my parents know I am all right and I love them." She snapped the top on and partially ran, then slowed down, back to the table.

"That didn't take you long at all," Dan said,

"No sir, I told you it wouldn't take long."

"It's a good thing you decided to cooperate for your own sake. It will make things a lot easier on you," Dan said to her. "What made you change?" he asked her.

"Well sir, you are a police officer and I respect them," she said. She did not say anything more, she was bolstering their egos. If he felt good about himself, felt confident, he would slip up sooner or later. April finished her burger and a third of her fries, "Would you like to have my fries, Dale?" she asked him.

Dale took them greedily laughing and looked at Dan, "You want some too, Dan?" he asked.

"No, Dale. You feed your fat face and enjoy them," Dan disgustingly said.

Soon they were finished, and Dan stood up and went to get a room. He told Dale to stay with April. April chipped away towards her plan. She complimented Dale at his size - he was so big and strong, with big hands.

"Yes, I have always been big. I was teased a lot by it too," he drooled. "The girls never liked me. They called me names and stuff," he said looking down at his plate.

April touched his hand and said, "I would never have made fun of you or called you names," she winked at him.

"You're real nice. I hate in a way what we are going to do to you. Maybe I can change Dan's mind. Don't say anything to Dan. He gets real mad you know," Dale said.

April knew it was only a matter of time. She had to work on chipping away at Dale. Dan came and motioned for April and Dale to follow him. They met him at the door, and he handed Dale keys and repeated the number to him four times. Dale took the keys and April's hand to search for the room. It was a no brainer for April, but for Dale it was a struggle, so she helped him a little.

Dale was real impressed that April said she could never have found the room number without him.

He liked this girl. She was real nice to him. She was nicer than his sister was. She was pretty and seemed to like him too. Maybe he could talk to Dan, and they could let this one go. She was not like the others.

Dan came in the room and told April to lie down on a bed. April was afraid when Dan cuffed her ankle to the bottom bed post. "We're not going to do nothing to you right now. Dale is going to take good care of you. Aren't you, Dale?" he said sarcastically. April looked at Dale with tears in her eyes. She poured it on. Dale asked to see Dan in the other room.

"Are you out of your damn mind?" Dan screamed at Dale. "Right now we are guilty of kidnapping, and a slew of other things, and you know what I mean. We are not letting her go. Get that through your thick, stupid noggin. Do you hear me?" Dan said very angrily to Dale.

They came out of the room and Dale lay beside April on the bed he turned her on her side facing him and whispered to her.

"Don't give up hope. Dan is like that. I know him good, and he might listen to me."

April whispered back, "I don't want you to be screamed at like that anymore. You are too nice a man for that," she said sympathetically sniffing her nose. Dale laughed a little making the bed jiggle

"I am not a scared of Dan. He and I get into things sometimes. He likes to scream at me. I don't mind, but he doesn't push me around. I am not married. He is to my sister. April sniffed and whispered "You deserve a really nice lady, Dale. If I were older I would be proud to be your wife." Dale was flying high inside.

All of the other girls and women they had abducted, none were ever like this.

They all screamed at him, spit on him, slapped or kicked at him, making his job of watching over them real hard. Dale would become meaner than a hornet. Dale never cared about any of those women. When they died, he felt relieved. But now Dale was worried about this pretty girl. She was really kind and thoughtful of him. She was cooperative and liked him and not many liked him. One look at his face and people usually turned the other way, but she was different. She smiled at him, laughed at his jokes and held his hand. Yes, she was real nice. It would be such a shame to kill this one. He would just have to work on Dan more.

Dale snored worse than April's Dad did. She had to concentrate with her mind and relax her body to sleep.

During the night she felt someone tug at the cuff on her ankle. April assumed it was Dan. He snuck around in the night, like a man who was guilty. He looked out of the window and over his shoulder all the time.

In the morning Dan said he would pick up some food, but not much so make it last and load up." He disappeared and April sat halfway up because of the cuff on the post.

"Oh darn, he forgot to unlock that cuff," Dale said.

"It's all right," April said. "It will give us more time to talk. I don't think Dan likes it when we talk and laugh," She told him.

"No, he don't, not at all," Dale told her. "Why do you like me? No one else does," Dale blurted out.

"Well, then they are stupid," April said. "I think you are funny, kind and just a really nice man."

Dale smiled happily. Usually people called him stupid. Yeah, he liked this girl a whole lot.

Soon Dan was at the motel door to their room "What are you doing still in here?" Dan yelled at Dale.

Dale turned slightly and pointed to the cuff on the post with April's ankle in it. "Need the key," Dale said feeling superior for a change.

Dan said, "Oh hell, here it is. Now make it snappy," and he left for the car.

Dale unlocked the cuff. April's ankle had a red mark and was a bit swollen, and Dale rubbed the swelling. "This will take the puffiness down," he said looking at her.

April leaned forward to kiss Dale's bald head. "I like you just like a brother. I don't have one. You know, maybe you could be my brother," April said.

That made Dale's heart happy. He did not have a brother. He was never close to his sister. He never had parents either. Dan was the closest thing he had to a brother, and he was never as nice as April was.

Back in the car, with everyone at place when suddenly Dan reached into April's side and repeatedly punched her ribs with thunderous blows. April could only sit there and take it.

Dale panicked. He ran out trying to pull Dan off April, half screaming and crying for Dan to stop.

Then Dan turned on Dale. "You, too, you stupid idiot," he said as he pummeled Dale's head. Dale became instantly submissive. Indicating this was a common occurrence in their relationship. "Get back in the damn car and do not talk to her," Dan screamed.

April sat there with pain in her side. She felt a sharp pain and guessed Dan had broken a rib, or maybe several. Dale looked much worse. His head was bleeding and Dan had broken his nose. The two injured knew not to talk to each other and they watched Dan fume as he drove the car. They drove for a long while, but no words were exchange between any of them.

April realized that the newscast meant her parents knew about what had happened to her. Her parents, the judge and everyone who knew her, and her thoughts went to her dear Larry. She hoped he would not know. He was usually so busy he rarely watched television. For the others, it was answer to prayer, they would all know and it grieved April. There was nothing she hated more than to bring grief to someone due to her actions. And that was the truth. This was her fault. She had not listened. Not to her gut instincts, not to Eddie, not to her father or her Father's blessing. April did not like sitting on a problem and not doing anything about it either. Both at home and in her military training she was taught to problem solve.

For now she was doing all she could, picking an enemy to side with, to protect herself as best as she could. Granted he was the weaker of the two mentally. No way would she have any chance to sway Dan. This was all his idea. Dan was the predator, the hunter. Dale was the follower. Both were guilty, but to April's way of thinking, Dale was less guilty than Dan.

Her ribs hurt excruciatingly. All she could do was to sit as still as best she could. Every bump of the car on the road caused her pain. Dan did not stop that car until it was nearly out of gas. As they traveled speeding most of the way, some of the sights were vaguely familiar to April. She guessed they were in Colorado, so she knew they were heading east. "I have to stop for gas soon. You two stay in the car," Dan gruffly said.

"I have to go to the bathroom, and I am going to wash my face," Dale replied. Dale's blood had dried all over his face and it was hideous.

"Well then, you take care of her and DON' T TALK TO HER!" Dan screamed at Dale.

Dale didn't care, screaming did not bother him. But he was not going to let Dan hit him anymore. At the gas station Dan went into the restroom first as Dale turned sideways to ask April if she was all right.

"I am all right," she whispered. "But just look at your face," April said with forced fake tears running down her face, "I am so sorry Dale. I never meant for you to be hurt," and she put her face down to force more fake tears.

"Oh, I am all right. I am just worried about you, April."

He said it. He said her name. That was the first time he said her name and now it was sinking into his head. She was a person, someone he could identify with, someone he cared about and hopefully can protect.

"Is your side real sore?" he asked her. "Yes, it is. I think Dan broke my ribs," she replied.

"Oh, that Dan. He is a real mean one. We have to be real careful around him."

"I think it would help if I could wrap material around my ribs to keep them in place and not move. With every bump, they move, and it hurts me," April cried more tears.

"When you get out and go into the bathroom, I can help you, April," Dale said. "I can pull material real tight for you. We just need to find something to use."

April told Dale that any material would work it just had to be tight to support her ribs from moving. When it was their turn to get out, Dan went into the garage area to pick up some food. Without his knowledge Dale went into the women's bathroom with April. When April lifted her shirt Dale winced at the red area at her side. "Oh. Dan hurt you real bad," he said. He had brought along one of his T-shirts.

April folded it in half and held it against her torso and told Dale to pull it tight. Yes that hurt, immensely, but it had to be tight. When in place, Dale handed April large horse blanket pins he had kept on his outer jacket pocket flap. With the make-shift brace in place April felt better. Now she could move easier without as much pain. "Oh, Dale, thank you so much," she cried looking into his eyes.

"Don't worry. I will take care of you," Dale said. They came out and went into the station's grocery area to pick out what Dale wanted. April was dying for fruit.

Dale picked up what April asked for and Dan looked at him curiously, "On a diet, Dale," he asked.

"It's none of your bees wax" was all Dale said.

Dan never noticed the wrap under April's clothing, but he did notice the missing pins from Dale's shirt. Dan also picked up a map and they all went back to the car and got in.

Dale casually tossed the bag with the fruit into the back seat. Dan pretended he did not see that.

They headed out on the highway speeding along. There was little traffic on the road. As they traveled, Dale was to read the map, and being simple, he often blurted out towns and routes along the way. Then he blurted out, "Look, Dan, we have from here to here to get to Wisconsin."

Dan slugged Dale in the side of the head. "You stupid idiot, don't say that."

Dale was angry, "Don't you hit me anymore, Dan. I don't like it, so don't do that ever again," Dale said drooling profusely.

"What are you going to do, Dale? Shoot me?" Dan lifted a Colt 45 revolver. He cocked it and aimed the gun at Dale.

Dale covered his head and screamed, "Dan, stop it. Dan, you're scaring me. I am your brother-in-law. Did you forget that, Dan?"

Dan un-cocked the revolver and put it back in the holster at his side.

Dale's chest was heaving, and to tell the truth April's heart stood still. Dan was unpredictable, and a very unstable human being.

"I noticed you lost some of your pins there, Dale Boy. What happened to them?" Dan said.

"Ah, I must have lost some on this trip," Dale replied.

"They were your trophy pins. Do you remember that, Dale?" Dan asked.

"I do remember, Dan. I don't want to talk about it," Dale said.

"No, you never want to talk about it, not when it's over. But when you are in the driver's seat, you love the rush. Don't you, Dale Boy?" Dan teased.

April was putting two and two together. They kidnap a woman, take her to a secluded place, a hunting cabin, and then have their way with her. They enjoy the struggle, the fight and then they do away with her.

"Not this time," she thought to herself. "Not this time." This time she would divide them. She would make one her best friend, and maybe by the grace of God and angels, she might be able to get away from the instigator Dan.

Suddenly there was a siren coming from behind them. "Oh shit," Dan said. The trooper came along side of their car waving for them to get over. "Don't say nothing, Dale, or you either," as he looked at April from his rearview mirror. April thought this would be her chance to get away and she waited patiently.

The officer walked up to the driver's side and said, "License and registration."

Dan handed over the information.

Then the officer turned his back to check the information in his computer. He did not get more than five steps towards his car, when Dan opened his door and shot the officer three times in the back.

April nearly jumped out of her seat and Dale screamed.

"Get our stuff out of the car!" Dan yelled at them. "Hurry!"

Dale got out everything from the front of the car and while he was doing that, April took the highlighter and half scribbled a note on the back of the front passenger side. She held onto the marker as Dale helped her out, nothing was in the back seat but her. As Dan emptied out the trunk, he had Dale help him put the dead officer in the driver's seat of their old car, removed the license plate, and left.

It took Dan a little while to learn how to turn off the overhead lights. After he did he looked proud as a peacock, "I promised you a good time. Didn't I, Dale?" he said with the biggest smile. April didn't think humor was possible from this man.

They flew down the road. Dan was testing out the *new car.* "Man, can this baby ever go," he said like a kid. He was free, having the time of his life. While an officer of the law lay dead, gunned down by the coward Dan. He may have been someone's husband, someone's daddy, a son, a grandson, or a cousin.

April was so angry she cried. She kept as quiet as she could to not allow them to see her. Karma will have its due. "What goes around, comes around," she thought. These men were not obeying any of the commandments, and sooner or later it would all catch up with them, Karma!

They made much faster time now. Eventually Dan pulled out the computer tossing it out of the window. He did not like the constant chatter, and lights going off.

They arrived at night time at another diner. This was an old streamliner, all stainless steel. They had the old type jukeboxes, where you put in a quarter and play four songs. It was a little dirty, but not too bad, and April was starving. The last time they ate was when the officer was shot at about 10 a.m. that day. She counted the days they had been on the road for three days. She imagined they would arrive at their hunting spot within a day or two, so they could be home in a week.

As April thought quietly and ate her rice pudding and toast. That was what she was allowed. She really did have to go to the bathroom and was afraid she would have to strain, and her ribs were sore. She asked to be allowed to go and Dan nodded his head. April thought maybe a television might tell her some updated news, but they had on a football game. She went through the wooden bathroom stall, and it took her a while, but she was all right.

Dan came in throwing open the door while April was still on the pot. "Writing more notes," he said sarcastically.

April told him she did not know what he was talking about. She was going to the bathroom.

He used his foot to kick her, knocking her off the toilet. He stomped on her wrist, kicked her ribs, and April snapped. She grabbed his foot and pulled.

Dan fell unexpectedly backwards onto the floor. The wind had been knocked out of him and he had hit his head hard.

April pulled up her pants, flushed her toilet, stepped over Dan, and walked out. She joined Dale at the table and asked him who had the car keys.

"Oh, Dan has them. Why, April?" and April told Dale what she had done. "I am tired of him hurting me when I have done nothing to him." April said touching Dale's arm.

"I know just what you mean, April. I don't like it either. Dan maybe real mad at you, but you put him in his place. He might leave you alone now," Dale said.

It took Dan almost twenty minutes before he came to. He sat at the table calmly which unnerved April. He looked at her and said "You ever raise your arm to me or do shit like that and I will shoot you dead, bitch. Do you hear me? Dead!"

April pushed the table as tight as she could to Dan's chest. She really pushed it tight and said, "You plan to kill me any way, Dan. You are a monster. Dale is not. He has a good heart. He is nothing like you. You egg him on, abuse him, and then blame him for your problems. I am not afraid of you. Do you hear me. I have not done anything but obey you and still you hurt me. I will never be afraid of you no matter what you do to me." And she shoved the table tighter. "Behave or you might be begging one day, Dan." April stood up to go out, with Dale beside her.

Dan pushed the table back and gasped. That damn woman choked the air out of him. He would fix her. No, no, he can't do that. He just wanted to get to the cabin and get this over with. This was not like the other times, not at all.

They always cried or begged. But this one, she was like his bitch wife. She too liked his ugly brother-in-law, and she was not afraid. Yeah, he just wanted this over with.

He paid the bill and came out to the car smoking his cigarette. He dashed it out on the ground before getting in. Not one word was spoken, not one.

Prior to Dan coming out, April was concerned about her wrist. She thought it was broken, but Dale of all people told her to try and move it. If she could move it, it most likely was not broken. He knew that because one of his friends had fallen down an embankment one summer while camping and jammed his wrist really bad on rocks. It swelled up but was not broken. "I hope it's not broken, April. A wrist would need a doctor and Dan would never take you to a doctor. It's not as easy to fix like your ribs." Dale was clearly worried about April.

April looked at Dale with tears in her eyes, "Are you going to kill me, Dale? Are you going to let Dan have his way with me and then kill me?" April asked him.

"No, April. I can't do that," he said shaking his head "You are nice to me, and no one has ever been nice to me. I promise never to hurt you, and I will do my best to stop Dan. Even if I have to kill him," he said.

"Dale, think for a minute. Dan is taking me to this hunting cabin and what do you think will happen to me?" Then she reached for him.

Dale hugged her from the front seat. "Nothing. I won't let anything happen to you, not like the other girls," he said. The two were facing front, not talking when Dale looked out from the diner. "About time," he said to himself. I want this over with.

Back home, Gordon tried to shield Miranda from the news from the beginning. The officers and FBI were told to strictly call his office, not anywhere else! This was an investigation he did not want Miranda involved in. He knew this would most likely kill his wife. But Miranda did find out.

One evening as they were watching TV, even though Gordon tried to keep television watching at a minimum. And there it was, a ticker tape that ran information along the bottom of the screen that read: "NEW LEADS ON THE DI ANGELO CASE SURFACED AT A DINER IN OHIO. A MESSAGE WAS

LEFT BEHIND BY APRIL DI ANGELO DETAILING HER CAPTORS' DESCRIPTIONS AND THE DIRECTION THEY WERE HEADING. MORE INFORMATION WILL FOLLOW AS GATHERED."

Miranda looked at her husband in disbelief, and she began to cry. Gordon could not console his wife, no matter how he tried to give her hope. He had to call their doctor to give Miranda a sedative or she would work herself into a frenzy. He also called the Bishop to ask if a sister would be willing to come out and stay with Miranda. Her visiting teacher was there within a half hour. Gordon spoke with her, and she understood what was happening and said she would do all she could for her.

This woman was married and had three teenage children, yet here she was giving of her time to console Miranda. She stayed with Miranda for eleven days straight. They did everything together: they cried, folded laundry, and cooked together. Lena and Nora visited and all of them had difficulty coming to grips with the fact that their girl had been taken. "But she is strong," Lena counseled, and they would nod their heads.

After eleven days or so they all had grasped the reality of what was happening. They prayed more than ever, and April was never out of their mind or thoughts. They all worked and did the daily activities they used to do, but it took so much more concentration.

Miranda was so thankful for Remi who distracted her and consoled her. He was such a blessing to their lives.

Gordon Di Angelo would go almost crazy without news. He wondered if the officials out there were qualified to do a good job at the crime scene. Surely there had been fingerprints left behind and they would know who they were. Surely they had some idea and could be at the destination before April and her captives were. How he wished he could go and be there. He knew he and his deputies could do a much better job than any of those officers. It was so frustrating to wait and wait for information.

Each day an FBI agent would call Gordon. His name was Danny Pacino. He was a city-raised New Yorker. Born in Brooklyn. All his life he wanted to be a police officer, like his dad and grandfather before him. A tough Italian, who had to fight his share of street fights. No man ever bested Danny, not ever. He worked his way up the ranks and was the best detective in the agency.

More than that, Officer Danny Pacino had a heart, and compassion for the families. He was like stone to criminals and putty to families who had felt loss. He could be berated, spit upon, but it did not matter because he took it, he understood.

When he was six years old, he and his mother were out shopping when she was gunned down right in the street in front of him. The scum robbed her of ten dollars and left her to die.

His grandparents raised him. His grandmother was stern and demanding, but his grandfather not so much. The two of them saved him in every way. They taught him about people, to be compassionate, responsible, and caring. His father lived with them, too. He immersed himself in work after the murder.

Danny told Gordon that April was not taken for money or ransom. There was no indication of that. The abductors were smart. They either smudged their fingerprints or used napkins or gloves to avoid prints. Their best lead came when they found the dead officer in the older squad car. In their car the prints were wiped, but not cleaned. The agency had the fingerprints, and they were waiting for results.

Gordon groaned. He felt this case was botched from the beginning. Agent Danny agreed with Gordon. The local police were not experienced or prepared for something like this, and the first few hours was a very critical time. The "offenders" were experienced, they had done this before. Of this he was certain.

The Di Angelo family was having their faith tested. They prayed even more than before. They read scriptures more and spent more time together. They knew if they did not do this their marriage could fail. They were aware that staying close, confiding in one another, and keeping the Savior close was the only way they would make it intact and sane. All who entered their home at that time left more whole. No one could put a finger on it, only the Di Angelo's and their closest friends could. They set a tone of reverence in their home. They played light music throughout their home daily. Meals were strictly at their table after prayer. They talked openly with one another, as did Remi. They had a right, as needed, to express what they were feeling, good or bad. With Gordon as head of their home, he had to step up and give counsel, direction, blessings, and see to their needs.

Gordon Di Angelo grew more spiritual during that time than ever before in his life. He thought he knew what being a priest holder meant, but only now were his eyes fully open. It was a lot of work, a huge load that he shouldered willingly and valiantly.

Gordon's dear friend Judge Du Val was there for Gordon at any time of need. He too was crushed by the news that April had

P. Costa

been abducted. He wanted to donate money to send a team to find her, but he also felt too much time had passed. It was humbling for Du Val to have those feelings and know that all he could do was pray and trust God.

It was a time of growth for all those who were close to and knew the Di Angelo's. Their home teachers and visiting teachers, who come once a month, were acutely aware of their needs as was their Bishop. The president of the Young Men's group made a huge sacrifice to personally pick up Remi so he would be at all of their activities. It did not matter if it was a lesson, a basketball game, or an outing with the boys, Remi was always there. He made sure of that.

Extended family members called on them and found themselves uplifted by their words of cheer and comfort. They did not know how, but somehow they did it with the aid of a kind and loving Father in Heaven who knows all of us are his children.

Agencies began to volunteer their services, people like Russ Bondsman. Over the years when April was racing, it was not uncommon for her to put someone in touch with Mr. Stevens. For instance, there had been a young man who had approached April one afternoon at the racetrack. His name was Russ Bondsman. He was training dogs for tracking, not for hunting, but human tracking. He had five dogs trained and wanted to know if April would help him financially to build the business. April was interested because she knew the value of finding people lost during vacationing or as a result of human trafficking. April willingly gave Russ the telephone number of Mr. Stevens.

Over a period of time Russ's business grew. He built a kennel with large runs and a training area. D farms helped him with finances all during that growing period. As time went on Russ's business flourished with his well-trained dogs and their successes.

Late one afternoon, as he usually did, Russ Bondsman gathered his meal and sat in his living room to catch up on the news. When he heard of the abduction of a student in Pittsburgh PA, he perked up. When he learned who it was, he put down his dinner plate and went to get his cell phone. He called station after station wanting information on how to help. Finally at wits end he called Mr. Stevens who sent the D Farm's Twin Cessna to pick up Russ, three of his men, and eight of his dogs.

It was people like Russ who came forward from all walks of life. People April had reached out to and helped in the past. Many from the D Farm program who had graduated and entered various careers also turned to D Farms wanting to help. People in key government agencies, private detectives, bounty hunters, and the list was endless. They all came forward putting the FBI in a tail spin.

Finally Gordon Di Angelo told FBI agent Pacino that he had to allow these people to help. They were motivated and passionate. You cannot hire passion. They were all expertly trained in their fields and the more help the better.

FBI agent Pacino told Gordon he was afraid too much information would get out putting April in danger.

"She's already in danger. The sooner we get these people out there, the better chance she has," Gordon replied.

FBI agent Pacino sighed. This father was right. His agency did not have all the resources that was being offered to the Di

Angelo's, so he agreed. That is so long as they all kept him informed as information was gathered. So basically FBI agent Pacino lived on his cell phone.

Mr. Stevens was a mess. He knew himself well. If he could throw himself into work, he would be all right. Without April's permission he went full steam ahead to get the dairy up and running in Hawaii. He only took one trip after completion, and he had to admit to himself this was the most beautiful of all the dairies in D Farms. The cattle produced more than others mainly because of the lush grass and available water within a short distance. Again this dairy was modeled after all the others with a few exceptions. Mr. Stevens knew that April would indeed be pleased.

Mr. Stevens had been home for three weeks and could not sit there anymore. He picked up his telephone and called Gordon Di Angelo at the police station. "Gordon, Mr. Stevens here, I know you have your hands full, but I was wondering if I could meet you at Flo's Diner for lunch today. It will be just a brief lunch if you can." Gordon agreed and met Mr. Stevens at noon at Flo's Diner.

Mr. Stevens was sitting in the back, no papers, just him sitting there. He stood when Gordon reached their table. "Thank you for meeting me," he said.

"No, thank you. I needed this diversion. There has been so much going on."

Mr. Stevens stopped him by touching Gordon on his sleeve. "I completely understand, and in part that is why I am here," Mr. Stevens said. "I want to help. However, I am not a police officer.

I don't know how to track as much as our own dog when she runs off for an adventure. I do know numbers though, so I wanted to talk to you. I was at the Hawaii site and was so impressed. It is doing wonderfully. And now another opportunity has come up in Alaska, and I wanted your thoughts on this," he said.

"Alaska, it's kind of cold there, not suitable for a dairy," Gordon said.

"You are right, but with a good building, it would be very good for raising steers."

Gordon did not comprehend, "So are D Farms now expanding to steer barns?" he asked.

"Well, we always have been. Each dairy raises the bull calves. They are castrated and if there is enough room they stay there in pastures during spring, summer and fall. They are put in barns over the wintertime. But often there is not enough room, so the steers are hauled to other farms. There would be only steers, anywhere from five hundred to a thousand."

Gordon sat there and remembered April raising all of the cattle on all of the farms when she was younger, it was a lucrative business.

"Well, I can see your plan," Gordon said. "But Alaska is a long way off."

"Not necessarily," Mr. Stevens said. "If steers were transported, from farm to farm, picked up along the route, it would be feasible and practical," Mr. Stevens said.

"Well, I suppose you are right," Gordon said. "I am not the one to ask though, you know April had the nose for business and she is not here," Gordon said tearing up.

Mr. Stevens nodded, "I will take care of all the details. I want to reassure you this is a very good deal. One that I believe April would want and we are standing on very good ground with all of the dairies. They are all turning profit. I don't know why but many, many alumni donate money, large sums of money along with testimonial letters of gratitude," he said.

"Well, I can see why," Gordon said. "I remember many of the letters April had read to us. D Farms gave them a chance when they had nothing and nowhere to go. So yes, I can understand them sending money when they reach a place they never thought they would be," Gordon said.

By now the three in the stolen police car were entering into the state of Wisconsin. It would not be long now until they reached the hunting cabin Dan thought. The sooner the better.

He was losing Dale somehow. Granted, Dale was not smart. He could not reason things. He could not figure out what to do. Dale always followed Dan ever since they were kids. When Dan beat up a kid in school it was Dale who was always close by. Dan loved to torture animals. He would tie cats together and watch them fight until they were dead. Blow up dogs with firecrackers.

Throughout the years these two were thrown together all through grade school and high school. After that Dale got a job at the local Goodwill doing various jobs while Dan left for the police academy.

Dale was very proud of Dan, well almost everyone was, all except for Jenny who was the apple of Dan's eye. He had asked Jenny to go out on dates so many times that he lost count. But he never gave up on her. After graduation, Dan secured a spot on the

Georgia town police force and sought out Jenny again. She was working at the factory as a sewing operator. He knew she was off at 3:00 p.m. So he waited for her. As the line of women exited the factory, Dan approached Jenny. They talked as she walked to her car. Jenny never liked Dan because he was too rough, pushy, and mean. She had seen and knew of Dan beating up kids in high school and she did not like that. Dan asked Jenny if she would like to go out for hot chocolate or a movie some evening. Of course Jenny said, "No, I am too busy."

Dan leaned into Jenny's body, "Come on, Jenny. I can show you a real nice time."

Jenny pulled away and asked Dan to leave her alone. She was seeing someone now and just wanted Dan to go and find someone else.

"Come on Jenny, just one date, you don't really know me" Dan continued. "I know plenty about you, Dan.

"I am not interested in you, so just go and leave me alone."

Dan did not like that, not at all. He left Jenny alone, but he never stopped watching her.

Dan made it part of his routine to drive by the factory at lunch time to wave at the ladies. Dan looked for Jenny, if she was there she would turn her head away purposely and not look at him. When she was not there, he would drive around looking for her.

He caught up with Jenny one evening when he was on the night shift. She was coming out of the grocery store with a cart of groceries. He parked his cruiser away, got out, and walked to Jenny's car. "Here let me help you with those," he said taking her bags out of the cart and putting them in her trunk.

"Thank you, Dan. I have to be going now," and she walked away with the cart to put it into the cart stall and leave.

Dan caught her by her hand and said. "Now, Jenny, you know I am sweet on you. Why don't you give me a chance to show you, to treat you right."

Jenny pulled her hand away quickly and said, "I can't, Dan. I have to get going. My mom is expecting me," she shakily put the key in the car's ignition and left.

Dan was not happy. Everyone was proud of him. He had come a long way in life. Now the person he wanted most refused him. He would just have to show Jenny what kind of man he really was. Dan knew that Jenny's family liked to go fishing and they had a small camp just outside of town at Hartwell lake. When he was not working, he would drive out to the lake and walk around. Sometimes he saw Jenny with her brother or her family, but it was difficult to talk to her.

One evening he went out to the lake and there was Jenny all alone fishing on a small spot near a sand bar. "Catch anything?" Dan called to her.

Jenny quickly reeled in her line securing it. Then she gathered up her things in her tackle box and began to walk as fast as she could back to her family's camp.

Dan could not believe it, so he jumped over the sand bar. Then he swore because now his pants were wet. Dan ran to chase after Jenny. He knew she was going to her family's camp. So he went around in another direction to stop her before she reached her parents' camp. He caught up with her one hundred yards or so before she reached her destination. "Surprise!" he said to her as he grabbed her waist in the dark.

Jenny was frightened and screamed.

Dan put his hand over Jenny's mouth, "the cabin. I am not going to hurt you, Jenny. I just want to spend some time with you alone."

"Please. Please, Dan, let me go. I just want to take these fish to Momma for dinner." Jenny tried to get away, but Dan refused to let her go.

"Now settle down, Jenny. I just want you to see who I am. I have a good job now, am respected in the community, and I want to settle down with a nice girl like you."

Jenny began to cry, "I don't want you, Dan. I am sorry, but I am dating someone else and I promise, to be true."

Dan was not happy, he fully intended to have Jenny. Dan just could not see how Jenny could be anything but his. He laid her down, raped her, and was proud as could be.

Jenny stood up and spit on Dan and went to walk away.

Dan grabbed Jenny and kissed her. He kissed her so hard that he hurt her.

She could not breathe. Jenny pulled away but could not get away. She hit Dan and tried to kick him. When he finally let her go from his brutal kiss, Jenny slapped him.

Dan dragged a screaming Jenny to the water and drowned her. If he could not have her no one would. Then Dan picked up Jenny's dead, limp, wet body and hoisted her over his shoulder. He gathered up her rod and basket and headed back to his car. He put Jenny in the trunk on a thick blanket and drove one hundred miles south. Dan then placed Jenny's body and her things in a murky swamp. No one would ever find her. She would forever be his.

Jenny's body was never found. It was believed she had drowned fishing. Jenny's family never believed that, they knew Jenny was a fine swimmer. They all felt something was not right but since no one listened to them, and there was no body or trace of her, they had to let it go. They felt some day, maybe the day of reckoning, what happened to their beloved beautiful daughter would be known.

That was the beginning of Dan's trophy casing. After Jenny it became easy. No woman ever said no to Dan.

Dan did marry a woman when he was so drunk he could not stand up. He married a lazy, good for nothing, low account, penniless layabout. They fought really well and that was about it. No matter how he hit her, she hit him back worse. In the 32 years of their marriage she had broken many of Dan's bones. He learned to stay away from her as best as he could. He was submissive and a coward in his own home. Her uncle was a senator, and she used that against Dan every time. She rubbed it in his face that her uncle had to help to support them financially.

So Dan found another source of fun which he pursued yearly on his vacation, going hunting. He found a woman that resembled Jenny somewhat and consummated his love to her over and over every year. He even took pictures of them with him in cute poses. They cooperated because they were dead. Never did it dawn on Dan that these people had a life, and people who loved them. Dan thought whomever he chose would be his and his alone.

As they drove along April noticed a small brown briefcase under the driver's seat that from time to time would slide towards her. Sometimes Dan would feel for the case and panic if he could not feel it. Several times he actually stopped the car to put the case back under the seat again.

On this particular day, Dan was being a jerk. He drove the car as fast as it could go until the car shook and the briefcase wobbled towards the back seat. It opened, spilling enough of its contents out so that April saw what was inside. There were photos, black and white photos, of dead women. One had a rope around her neck in a straddled position with Dan standing over her. Another was face down with Dan standing over her. It was as if these women were his hunting trophies.

April said nothing. She looked then looked away. She fidgeted with the ring on her finger and as she turned her ring. At one point she felt like, well she didn't know what she felt like, but she wanted to fly away. This was nuts! She was sitting in a car with two murderers. She knew to cooperate somewhat to stay alive since one was also armed. But she just could not wrap her mind around what they had done over the years. Finally April vomited over and over in the back seat.

Dan pulled over in a hurry. "Now what in the hell is wrong with you?" he asked angrily.

"I don't know. Maybe I picked up something," she said as she vomited more. "Something from someone."

"Oh hell!" Dan said kicking his car tire. "Dale, what'd you say to us ending this trip right here and now. We can throw her over the bank. She would roll down the side and not be found."

Dale felt his blood boil, but he knew not to argue with Dan. "Well, Dan, I would not like that at all. You promised me fun, you know, at the cabin we rented, another hunting party."

Dan looked at him. He wondered if he meant it, but from Dale's gaze it was evident Dale wanted to go through with their original usual plan. "Well, then we have to get something for her vomiting, Pepto Bismol or something at the next stop." Within minutes they came to a roadside store and Dan came out with the bottle of Pepto Bismol. He threw it in the back seat and said, "Here." He got back in the car, and they drove off.

April did drink almost half of the bottle, and she never looked at that underside again. She blocked out what she could and paid attention to where they were going.

It snowed almost every day. From Ohio to where they were now, there was snow. They were crossing into Wisconsin. And wow, there was enough snow for everyone. April had not seen snow growing up in California. She saw it for the first time during the Olympics, but not since then that she could remember. It was cold. Even with a coat on April was cold.

As they drove Dan punched Dale's arm, "Almost there, buddy boy. In about an hour we will be there," he said.

Dale turned sideways as if he was looking behind them for traffic. He looked at April. She was sick and her color was pale bluish green. He knew they had not fed her much. Her ribs were broke and her wrist was really sore. Maybe she had an infection or was really sick with the flu. Dale turned back and said, "Dan, she doesn't look so good. Maybe we should give her a couple of days to get better, stronger, or it will not be near as fun."

Dan was almost insane with Dale because on this trip he actually cared about this woman. "Dale, we have to be back at home in six days. We can't afford that kind of time. Do you understand me?" he said.

"I do, but, Dan, when we get there can we just let her have one day to rest. Please, Dan.

"I don't give a shit. This one is yours to do with what you want. I am not touching her," and he spit on the car floor.

FBI agent Danny Pacino was the best, but each time he checked out another lead, they were gone. No one offered any clues except April. There were helicopters watching certain highways while on road patrol. There were other volunteers when a lead was secured. They would go in that direction to find her. They were illusive and that frustrated FBI Danny, but he would not let anyone see it.

What puzzled him the most was here was a young woman who was strong and brave. She just came out of the Marines as a Frogman where from his understanding she was extremely cunning. Often she used her mind more than a gun. He could not understand why she did not run from her captors. It all came down to the car and the uniform. April's father was the Sheriff of their town. He was loved and respected. FBI agent Pacino concluded that April did not fight back either due to respect for the uniform or she was waiting for her chance. The more time that passed, it lessened her ability to escape. Unless, unless she was cunning enough to somehow get between the abductors. It was highly likely they would fight over her, even if they did not know her value.

What he had learned from her Commanding Officer was this: "She was an honest, dependable soldier. She had the ability to think through a situation, as she did in the jungle. She had not been there before, but she navigated through it all. She found the missing men, and without one bullet she overthrew the entire village by putting them to sleep and escaped. She is not stupid, and I can't imagine she has given up. Give her time, and she will come through. I have faith in her," Sgt. Bob said.

"So you feel that confident about her? You believe she will be all right?" the agent asked him.

"Hell, I don't know. There are nut jobs out there that would not hesitate to pull a trigger, but if she has any chance at all, she will figure it out."

Dale was elated. "THIS ONE IS YOURS!" He said it. Dan actually said it. Then if that was true, Dale could let her go. He could just open the door and let her go. That's what he would do. Dan said so, it must be true.

That hour went fast. April tried to refresh herself as best as she could. She really was sick, and it was not just from the disgusting horrific photographs.

They pulled into the lane of the cabin but could not go much further than the entry because the lane was full of snow.

"Come on. Let's go!" Dan yelled as he slammed his door. "More crap to put up with," and he trudged through the snow to the cabin.

Dale got out and turned to help April who was already out of her door, vomiting in the snow. She stood and her nose was running, and she had tears in her eyes. "You really are sick," Dale said.

"I am and I hope it is a contagious disease that Dan gets and kills him. Then you and I can drive away. I can stay with you," she said.

That made up Dale's simple mind. He would stay with her forever. She was the girl for him no matter what Dan said or would do. Dale helped April by supporting her arm on one side and carrying their bags on the other - four bags with straps, and a big bag handle. "Easy there, April. Don't fall or that will hurt your ribs."

April was glad Dale helped her. She was weak. She was really sick. She prayed for an advantage like this, but not with her so sore and sick.

As they made their way to the cabin, up the steps, and onto the porch, Dale dropped his bags and helped April through the door where Dan was building a fire in the fireplace. April took one quick glance around the room and saw a fireplace in front of her, and to her left was a picnic table to eat on. There was a small sink on the wall, and beyond was another room. To her right was a chair, a couch, and an old TV that sat along the wall unplugged with a VCR on top of it. There was a bed at the far wall with blankets folded on the seats.

"It's really cold in here," Dale said.

"No shit, Sherlock. I am building a fire," Dan angrily said.

Dale helped April towards the chair, and she wanted to go and sit on the couch. "Okay, April, you stay here, and I'll go and get the bags," he said and left.

Dan looked at April and said, "This is your last stop, girlie girl, home sweet home. The last thing you are ever going to remember. Oh, I am not going to touch you. You are all Dale's Sure, he is all sweet and nice. But you have never seen Dale in action." With that he turned his attention to the fire that was now beginning to take hold and burn.

Dale came inside exclaiming "It's snowing more out there. It must be coming down inches a minute."

"Oh, Dale, don't be such a dumbass, snow does not fall that fast," Dan replied.

"Just look outside. You can't see the tracks we made coming in," Dale said.

Dan got up to look and sure enough their tracts were gone, covered up by fresh snow. "Great! We might be socked in here for days. I should have just greased her the other day. By now we would be on our way home and not bothered by this snowstorm," he said.

Dale looked at him and said, "We have time, and we can get to know her better this way. Right, April?" Dale said.

April wearily nodded her head. She had a fever. She knew it when she touched her cheek. It was warm but her forehead was burning. April looked at the two men and asked, "Would it be too much to ask if either of you might have aspirin on this trip?"

"I have baby aspirin that I take every day," Dale replied, and he began to root in a bag. Dale found his medicine box and took the small bottle and some water to April. April took six pills and water and hoped for the best. She leaned back and rested and then she vomited the aspirin too. She turned on her side with her head lying on the couch arm. She was overwhelmed, sick, with fractured ribs, and possibly a broken left wrist. Her eye bulged, was bloody, and she had a God-awful headache thanks to Dan's last beating.

As she lay there, she did not cry, but tears ran out of her eyes. And low, she saw an angel sitting there near her. The angel was crying, clear tears ran down her cheeks and in each tear April saw what she wanted most. She saw her mother and father kneeling on their living room floor praying for her. She saw Remi crying clutching his pillow with Ruby lying worriedly beside him. April saw her grandparents' faces etched with great worry, all of them, and then she heard them.

There were many voices all in prayer. She could recognize them individually. Her parents' prayers had tears and choked voices. Manny and Contessa sat praying in church for hours and their prayers were tears. Her other grandparents did the same as they lit candles and cried silently. Her brothers were so angry, they wanted to kill whoever did this to their sister.

To Live or Die

THEN SHE HEARD SGT. BOB CALLING HER, "GET UP D. DON'T TAKE this shit. You are my recruit, and I expect more from you."

Yes, April heard them all. April knew she had to reach way down and pull herself together. She did not want to die. She wanted to live to go to those whom she loved most. She was not willing to let that go. Not yet, not for a long, long time.

Slowly April determined in her mind to receive the strength she needed. For her heart would receive those messages and her hands achieve to them do them, whatever was necessary.

Dale sat beside her and watched her. "There is your prize, Dale. Isn't she lovely?"

"She is, Dan. She is just sick, and I think it's your fault."

"My fault. How is this my fault? Dan said.

"Because you broke her ribs. You are always hurting her, and she didn't try to run away for a long, long time."

"How do you know I broke her ribs?" Dan pushed.

"I just know it. That's all," Dale said.

"I know it because I asked you what happened to your lucky pins, and I know where they are," Dan said as he got up and walked across the floor to where April was sitting. He lifted up her shirt so hard he lifted April up off of the couch. "Here, here are you lucky pins," and he dropped April like a stone."

That started a fight, a real fight. Dale had had it. He got up and slugged Dan so hard Dan flew back onto the floor. Dale got down and pummeled Dan's head and chest and he did not stop.

April wanted it to stop. It was a horrible, violent fight. She wanted to call to Dale and have him stop, but part of her also wanted Dan dead. Finally when Dan was out, literally lying flat out sprawled on the cabin floor, April faked a deep cry for Dale to stop. She had difficulty getting up and she walked to Dale putting her hands on his shoulders asking him to stop, and he did. Dan's face was bloody. There was a lot of blood loss and Dan had blood coming out of his ears. April pulled at Dale pulling him to the kitchen area.

She ran water on a towel she found and began to wipe the blood spatters off his face and hands. Dale was like a small child and let her, never wanting to get up and wash himself. "I did it, April. Now we can be together forever," he said.

After Dale was clean April put more wood on the fire and told Dale it might be a good idea to move Dan from the middle of the floor. Dale dragged Dan's limp, lifeless body to the room at the back of the kitchen. It was a small bedroom with one twin bed. Dale put Dan in a sitting position and left him there. As he was busy with that, April kicked in gear and grabbed the small brief case Dan kept so near him and put it in a backpack.

As Dale came out she turned to him and thanked him. "I am going to make you a nice dinner, Dale," she said.

"You will? For me?" he said happily. April pulled out the potatoes that were in one of the bags along with an onion and green pepper and made fried potatoes. They had eggs she could make as well. There was no toaster, so she took a stick and asked Dale to brown the bread in the fireplace and he was thrilled like a child to help.

They ate better than they had in a long, long time. Dale was getting sleepy, but April wanted to keep him going. If only he would sleep, she could walk out the door and be free. "Dale, let's play a game!" she said excitedly. "You go in there," and she pointed where Dan was "count to sixty, come out and guess who I am," she told him.

"Okay," he said excitedly. Dale got up and lumbered into that back bedroom.

April worked quickly. She rifled through the bags and cupboards. First she put on big heavy wool socks that were Dan's. Then she saw a pair of split coveralls and boots. She found an ax in the corner and put some coal ash on her lip. As she did all of this she gathered matches, lighter fluid, candles, beans, rice, and dried fruit that Dan loved. And then Dale came out. "Can you guess?" April said with a big smile on her face.

Dale looked and looked, "I am not sure, April," he said.

"Oh, you must know. He had a blue ox he called Babe," she said.

"Oh, Oh, I know, Paul Bunyan," Dale said excitedly.

"Yes, yes you are right," April praised him. You are so good at this. Good for you, Dale."

"Now you go back in and count again, slowly this time. I need time to change around."

"Okay. I will. This is fun, April. No one ever plays with me," Dale said.

April scrounged for things she would have taken on a mission, a good knife from Dan, a canteen, a plastic bottle would have to do, gloves, and a hat. She packed faster than a thief.

"Are you ready?" Dale hollered.

Dan's swollen eye opened, he was barely aware of someone in the room with him. He felt like he had been hit by a truck and had no feeling in his legs. Not in his left arm or right hand. His one eye was swollen completely shut. As he opened his left eye in the dark room he was aware the figure was Dale. That son of a bitch had beaten him to a pulp. This was the last straw. He would kill him and that bitch and go home. He could make up a story, and who would care? Dan slowly and quietly reached for the revolver in his side pocket. He slid it out and cocked the arm and pulled the trigger.

"Give me a few more seconds," April said. And then she heard a huge boom and out walked Dan with his revolver in his hand.

"Now Danny is playing a game. Thought you were smart, eh. Turn Dale on me, eh. Well, Dale is dead, and you will be joining him shortly."

April did not hesitate. To her Dan was the enemy. She felt at her side for the hunting knife while rushing him with all her power. She used her right arm with all the strength she had, stabbing him in his left eye. The knife went in so deep that it went right through Dan's skull and embedding it in the wooden wall behind him. Dan's legs quivered for a minute and then he was dead, really dead.

April had mixed emotions. She did not hate Dale, but he too was a predator motivated by Dan who was an insult to all police officers. He had taken many lives for fun. April stepped back, weak, sat down, and mourned for all of them.

As Dan hung there against the wooden wall, his blood leaked out, towards April on the floor. She threw the rug in the living room over the blood soaked floor to stop blood from spreading.

April was in a bit of a daze. She sat there staring at the most evil man she had ever met. "Satan's Spawn!" she said out loud. Then it hit her, she was free! She knew she could not sit there. It was time to move.

In no way did she want to stay there. It felt evil. April was in a daze. Her head was fuzzy, but she had been trained by the best. She knew she had to concentrate and gather up what she would need. She had no idea where she was or how many days it would take for her to return home. Oh home! What a lovely word that is.

Thank God, Praise Him, I Am Free

APRIL GOT UP AND CONTINUED TO PACK TO LEAVE. SHE FOUND Dale's hunting knife still in the leather carrier. She knew she had to travel light and be prepared for snow and this bone-chilling winter which was something she had never done before. She was dressed, had one pack on her back, a small duffel bag in one hand and the car keys in the other. April opened the door, looked back around her and walked out, closing the door behind her. She breathed in the cold air and for the first time in weeks she felt free. Somewhat broken and bruised, but free. She stepped down the snow covered steps one at a time heading to the police cruiser.

April reached the car and opened the driver's door when she heard a bullet whiz past her striking the opened door. She quickly looked up in the direction of the cabin and froze. There was Dan standing in the doorway. April was shocked and stood there in disbelief. Another bullet came her way, and she ducked that one as it went over the car roof. Dan stepped down one step and fell. As he fell, he shot the last bullet of the gun into the starlit sky. April did not move. She stood there waiting to see if Dan would get up. He did not, not for over ten minutes.

April got in the cruiser and started the engine. It turned over with a roar. She put the car in reverse, but it just slid to the side of the driveway. It was stuck solid. April gathered her things, put them on, or in hand, and began to walk. She had no idea where she was, but this road had been plowed at some point the snow was not as deep as it was in the driveway to the cabin.

April turned right. She wanted her life to turn out right. And as she walked, she thanked her Father in Heaven and asked for his guidance. She vowed to never be so ignorant and evasive again.

April walked close to five miles in that deep snow when she saw lights coming her way. She was afraid and did not want anyone to catch her again. She was out here in the unknown and did not want another predator to find her. April hiked over the bank and slid down the other side. She waited until the lights passed. It was a snow plow clearing the road. April knew she would not be able to get back up on the road, so she hiked out in that same direction through the woods. She walked until she did not feel her feet anymore. She looked ahead of her and there covered in the snow was the opening of a small cave.

April walked to the opening. She did not see any footprints, but that did not mean there was not something already in this cave. April rationalized she would take her chances. She had already escaped the monsters of hell's grasp.

April entered the cave feeling the left side wall, and the ceiling as she walked in. She reached for her matches and lit one. It was a small cave, six feet high, about eight feet deep and four feet wide. Relieved, April shrugged her pack off of her back. Then she went back outside and found a tree that had fallen close by. She hacked off several of its branches, went inside, and built a small fire. She took her feet out of the boots to warm her toes and when they were pink and warm again she knew she did not have enough wood for the night.

With her boots back on, she went back outside. This time she took the axe and hacked larger pieces of wood. She carried each one back with her and split them. With a sizable amount of wood, April began to undress to get warm. She wanted to let her outer clothing dry and take care of her wounds.

She pulled out a small towel and dipped it in the small amount of melted snow she put in a metal cup to clean her face and sooth her wounded eye. The cold water felt good. She felt around her eye and realized her eye socket had been broken and she could feel the separation of bone.

April sighed. "All things happen for a reason," she said aloud. "And you were stupid!"

Very slowly she removed her clothing, right down to her skin. The small cave was adequately warm with the fire now blazing and she welcomed the cool air. Her ribs were sore, but not as bad as two days ago. She hoped they would knit and hold. She was not sure how long she would be walking. Her wrist was broken, she was sure of that. Her left hand went slightly in the wrong direction and her wrist hurt like crazy. She knew to divert the pain by concentrating on something else, so she picked up a pebble, rinsed it well, and rolled it between her teeth. April was not hungry. She was thankful she made a decent dinner for her and Dale.

The cave was ideal. The opening was out of the wind, even with a fire inside it was not noticeable. The cave had a small hump going in that prevented looking straight inside. April put some logs on for the night and curled up without clothing in the sleeping bag. She tied the bottom of the backpack she had taken out of the cruiser's trunk to the sleeping bag.

April slept off and on, until she heard a noise that she thought was Dan coming for her. But she knew Dan was dead. "I have to get these monsters out of my head," she said to herself as she focused on the moment as she had been trained. She closed her eyes and slept for a glorious five hours. When April awoke it was daylight. The birds were busy. "And so should I be," she said.

She got up and dressed. She was just wearing a shirt and underwear as she went outside to relieve herself. She had her bearings now. She realized the road was about two hundred yards above her. She had been walking in an abandoned meadow that had been overgrown with trees and shrubs.

April looked around in the far distance and she saw a barn. The snow was deep, and she felt there was time to get to it. For now she wanted to rest. She reached into the pocket of the backpack and pulled out a can of beans. She got more snow to melt for water to boil and added rice. That meal was the first meal April had out of captivity.

April sat there in her heavy shirt, underwear, and boots. She was not sure what day it was or how long she had been gone. For now she was grateful and happy for the little life she had.

As she sat there a small raccoon entered the cave, looked at her, and scurried to the far side sitting in the back in the dark. April said nothing. She only watched. Soon the little critter came closer and closer. It was hungry, and April offered him some rice. The hungry raccoon used his paws to scoop the rice from the rock where April had placed it. When finished, it looked at her for more.

"All gone," April said looking at it. Surprise! It was a young female. The raccoon seemed much more friendly than she should have been. April wondered if there was someone living nearby who had tamed her.

April was in no hurry to leave her safe spot. Here she could eat, sleep, do what she wanted without fear.

From what April remembered she had been taken in November, about the 11th, she was not sure what the date was. On the fourth day, April decided it was time to move out and continue on. She packed up and crossed the meadow working her way through the deep snow to the barn.

On her way there, she heard animals begging. A cow was mooing, a horse whinnying, and a dog and cat making their needs known. They all talked not in greeting but in great need. April pulled the latch and opened the door. None of them had water or food. She took a pitchfork nearby and gave the horse and cow some hay. She looked for dog and or cat food, but it was gone. They had torn apart the bag looking for more. "Hold on. I can help you," she said to them.

April stepped out for a minute and saw a hen house with chickens. She walked to the coop, and they did not have water or food either. It was a free for all filling the feeder. April gathered eggs and took them with her. Outside of the barn she built another small fire. She took her pan and cooked the eggs offering them to her new companions.

The cow had a calf. Their pen was full of manure as was the horse's. No one had been here for quite some time.

April walked out of the barn to a one-side-open shed. There she saw a tractor with an attached front end loader. She knew how to operate it, since they had one at home. April climbed up and started the engine. It was slow but started. She let it sit to warm up, got off, and checked the oil and gas. They were full.

April pushed the throttle forward and the tractor began to move out slowly. She knew they were not the best on ice, so she had to clear out the snow as she went forward. This uncovered dirt on which to drive the tractor. It was like being home, moving gravel, only this was snow.

April cleared snow from the shed to the barn. She went behind the barn and opened the twelve foot gate. Then she cleaned out the area so the animals could go outside. When that was done, she closed the gate and cleaned the driveway all the way to the road. Then she parked the tractor by backing it in the shed.

April found a shovel and cleared the walkways to the house and its porch. She knocked on the door, but no one answered. "Maybe they left before the storm so they would not be stranded," she thought. She left the shovel on the porch and tried the door. It was not locked.

April felt a bit guilty, but she entered the room and removed her boots. It was an older country house. Quiet as ever, the faucet dripped, and the clock on the mantle chimed at the stroke of 11:00 a.m.

April looked in the refrigerator. It was full of food, cheese, lunch meat, and there was a cooked chicken. She pulled the chicken out. "Ewww," it did not smell so good. She put it on the counter to give to the cat. The milk was spoiled but the rest seemed good.

April took off her outer clothing and looked around. From what she could determine there was an older woman living here. There were no recent pictures of a family. Old ones from the

1900s to 1950s. She did not want to be nosey, but she wanted to know who lived here to thank them someday.

There was a neatly folded shawl lying on the rocking chair in the kitchen. There was an open fireplace hearth that was stone cold. There was wood on the porch, but she declined to build a fire since this was not her home. April opened the door to go upstairs, but it was evident that no one had gone up those stairs for years. Cobwebs lined and crisscrossed the stairway, so she closed the door.

April looked around the corner and to the left of the kitchen was a bedroom. It was very neat and tidy with no rugs on the floor and a nice coverlet quilt on the bed. There was a door to the right that went into the living room, then back to the kitchen. So who ever lived here lived on one floor, which meant the owner was either someone older or with limited physical conditions.

There was mail on the table. April picked up one letter and noted the name and address. Now she knew for sure she was in Wisconsin. The postmark told her that, but the date was December 22. Could that be right?

April looked around for a television and there was an older floor model in the living room. She turned it on, and at first the screen was full of snow, then the black and white screen appeared. She almost jumped when the volume warmed up, it was extremely loud. She had to turn the sound way down.

There was a game show on, so she changed the channel. This television only received four channels. April let it on, hoping for news. As she made herself a sandwich, she waited and waited. Then she realized there would be no news for quite a while since the clock on the wall said 1:00 in the afternoon.

Next she went into the kitchen and there she found an older brown radio. She clicked the knob to the right, and it turned on. As the radio warmed up the orange glow appeared. The station that the radio was turned to was clear, so she left it there. From time to time news was announced, also some commercials. Then the station's announcer identified the station's call letters, the time, and the date. She could not believe it. She stood there shocked, in disbelief. It was January 23rd. "How could that be? I could not have been missing for three months," she said out loud.

Again April looked around the room. There was a telephone. It was an older type and seemed like it could have been from the beginning of time. It had a receiver connected to a coiled wire and had a face dial. She picked up the handle of the receiver, but there was no dial tone. Either the lines were down from the storm, or the phone was shut off. "Oh well, that's that," she said to herself.

Then she went into the bathroom which was next to the kitchen and ran water in the tub. At least the hot water was hot.

She went to the mirror and medicine chest. She could not believe that it was her looking back.

April reached up and touched her eyebrow area. It was swollen and very sore. Carefully, lightly she touched the arch bone and realized it was broken. She did not know if it was a line fracture, or how far the crack went. Now she remembered why her headache was so bothersome.

She had not had a shower in months. She stripped and stepped into the tub with the shower running glorious warm water. She scrubbed with the soap that was on hand and the water turned brown. It was so wonderful to feel clean. She carefully, slowly touched all over her body to discover what areas were injured. There were sore spots on her back, her buttocks, her thighs, and her right foot was all black and blue.

Next she washed her hair. It had grown out somewhat since being shaved by her abductors and was now like a bob cut. She took extra caution not to get anything near her right eye.

After she washed, she wrapped herself in a clean towel. She doubted anyone would understand how wonderful it was to take a shower and dry off with a clean towel. Such a simple thing and it meant the world to her.

She hung the towel on the wooden dowel rack in the bathroom to dry since it already had other articles of clothing on it.

April dressed and headed back outside taking the semi-spoiled chicken with her for the cat. Then she opened the back doors to the animal pens so they could go out. Next, she got the tractor again and cleaned out the animal pens. All together she took out eight scoops of manure and put them on an existing pile by the back of the barn.

Then she gave the cow and horse more hay and water, fed the dog with dog food she found on the back porch, and went back into the house. She left the lights out for fear someone would investigate. April found food in cans and made herself a good meal for dinner.

She sat on the living room chair and fell asleep. She did not wake up until she heard a loud crashing noise. It was the snow plow on the main road.

April had found a woman's wrist watch lying on the table near the television earlier in the day. It had a back light and when she pressed the button the light revealed it was 10:00 p.m. She hoped whomever the watch belonged to would not mind her taking it. She would replace it and pay for what she used in the house. April yawned and stretched a little, making sure not to re-injure her ribs. Then she leaned forward for a prayer. She was tired but would not go to sleep without a prayer to her Father in Heaven. She owed him everything.

April went to the bedroom, laid down on the daybed, and was out like a light. She did not wake up until dawn the next morning. When she awoke, she slid to the floor to have a long thankful conversation with the Lord. She did, and had he not provided an angel to show her what she was missing, she might have given up. She also told Father how grateful she was. She had no idea, until now, that there is nothing like freedom. "You gave that to me. Well, you give it to everyone really. We all have the ability to choose, but we have to choose wisely."

April did not want to dwell on the past. What had happened? Happened! Her only concern was that she killed a civilian. It didn't matter how wicked he was. She did it.

April was dressed and went to check on the animals. The dog and cat were sitting on the porch waiting for her. "You crazy buggers. It's wet out here and cold. Why are you not in the barn where it is warm?"

The cat meowed at her, pawing the air, wanting to be picked up.

And then April saw the female raccoon. It was scrambling through the footsteps she left in the meadow and was now headed to the house. "Ah ha! So you knew where to go when there was no food there, eh?" April petted the raccoon who was chattering at her. Then the raccoon jumped on April's back which took her by surprise, and the cat was already in her arms.

She looked at the beagle dog and said, "I have no room for you, Doodle," and they walked to the barn.

The horse was outside waiting for hay and the calf was suckling at its mama. April pitched hay and found some grain in a barrel for the mama cow. She gave the beagle its dog food and the raccoon jumped off to join the dog. That raccoon was not particular about what there was to eat, so long as she could fill her tummy.

It was then that April felt compelled to write a note in the event she had to leave soon. She did not want there to be any misunderstanding about why she stayed there and that she would reimburse the owner for anything she used. After all, she did not want to be turned over to the authorities and be rough handled. She just wanted to go home. She no longer trusted anyone!

April found a feed bag to write on and she told her parents what she had done. She was sorry about what she had done, even though they were evil, they were humans. She did take the life of Dan, but it was Dan who shot Dale.

April told them a little about her injuries but reassured them she would be fine. She filled the entire side of the feed bag. When she was done with her writing, she hung it on a nail high enough on the wall to be noticed and safe as not to blow away in the wind.

She noticed smoke coming out of the chimney of the house and thought she should go and check on it. April went in the house and discovered the door to the basement was bolted and locked with a turn lock. She wondered why. When she went to turn on the light, it did not turn on. So she closed the door, got one of her candles, and lit it. As she opened the door, she learned why the door had been locked and bolted. Up on a shelf, was a huge boa constrictor snake. It hissed at her which almost made her fall down the steps. She ducked out of instinct then continued down the steps to the basement.

The furnace used oil, so she checked the gauge. The tank was half full. She knew she would be long gone before it needed service.

She inched her way back up the stairs keeping as far to the right side of the wall to avoid that boa. She closed the door, bolted and locked it, placed the rug in front, and got a chair to put under the door knob. April did not like snakes, not at all. If she did see one, she left it alone. If it came towards her aggressively or even defensively, she killed it. Snakes were to be left alone, but she did not like them.

"Well that was interesting. I wonder where he came from, especially living with an *old gal*," she said. But she never went down those steps again. She left a note on the table to forewarn others about the snake. She would not feed it. Surely there were mice in the basement.

April stayed at the farmhouse for five days. She ate well, worked out in the snow, showered, and took care of her body. The bruises were yellow now and even her ribs were not as sore. However, her wrist looked awful. It had turned in the outer direction. She could use her hand but not turn that wrist with ease. She was concerned it would stay like that.

Her eye worried her the most. Her eye socket was broken on the top at her eyebrow. She could feel the split and what concerned her was that she did not know how far that split went.

Her headaches were not as frequent or as powerful and for that she was very thankful.

Too many days of resting were not good. April was not sure how far she would have to go. She did her laundry, packed some food, and when she was ready to go on day five, as usual there were her companions waiting for her. "Nope you have to stay," she said. April put the three of them in a small shed that held gardening tools to keep them from following her.

I Am Going Home

APRIL HIKED OUT OF THE DRIVEWAY. HER PLOWING JOB WAS pretty good. There had not been any new snow and the drifting was minimal. The lane was not closed at all. Out on the road she was able to pick up her pace. April was a good three miles from the farmhouse when she heard barking. She turned slightly and behind her came the beagle, followed by the cat and the raccoon. April's heart sank. "I can't take you with me," but the beagle did not hear her.

The dog was all over her, rubbing her, and licking her. The cat meowed loudly, and the raccoon chattered.

"Oh well, it seems I have no say in this one. You all stay with me you hear? Don't wander off into danger or make me chase you," she said.

With that the raccoon jumped on top of the backpack as did the cat, and away they went. April was glad the cat and raccoon were young and small. She would look funny to anyone passing by with such curious creatures as passengers. And she was so right. A pickup truck drove by, the tires had chains clanking slowly. He waved to April expecting her to be someone he knew. He drove very slow but kept going. Of course if he saw her face. Her eye, in particular, was enough to scare anyone off.

April knew she could not stay on this back road forever. Walking with all the clothes and backpack was making her feel hot, even in the cold weather. The only thing cold on her was her nose.

There were no cars for a long, long time. Then a snow plow came along, and he stopped. "If you are going my way, I can give you a lift," he said.

April climbed up, the raccoon crawled into her coat, but the cat stayed on her back pack and she hoisted the beagle.

"You don't need to sit out there," the plow man said.

"Oh, it's okay," April said. "My companions don't like it inside a cab."

"Okay then, hold on."

With that he stepped up the speed putting his blade down every now and then. The snow folded around them on the side like wings. It was an exhilarating experience. The plow went all around on back roads and within minutes they pulled up to a "T" in the road.

"I am not sure how long you want to ride with me. If you get off here, straight ahead is our town in about ten miles. Go left and it is winding all around on the back roads. Go right and you head to the state game lands, but I would not want anyone to go that way."

Promptings from the Holy Ghost

APRIL HOPPED OFF THE PLOW WAIVING THANKS. WHEN HE WAS out of sight, she knelt down right there in the snow and prayed. April wanted to know which path to take. She knew everything happened for a reason. If she walked ten miles straight she would be home in days. If she walked left she would be lost and to the right really lost. But his will was hers. As April prayed she felt strongly she was to go right.

April was confused, and asked again and repeatedly she had the same impression. She was to go to the right.

April stood up looking at her companions wondering how she would take care of them or provide for them. So she asked them, "It's going to be a rough trip. I am not sure how long it will take, and I don't want you to get hurt, starve, or die. That said, I would rather you go to a safe place." The little raccoon pulled April's hair. "Hey, now don't be mean," April said.

The beagle sat wagging her tail like a broom sweeper in the snow and the cat pawed April's face. "I know this might be hard, so if you want to go with me, let me know," she said. The beagle barked, the cat hit April on her head twice, and the raccoon chattered at her as if lecturing.

With a sigh and a prayer in her heart April began trudging through the snowy road on her right. The snow was deep, easily shin to thigh high in spots.

Back home FBI agent Danny walked up the steps to the Di Angelo home. He saw Miranda in the kitchen. She walked to the door opening it for Danny. "Want something to drink or eat?" she weakly asked.

"No I drove through town and did not see Gordon. Is he here?" he asked.

"He is. He will be in soon. He is doing my job, taking care of the ponies," she said. Then she sat down abruptly at the kitchen table and began to cry. "I can't take much more of this you know. I try to be strong for him and the boy, but this is killing me. I never ever thought she would disappear out of our lives," Miranda said.

"I understand Mrs. Di Angelo, but there are thousands of young women and children abducted every year. Some right out of their homes or yards on the way to school. In your daughter's case we now know it was by a rogue police officer with a shady past. His companion is his brother-in-law who has Down Syndrome, a usually quiet soul, but a follower."

Just then Gordon came into the kitchen, greeting agent Danny. "Hello. Any news?" Gordon asked.

"Yes. There is a huge lead that I wanted to discuss with you," he said. Gordon sat down. "We have learned your daughter was taken to a remote cabin that had been reserved eight months ago for hunting. The snow plow spotted a police cruiser sideways with its door open in the snow-filled driveway. He felt something was wrong and called the state police."

"When they found the car, the state police knew right away this was the reported stolen police car. They waded through the deep snow and found a man dead on the steps. He had been impaled, and inside the cabin was another dead from a single gunshot wound to his head."

"We believe your daughter killed one of them, but the story is not complete. It may not be until she is found. She may be on the run still afraid she is in trouble with the law," he told them.

He continued, "Further down the road, one fellow from town had brought his mother to his house to avoid the storm. They left in sort of a hurry. The storm came fast and yet when he went back five days later, someone had plowed open the lane and all around the buildings. They cleaned a large area for the horse and cow to go out. They fed all of the animals and left a note on a feed bag in the barn and one on the table. Here is the note on the bag in the barn," he showed that to Gordon on his cell phone.

Both of April's parents began to cry in relief and gratitude. She was alive. "We have a helicopter heading out that way if you would like to come along. I sure would like your input," he told Gordon.

"I would like to go. Will you come along Momma?" He asked his wife.

With big tears falling down her face Miranda said, "Yes. I will go. I want to see where my daughter was and pay her debts."

"There is one thing," Danny continued. "There was another plow driver that picked up a person. He could not say if it was a man or a woman. It was just a thin person who had a raccoon and a cat in a backpack accompanied by a beagle dog. And those are the same animals that are missing from the farm house. That is where it is believed your April had stayed."

Gordon's eyes smiled. That was his daughter all right. All animals loved her. April had a kind heart, and all animals knew it.

They took the flight out at 1:00 p.m. They were at the farmhouse by 4:00 p.m. There Miranda greeted the lively old woman who lived there who insisted they not pay her. The older woman was glad to have been of some help. Miranda walked into the barn with Gordon and looked around. This is where her daughter went for safety, for refuge. She looked around and the pens were clean as if April left her signature. Miranda looked at Gordon. "She is so old fashioned, animals come first, and she turns to a barn for safety."

"I don't know when our girl last had a shower or a decent meal," and she cried.

Gordon hugged his wife with one arm around her. "Now, Honey. You know April as well as I do. She is not interested in that. I think she helped here. Let's stay positive and wait. We can do that. It's been almost six months, but our girl is coming home."

Just then cars pulled into the lane to pick up the Di Angelos and the detectives for the ride into town for the night. It was too late to return. It was time for a meal and a decent room to stay in.

Miranda went reluctantly. She knew her daughter was still out there, somewhere. She had no meal, it was freezing cold, and she did not have a bed.

As they all sat in the dining room, an officer approached their table and asked to speak to agent Danny.

"Excuse me please," Danny said as he began to get up from the table.

"No, no. Don't do that," Gordon said as he stood up. "We are all here for the same purpose. Please share your information with all of us," and Gordon sat back down.

The officer looked at agent Danny and he nodded his head and sat down.

The officer told them that a snow plow driver told them he had taken a person with a raccoon and cat in a backpack, holding onto a beagle to the last intersection to town. On his pass back around he noticed that person had walked up the incline to the overpass."

Danny was shocked.

"What does this mean?" Gordon asked gripping his napkin.

"It means your daughter has decided to cross over a major mountain range in the wintertime." Mentally he said to himself, "Others have tried this, but no one has ever come out."

April hoofed up the incline until it leveled off. Her legs were getting stronger, and she felt good. Her eye was not good yet and she did not depend on it. Her wrist was sore, but she was able to use both hands to grab onto trees to steady herself and keep on track. At the top of the hill April looked far below. They had come a long way. She looked around and in the distance she saw what looked like a cabin, so she struck out heading toward it.

By now April began to call the beagle Happy, as she was the happiest little dog. She bounded after April jumping from her foot step to foot step always looking at April as if to say, "What's next?"

April knew she had to find shelter for her companions, so they kept going. That cabin was much further than April expected.

The Cabin

THEY DID NOT REACH THE CABIN UNTIL AFTER NIGHTFALL. APRIL turned the doorknob, and it broke off in her hand. Then April shoved her shoulder against the door. On the third try, the door flew open.

Inside was a small table and two chairs, one had three legs that leaned against the wall. In the center of the room was a pot belly stove that looked rusty, but April hoped it would work. There was wood inside, dry and ready to burn. April cut some of the wood to make kindling and used some newspaper she found from 1942 which she cut into strips to help start a fire. Slowly the fire lit, and April was able to cast light in the small cabin. She realized there were louvers inside the stove with tampers on the backside. Her Grandfather Manny had a pot belly stove just like this and often she had helped him make a fire or tend it adding wood. With a fire started, April put down the backpack and her companions crawled out to chat with her. The beagle faithfully stood steadfast at her side waiting to be asked to do something.

April stood up and found a small lantern that had some oil in the bottom, and she lit the dirty wick. The wick sputtered and lit slowly. It shone light all through the small cabin giving April a way to see what they could have for dinner. She had a can of tuna which she divided between the cat and the raccoon. She had a can of hash that she shared with the beagle along with a piece of bread toasted by the pot belly stove. The companions took their time eating.

April put her hand on her new companion's back and Happy wagged her tail, sweeping the floor. April got up and pulled out the sleeping bag shaking it out to lie down on.

She then loaded the little stove with three good size pieces of wood and set the draft down so the wood would last until morning. There was an old bucket she found that had no holes. She wiped the dirt out and filled the bucket with snow, so they would have water in the morning.

April lay down and Happy lay beside her, while the cat preferred to sit on her head with the raccoon between her legs curled in a ball. April smiled and thought that it was so true. The greatest power on this earth was love. April realized she had forgotten to pray, but she knew she could not get up. So she prayed right where she was. She felt God would understand. These little critters were his too, and she knew that God knew what they were doing. She felt that with her first turn to the right, or she would not be here.

They slept. They all slept. April did not hear snoring from Happy, and never needed to push the cat off of her head. At one point April moved her legs and the raccoon growled at her. She did not move again. Not to accommodate the raccoon, April was exhausted. This was as free as she could be with companions that wanted to be with her. Not one was aggressive. Well, maybe one was, but that raccoon depended on her. They all did. And it was nice, really nice.

April woke around 4:00 a.m., slid the cat off with little protest, and carefully got up not to disturb the raccoon. She slid those two together for warmth and checked the stove. There were hot embers inside glowing, so April put on a jacket and boots to bring in more wood. To the side of the cabin there had to be at least seventy or more pieces of wood, but most of them were too big to use, and were also frozen together.

April struggled to bring in eleven large pieces of wood that would need to be split. She was unsure if she could do it with her wrist so sore. She did not want to aggravate it, but they had to keep warm. One by one the wood split – the wood gave, or so it seemed to her. Within a half hour the chopped wood was stacked in the small cabin, waiting to be used.

For breakfast they had canned meat and some fruit, which the raccoon loved. After breakfast she went out closing the door behind her, much to the chagrin of her companions. Happy howled to be let out but April kept going.

She set some snares in hopes of catching dinner for tonight. April set six stringers and walked around the top and bottom of the cabin to about one hundred yards. On her way back, one stringer had been taken and in another she found a rabbit. In the last stringer was a pheasant. Normally she would never kill these animals, but for survival's sake she did. She roasted them both on a spit on the old stove. They were delicious, along with the potato she had brought along.

The second night April prayed on her knees and thanked God for his bountiful protection over them all. She was uncertain of where her journey would take her, but she told God she trusted him. As always, she promised she would obey and follow. She slept in total peace, all of them did. Happy was bound to her side while the cat and raccoon finally made peace and slept beside the stove, side by side.

The next morning April felt a sense of urgency inside her to get going. She carefully put out the last of the stove's embers. She packed up, was dressed, and ready to go while her companions ate their meat scraps for warmth on their upcoming journey.

Out the door, backpack on with two travelers tucked safely inside. She then hoisted up Happy and carried her for the haul of the day. How April wished she had skis. She remembered gliding along. How fast and efficient they were. Here she was struggling with each step through the deep snow.

She pushed on, through thick trees and forests, using the river below as a guide. As she walked she saw the mountains looming in front of her and prayed silently she would not have to go up or over them. On she walked into the night, there was no cabin.

April broke tree limbs to make a shelter from the wind. She made it sturdy and thick on three sides with the entry out of the wind. April bent down to enter their new accommodations. She pulled off the backpack and set it down. Then she spread the sleeping bag on pine boughs that she had laid for a bed. The two in the backpack scampered onto the sleeping bag to own it and sat up begging for food.

April had some Ramen noodles which she gave to them after warmed on her small cooking can. Then the four of them feasted on the noodles with dry eggs. The eggs almost made her vomit, but her companions loved them. So she held her nose and gobbled them down. April knew they were protein. She only wished they had tasted more like eggs. She tried to sleep, but it seemed the forest was talking, whispering to her. As her companions slept, she watched over them, and felt like something was watching them. Her sleep was on and off that entire night

The moon was ablaze, and April could have sworn she heard footsteps. But in the morning there were no foot marks around the boughs or around their encampment. She gathered the sleeping bag and shook it out, then rolled it back up, and tied it to the backpack. She pulled out some nuts for the raccoon, and some tuna for the cat and Happy. But she had an energy bar that would have to do for a while. She felt need to keep going.

The four continued on up the incline on a trail of sorts. The trail was well marked but very narrow. There were rocks that had fallen from above. If she was not careful, the rocks could trip her.

The snow was not as deep here on this trail. Some of the snow had been blocked by trees, and the mountainside gave good protection from blowing drifts. Along they went and it was soon evident why April felt so urgent to move out. The snow began to fall. It came down fast, and the four sought protection in a small offset ravine in the wall of the mountain.

April put the animals toward the wall to protect them from the heavy falling snow. As she watched the snow falling, April heard a small still voice telling her to move quickly! April reached for her companions putting the two quickly inside her backpack and grabbing Happy as she ran out of that ravine. April was no more than twenty feet away when the ravine crumbled even more, falling down the side of the mountain.

She kept going, keeping a steady pace. That brought to mind when she was skiing in the Olympic race. She controlled her breathing to save energy and kept moving on. The mountain was beautiful. From a distance no one could see the colors in the rocks or the trees growing out of them.

The ground was far, far away now and there was no turning back. April knew if she slipped or fell, that would be it for her. She was sure to be careful. Happy wanted to run so much that April let her but often called her close to her. Happy was too innocent and didn't know the perils.

About halfway through the day, with the sun overhead, she kept on. The snow was still falling. April accidentally discovered a trail that was partially secluded. It was alongside the mountain. Without thinking, she took that path and soon found herself in a cave like area, but it was not enclosed. The trail kept on to the outside that was visible. It was more like a hallway, but offered shelter from the snow and wind.

"We will stay here until tomorrow. Maybe the snow will stop by then," she said as she set her backpack down.

Food was beginning to be a problem. April knew she had to ration what she had left. So she sat looking in the backpack for a while and decided they could go for five days. The food should last if they were careful, and if April could find food, maybe a bit longer. She was not sure how long it would take to get to where she was supposed to go. "No sense worrying about what I don't know," she said. Training from her Frogman days, "Just have faith, trust in God and you will be all right," she concluded.

April pulled out more nuts for the raccoon and some dried fruit, "Two pieces, that's it for today," she told her. She then gave the cat and the dog the last of the hash leaving her with one third can and two crackers. Everyone seemed to know it was ration time. None of the travelers complained or begged for more. Instead they crawled into April's lap and cuddled with her.

Happy was content to have her head inside April's arm while wagging her tail. The cat and raccoon made a small competition to see who would rub April the most. "You are good companions. For some reason you are to be with me. I pray all of you are safe and make it out with me." April was worried about them. If not worried, concerned, as she felt responsible for them. They chose to be with her, and that meant a lot to April.

They settled in for the night. The weather was a bit damp and chilly, so April propped her backpack against the rock wall and leaned against it. She was most comfortable in a sitting position.

She opened the sleeping bag as a blanket so all four of them would have warmth. April was surprised at how warm she was with the three furry little bodies on her and next to her under that bag. All the while Happy had to have her head sticking out of the blanket to breathe.

It was quiet. You could hear the wind howling, but not much entered the hallway. April heard the snow falling. It was hitting the trees and the branches were making a scratching sound. She also heard predators hunting. She was not sure what it was, but something was out there.

April's sleeping pattern was much like when she was in the military, first off and then on. Fully awake and then out fast, like a light when she felt safe. At one point it sounded as if someone were knocking, April sat still. She knew she heard it because Happy had heard it with her ears alert. April patted the dogs head, "It's okay, Happy. It's okay. Be still and go to sleep," she told the dog.

The next morning April looked out at the other side of the hallway. There was no possible way they would be able to get through the snow or up the steep embankment to the trail again. They would have to go back.

After a light breakfast, but before making up her mind, April felt it important to find out. She knelt down and began to pray. "Father in Heaven, I ask thee to hear my prayer in the name of Jesus Christ. Father I am here. You know the trail before me is blocked. I may have to go back, Father. I am unsure and want to know what I should do. So I leave this in your hands, Father. Please know that I am willing and trust you in all ways. Lead me, guide me, and help me find your way is my humble prayer, in the name of Jesus Christ, Amen."

God's Grace Is Sufficient

APRIL STOOD UP, AND AGAIN HEARD THAT FAMILIAR KNOCKING AS she did during the night. She ventured to the opposite side of the hallway looking out and she held her breath. There on the top of the hallway over her were majestic mountain goats. They were all white with shaggy coats and brown horns. April was not afraid as one pawed the ground as if calling her out, not in a warning.

April cautiously stood looking out of the hallway, while Happy was ready to bark. She hushed her and reached up with one hand to climb as a pair of goat horns were within her grasp. She reached out and held tight. The horns pulled her hand to the top. There in front of them were the grandest, proudest mountain goats she had ever seen. The two that pulled her up bumped her leg and turned as if telling her to follow them. April hoisted the backpack and began to walk carefully. Then twenty or more mountain goats joined her with some at her side to keep her away from the edge. The goats littered the mountain sides and were barely visible from the new snow. April was in awe of their beauty. She thought they were regal looking. This is when one huge goat turned its head to acknowledge April's thoughts. "That's crazy," April said to herself. But then she knew, this was the answer to her prayer.

She also knew anything was possible. If indeed they could read her thoughts, she felt she could read theirs, "if" she weeded out all other thoughts. And she was right. They did talk, not in conversation, but in what needed to be known.

They continued on, at times some beside her and then some in single file, with warning of the narrow ledge they were on. They warned her of falling snow and of dangers on the mountain as needed. April trusted them with her life. Happy seemed to understand and the other two companions were indifferent. They slept most of the time, and when not sleeping poked their heads to get fresh air and see where April was.

They trudged on and on, over small hills, through ravines, and across huge logs while giving April assistance.

They were her caretakers, a mercy from God. "There has to be a mighty need for all this help," and April was glad for it. She had a direction in his Kingdom. For whatever purpose this was, it was for Him. They all continued along like this for two days, when she and her companions had to stop for sustenance and rest. The goats nibbled on brush that stuck up through the snow, they seemed to understand.

On the second day of traveling with her fearless, strong companions, they came to a place where there was an outcropping of rock that showed down into the bottom of the mountain. The goats looked down and then at April.

"You're kidding" she instinctively said, and then she wanted to take back those words. So she knelt down right there and began to pray. The wind took her words and often her breath. But she prayed and prayed for God's help and his guidance.

At one point when the wind blew, almost knocking her over, April was surprised to see some of the goats kneeling. All of them had their eyes closed. April ended her prayer and thanked her mountain companions. She bowed her head in thanks. They left her there. One by one they left to go on to the mountain side.

The Great Mountain

"WELL IT'S JUST US NOW," SHE SAID TO HER COMPANIONS AS SHE slowly descended the mountainside. Down, down to the depth of the mountain floor. This floor was covered with very deep, deep snow, easily waist high on April. She did her best to keep walking, while carrying a wiggling Happy. The other two had their heads out of the backpack sniffing the air, as if watching for something, maybe danger? On and on April went, deeper and deeper through this dark abyss. The trees had overhanging moss and vines which April tried to avoid. If only she could see better. Between the dark and the fog, visibility was very difficult.

April walked with her feet on the ground sliding through the deep snow. When her foot hit a rock, she moved to her right and there was another rock that almost tripped her. Happy began to bark and howl like crazy. April did all she could to quiet the dog and then Happy pulled out of April's arms and was on the ground barking and growling as if there was a monster. The two companions in her backpack began to hiss. April did not know what was happening when all around her the rocks began to rise. They stood with mist rising from their shaggy bodies and they seemed to have red eyes.

April froze! She knew not to try to run, because she could not. But Happy, silly Happy was still barking her head off. "Happy, stop!" April said commanding the dog. Happy did stop and she backed up sitting at April's feet.

There looming over them was a huge bison with straggly wool hanging from his sides. He was full of snow and there was steam all around him and snorting from his nostrils. "What do you want here?" he demanded. Not in words, but in their mental thoughts.

April stood her ground. She raised her right hand to a square and said, "I come in the name of Jesus Christ. I mean not to disturb you. We come in peace. I am to pass through," she said.

The old bison snorted looking at her. He was joined by thirty or more all deciding what to do. April did not move. Happy quivered at her feet and the two on her back seemed to want to hide. The bison seemed to be talking to each other and slowly began to turn to walk out. April felt a small calf at her side that sniffed her and sneezed. But the little one stayed beside her just like the mountain sheep had, guiding her.

The walking was much easier with the bison making mowed paths for her. Happy trotted alongside between April and the bison with not a care in the world.

The bison were leading her deep into the mountainside. For one fleeting moment April wondered how in the world she would ever get out of here or find her way back. That is when an older female bison behind her bumped her hard. They could indeed read her mind and April made sure she did not make that mistake again.

She found it easier to compliment them on their strength and knowledge of the forest and mountain. She also prayed prayers of thanks. It seemed like a long walk.

They walked until deep into the night. April looked above her and could see the bright stars in the clear night sky. Still they pushed on, until they came to an open clearing. They approached this place very slowly, carefully. The lead bison stopped and waited, they all waited, for what April was unsure.

And then they came like lithe spirits. They floated out of the mountainsides, out of the ground, and out of the trees. They seemed to be dressed in Native American apparel with loin cloths and face paint. They danced a spiritual dance as they edged closer. They were not of human flesh. They were indeed spirits. April could see through them. They were what most people would call ghosts. April was taught to be respectful and to call them spirits.

Why they were still here and had not moved on was curious to April. She was about to find out as the lead bison moved. Some bison moved left, and some moved right leaving April in full view of the spirit warriors.

They looked at her as if she was not real. They scrutinized her. Some walked or floated around her while others stood in front of her.

"I am not afraid," April said, and she heard laughter. Again April said, "I am not afraid of you. I am Chippewa or Ojibwa. I too am Native American. I come in peace having been sent by my Father in Heaven. I am not afraid," she said.

It was eerily quiet, as they mulled around whispering to one another. They looked at April not trusting her. That is when April heard the still small voice again, telling her to holler in her native tongue a welcome arrival she had learned from her birth mother and aunt.

April stood and yelled the welcome arrival as loud as she could. "Bi-zhaazhig, anamikaage, biindigen." It was said so loud it bounced off the walls of the mountain echoing. The mountain goats high above heard her voice as it floated up into the night sky.

The spirits stopped suddenly and came to her. They eyed her closely. They looked deep into April's eyes. They touched the scars on her eye, her side and wrist. They walked around her touching her hair and shrank back as if afraid. "She has come," one said and then another, and they bowed to April. April was confused and waited patiently to know what was going on.

"We have waited here for over three hundred years waiting to be found. We were warriors of long ago when this land was ours, and when the rivers teamed with all sorts of native fish. The great mountain sheep numbered in the thousands, and when the Bison roamed in great herds freely. We were to protect our lands when we were outnumbered and ran to safety here in our great mountain. We could not come out and as we stayed we began to become sick with something we had never seen or experienced before. We were trapped. One by one we died. Some of us went together three or four at a time. And still we waited here to protect our great lands."

"Until recently when an angel appeared to us to tell us someone was coming for us, to find us. To have us be accounted for, so we could go home. This is you," the spirit said.

April was astounded. They did not want to be lost and for whatever reason she was to be the instrument in God's hands, to record who these spirits were, their tribe, and their war.

April felt humbled and so she knelt right there in the deep snowy grove. As she knelt, so did all of the spirits and the bison. April bowed her head and prayed. Her tears flowed at this extremely spiritual happening in her life. She asked a blessing to be able to retain who they all were, for posterity sake. For them to be recognized and be able to cross over and go home. "Also

Father, help me find a way to protect their lands." Finally, when she ended the prayer many of the spirits attitudes had changed, it was now a feeling of love, trust, and hope.

And it happened one by one, each warrior came forward and said their name and handed April a small thin shale rock with their name carefully etched in the shale. Some were elaborately scrawled into the rock.

There were women warriors too. Some of them touched April's cheek out of gratitude. One touched April's stomach and smiled, "You are a warrior within," she said.

As they each handed April the rock with their name, they gravitated to others and slowly, ever so slowly, they disappeared. They all left this prison. They all left to go home, finally!

After the last spirit had disappeared and all of the rocks placed carefully inside of April's backpack, she stood up ready to leave. The bison led the way. They took April sixty miles through the mountain, down to feeding areas, and onto flat plateaus. They all went through forests, across rivers, and over ranges. They moved steadily and slowly, pausing to eat. April was able to snag a few rabbits and quail. Sadly she could not cook them, and as difficult as it was, she learned to eat the meat raw. After the fourth day it became easier, she did not vomit anymore. By now she did not mind at all, when a person is starving they will eat most anything.

They traveled on for another ten or so days, April had lost track. They all went slowly and steadily, until they came to a ravine that ran between the mountains. April walked forward to the eldest of the bison. "This is your stop," he mentally said. "This will take you back to the world. Go and be safe. Great thanks to you for releasing the spirits who mourned to go home. No more will we hear their cries," and they all nodded their great big heads. April stood there and she slowly reached out to hug the eldest bison, who did not move.

"It is I who thank you. I never would have made it out without you. I wish to do more to help you, and I promise to do all that I can to protect you. I have put my trust in you, now I ask you, if you can, to put your trust in me."

This was an amazing moment in her life, one that April would never forget. She bowed her head and thanked her big friends, who then turned to leave her.

"I will not forget you. I will keep my promise to you," she said. The trail down was steep, and snow littered. There were wild flowers blooming, crocuses, wild lilies, and others. Their colors were red, orange, yellow and white. All so beautiful and April realized it must be spring. She wondered, "Was I really on the mountain for three months? No way. That is not possible!" She also wondered what the lithe Native American warrior meant when she said April had a warrior too. She was not one, unless they thought she was one due to her heritage.

April pushed these thoughts out of her head to pay attention to her companions. "Do we stay out here one more night or do you want to try and go down the ravine? It will be dark soon, with walking down rough, but on the other hand there is precious little for all of us to eat."

Happy barked her happy bark and the other two were pawing the air, begging. There were three nuts left, some dried berries April had found. Eight crackers and a few bones she had saved. She had leaves full of sweet sap and that was it. April gave Happy the crackers, the raccoon the nuts and sap, the cat got the last of the bones and April got nothing. She did not want anything, not really. All she wanted now was to fulfill her promise and get these stones to a safe place. Take a shower and eat something cooked warm and go home.

That night they lay out on the sleeping bag, all together watching the lights far below. Cars were coming and going in their important lives. None of them had a clue about the beauty that was here on the mountain. April was so grateful she had the chance to experience all that she had.

She ruffled Happys neck and ears, and she sighed. She did not sleep. April was excited. She wanted to find someone who would help get these Native American signatures and the truth known out and into the world. This really had happened, and their voices would not be silenced any more.

As her companions melted into her to sleep, April lay there watching the lights. Then she looked skyward and thought those lights were the most beautiful of all. April remembered sitting out on the porch with her parents and at her birth mother's home on the porch with a view of the night sky, and it always brought peace to her. It was feeling a connection to something greater. As ominous as the night sky was, it made her feel content and secure.

April realized she had slept until the break of the morning dawn. She saw her companions still asleep as she stood to stretch and greet the day. She saw deer at the water's edge. They snorted when they saw her.

April relieved herself and wanted to get a start on this day, the day we find home. She wondered what to do with her faithful companions. Up and at 'em. The little group was on their way down the ravine, slowly, carefully. The ground was defrosting and muddy. You could slip very easily.

It took April quite a while to get all the way down to the roadside. There was an electric sign across the road at a bank which said it was 9:10 a.m.

April walked alongside the road carrying Happy, with the other two safely in the backpack. As she walked, she noticed this was a sizable town with many stores. There were places to eat, gas stations and there was a sign for a Chamber of Commerce. April crossed the road to enter there.

The woman gave April quite a look, asking curtly, "May I help you?"

April asked if there was a library nearby and the woman pointed to her left.

"Down that way about three hundred yards. I believe," she said.

April thanked her and walked out, scooped up Happy and to the library they went.

As she walked through the library parking lot there was a woman who was juggling papers and April caught several that had blown away. The woman thanked her and was not snooty like the Chamber of Commerce lady.

APRIL ASKED HER, "DO YOU DEAL WITH ARTIFACTS? YOU KNOW, from history? Learning about something that happened that no one else knows about?" That stopped the woman in her tracks.

"Why, yes. Yes, we do," she said. "May I help you?"

April liked her immediately and asked if there was a room they could go into for privacy.

"Oh, yes. There is. Follow me, Dear," the woman replied.

They went into the bottom of the building and April pulled off her backpack. "You two wait here," she said pulling out her two companions.

"Oh, my. Do they live in that?" the woman asked.

"I know I look homeless, but I have just been on an amazing journey. We", April waved to the three little creatures, "We just came out of the other side of the mountain. We came across these." April pulled out the many single-name stones from the Native Americans. "All I know is these warriors want to correct a story," and April told her.

She told her she found these stones (not how it really happened). They indicated they died from disease in the depths of the mountain having been pursued by soldiers.

The woman took one stone in particular holding it preciously. "Do you know who this is?" she asked April excitedly.

"No, I do not," April replied.

"This is the signature of the mighty chief Powhatan. This must be his son. See the II there as in second one? There was a story that the Native Americans attacked the soldiers' small outpost, and the soldiers hunted them down and killed them all. Now I know that story is not true. If you found these signatures on rocks, they were not dead after all."

April told her that the Native Americans had run to their mountain and had been holed up for safety and to protect their mountain. There were traces of bones, indication of necrosis, or disease.

"Oh, I would love to go there and have them preserved."

"You probably can," April said, and she drew a map to the place where the remaining bones would be found. "Before I give this map to you, I want you to promise to help me to preserve that mountain - no more bison hunts, no more hunting whatsoever. This mountain should not be disturbed. Let it return to the splendor it was long ago.

"I totally agree with you. Several years ago a man came out insisting that there was copper ore in that mountain. No one wanted him to dig, but they allowed him to take samples to prove if his theory was right.

Well, he was wrong! If there was copper there, he got his samples in the wrong places. All of us in town were thrilled the mountain would stay as it was.

"That's not good enough. We need to preserve that mountain so no one in the future comes along wanting to split her open, killing habitat, and all kind of wild animals there," April told her.

The woman looked at April and agreed. I just came down from the mountain and wanted to put these signatures in the right hands safely. Promise me that they will be recognized, and this lie corrected."

"Yes, I assure you. I have a lot of pull with the community and local elected officials. If you contact me in the future we will push forward on preservation," she said handing April her card.

"I can't thank you enough," April said.

"Oh, no. I thank you for these ancient signature stones and the knowledge that they existed and lived and thrived on the mountain. They did not initiate that war. It came to them, and they hid for refuge on the mountain. You bet I will see this through. It will make the papers," she said smiling.

April thanked her and called her two companions to go back in the empty backpack. "Wait a minute," the woman said. "Here, please take this and get a shower and a meal. You all look like you need it," April did not want to take the money, but the woman insisted. "It is the least I can do for what you did for our community," she said.

April walked up the street and saw a riding stable. She walked down that lane and no one was in the stable. She carefully set down the backpack. From the back compartment she pulled out Dan's small brown suitcase. April climbed high up a ladder and put that brown suitcase under some tin that was covered in dust. "Should be safe here," she said climbing back down.

She looked at her eager companions and thought they are going to hate me. She put the cat and the raccoon inside a large wire pet cage and said, "I'll be right back," she scrawled a note on the page of paper lying on the desk. April then walked out up onto the road and headed for a gas station that had a bathroom.

April waited at the counter and asked the clerk for the bathroom key. The young girl looked curiously at her, and April realized she was not only dirty but hideous to look at. She took the key, went inside, and stripped down while Happy watched her.

April washed herself over and over in that bathroom sink. It was glorious. She washed every inch of her body including her hair and she even scrubbed Happy who seemed not to mind.

Back in California, Gordon Di Angelo was at work flipping his calendar. They were last in Wisconsin that was in January. Now it was March. He did not want to believe his daughter was lost on that mountain. Three months in the dead of winter? How could she survive that? He shook his head and brushed the negative thoughts away. Just then Judge Du Val came in.

"How are you, Buddy? Want to go to lunch with me?" he asked his lifelong friend.

"No, I am not hungry," Gordon told him. "But I sure would like to talk to someone. I think I am going crazy," he told his friend.

They left the sheriff's office and walked they talked as they went and ended up in the park. At the park, mothers were swinging their children on swings and Gordon had to look away. "I am afraid to say it, but I think she is gone," he said starting to cry.

His friend hugged him, "Don't give up hope. April is one tenacious woman You know that."

Gordon nodded his head in agreement. "Yes. Yes, I do, but expert climbers attempted to climb that mountain and never came back out. What kind of chance does she have?"

"You are sounding a lot like your agent Danny," Du Val said. "Maybe she didn't go up over the mountain. Maybe she went beside it or through it. I don't know, but I am betting doughnuts, she is going to come back. I don't know when or how, but it's something I feel inside," he told Gordon.

"I wish I felt something inside. I am all torn up over this. Miranda's health is failing. You know the doctor had to put her on oxygen now. She had too many panic attacks. They felt that would help. And that darn foreigner keeps calling our home wanted to challenge Native Son in a race saying his horse should go down in history. Native Son did not deserve any titles. We just can't deal with much more," he said.

"You let me deal with the foreigner. You take time with Miranda. Can you get away for a while?" Du Val asked.

"No, she will not go. Miranda hovers near the telephone hoping to hear from her," Gordon said. "I would give my life to have her back," as he looked at his friend.

"I know you would, but I don't believe that is going to be necessary. I have no inside information, but when I pray I feel she is still out there somewhere," Du Val told his friend.

"I am about spent," Gordon said. "I try to put my day in and hope nothing goes wrong. I go home, and we eat some days. I have to coax Miranda to eat. Her parents were here, and they said Miranda should be put somewhere to get well. I can't do that to her. It would kill her. I love my wife with all my heart and my daughter." He paused to catch his breath. "I just want her back. I don't care if she was hurt or injured. I just want her back to help heal her."

Du Val had no words. This was like going through hell for Gordon. He felt his friend's pain. "I know you don't want visitors.

My wife used to go to see her, and Miranda would not answer the door."

"Yes, I know," Gordon said. "Listen. I appreciate everything you do, really. Don't give up on me. I am trying, however feeble, and I know the Lord knows. It's just a hard thing," he said.

The two sat there for a while and then they walked to Flo's Diner. Flo knew right away there was something wrong. Gordon was always so jovial and telling jokes. Today he was stone white and quiet. Flo prayed that the news was not bad. "What'll it be, boys?" she asked them.

"Just the lunch special for us, Flo," Du Val answered her.

"Okay, coming right up," she replied in a chipper tone. Gordon looked at his friend, "You know this is right where it all started. Right here where we are sitting. I was called and found the cutest little girl who was so afraid and thought I should cuff her," and he chuckled a bit.

Du Val spoke, "She is crafty and resilient. She made it on her own when she was six years old. She is a grown woman now with military training. That's where she used her cunning and the power of the Holy Ghost. Don't you think she still does? You know she got away from the two thugs. You know that! She could have walked straight into town, but for some reason that we don't know yet, she didn't. You know I believe she went up that mountain NOT out of fear. At that point she was free. She went up for another reason."

Gordon knew his friend always had his best interest at heart. As much as he held on to hope for April to return, he began to have doubts. But now this made sense. Gordon looked at his friend and said, "You're right."

98

Today lunch tasted good. Today the day seemed better. Gordon went home after work and he and Miranda made dinner together. They talked like they used to. Gordon told his wife what Du Val had said. They prayed together in the evening and Miranda felt better.

"Maybe you could go with me tomorrow to the grocery store?" she asked her husband.

"Sure I'll go along," he replied.

That night at bedtime they were closer than they had been in a long time. "We have to be strong and stay close dear," and he kissed his wife. "She will be expecting that when she comes home."

Miranda said, "Oh I have prayed and prayed and . . ."

"We both have. It's spring, a promise of new things. Remember that, keep that in your heart, and be happy. You know that happiness is just a choice, don't you?" he told her.

Miranda nodded her head. It was all true. How blessed she was to have a kind husband, one who did not give up on her, and for the first time in a long time Miranda felt hope.

In the morning, Gordon went with his wife to the grocery store, and they met many neighbors and friends. Nora and Lena were in one isle of the store, and they hugged Miranda and Gordon. Yes, there was hope all around. They just could not see it with all of the sorrow they had felt.

The bodies of the two kidnappers were transported back to their homes in Georgia.

Dan's wife had received horrible threats, and she had to move away from her home. The truth was no one knew what really happened. The only one who knew everything was April.

Gordon and Du Val put a call into the mayor of that town who told them that Dan's wife moved because she was afraid they would have harassed her and the children so much that there may have been a tragic accident.

There was much controversy in the media. They thrived on it. Some felt April should be made to testify about what had happened. She might receive jail time for murdering the two men. What she had experienced did not justify taking the lives of the two men.

Gordon could not watch it. It just made him angry. He wondered what happened to common sense. Right from wrong was all messed up.

Agent Danny told him that none of that was going to happen. They were only talk shows and the news media. They had nothing to do with the law.

"I surely hope to meet your daughter. She is the most resilient person, and the most elusive person I have ever had to track. I just could not keep up with her," he said.

Gordon told him that is what she was like in real life with them at home.

Agent Danny shook his head and laughed.

After her "bath," April exited the bathroom leaving it cleaner then when she entered it. She returned the bathroom key to the clerk. "Hey, you from around here?" the girl asked.

"No, I am not. I got lost hiking in the mountain," April told her.

The girl was about seventeen and she surmised differently. One look at April and she knew April had been beaten and abused.

She knew because she watched her mother in that type of situation all her life growing up. "Hey, you hungry?" the girl asked. "Hey, I'm Amy by the way."

"Yes, I am, but I am so hungry for a warm meal," she replied.

"I can make you a hot turkey hoagie if you want, some fries too. No charge," Amy said.

April was so grateful she almost cried.

Amy touched her arm, "It's okay. I understand," and that was that.

April ate it like it was a delicacy. That was the best tasting sandwich she had ever had. Then she asked Amy a question. "Hey, would you be interested or know someone that could take care of a beagle, a cat, and a pet raccoon?"

"Oh, wow. I'd love to, but I have a small apartment. I have little room. Not that the land lord would care, but they would be inside all day, unless I put one on the porch."

April told her, "Look I know you might not believe me, but I know I will be back. If you could watch over them for a week or so and then either I will get them or someone will pick them up, and we will pay you too."

Amy knew better, she had seen hard cases. Heck, she was one once herself. She never wanted a dog again unless she had the room, the time, and the money. It was so heartbreaking to lose her dog. Surrendering Biloxi to a shelter and worrying if he would be adopted by some kind soul. But she had no choice. She needed a place to stay. No way would she go back to a home full of fighting, drunkenness, and arguing.

"Sure, I can help for a week or so," Amy told April and don't worry about paying. I can give them scraps from here. The raccoon interests me anyway."

April told her the cat needed cat food. The raccoon was happy with fruit and nuts. The dog needed dry dog food and April handed Amy the money that was given to her by the library woman. "Oh, hey forty bucks is too much," Amy said.

"Keep it," April told her. "They will come back to me soon," The girl was told where the cat and raccoon were.

Then Amy gave her address to April who tucked it in her pants pocket. Amy's apartment was behind where she worked and she often ran home if she needed something, and others covered for her so this would not be a problem.

"I appreciate this, and I will make sure you are taken care of," April told her.

Amy knew better, she would be lucky if someone came for the pets at all.

April looked at Happy, "I need you to be a good girl. You are going to stay with Amy. Do you understand that?" Happy just sat there panting with her tongue out. "Oh, Happy, you are such a good dog," April hugged her and handed her to Amy who was going to slip out to put Happy on her enclosed porch with water. Amy was back in eight minutes. April hugged her and reminded her of the other two, giving her a note as the owner and then she left.

The Truck Stop

APRIL SPOTTED A TRUCK STOP AND WAS HEADING IN THAT direction. It was about a mile down the road. It was a good walk. There were more than eighty trucks in the parking lot. Most were here to fuel up. Some drivers needed showers, or to sleep as this rest stop offered all amenities.

April got to the truck stop and looked around. She shied away from all men, but that did not stop many from whistling at her or calling to her. April pushed all that out of her head. She was not like that, so she kept looking. She realized this was very confusing, so she began to pray as she walked.

"Father in Heaven, you know I don't look afraid, but I am. You know that I don't trust men anymore. Well, not much of anyone for that matter. Help me, Father, I want to go home safely. I don't know where to go. I just want to go home. Father, I beg you to help me," and then April heard a dog barking. It was a beautiful black and white Bulldog. The dog pawed at the passenger side window with his tongue out smiling at her.

"Hello, fellow," she said, and the dog barked happily. He had no aggressiveness towards her. April waited, not sure where the owner of the dog was. Surely he would not stay here and let his dog out here, so she waited. Soon the dog was up against the window again barking and scratching on the window to get to April. Then she heard the door slam, and someone say, "Get down from there. Have you gone crazy. You know you're not supposed to do that." it was a man's voice.

April went around the front of the truck to talk to him. "Hello, Sir. May I talk to you please?" she asked him.

He ignored her.

"Hello, Sir," and she knocked on his window.

Then the man yelled at her and said, "Get back or my dog will attack you. He does not like strangers."

April laughed, and the man pulled the latch of the truck to jump out and chase her away. That's when his dog jumped out and ran to April licking her hands and barking at her to pet him. The man stood there in his tan khaki pants, checkered tan and yellow short sleeved shirt, and cowboy hat. He removed his hat slapping his side saying, "Damn." He could not believe his menacing dog liked anyone but him. The dog was drooling and jumping up and down.

"What's your name, Sweetheart," April bent over asking the dog.

The man answered, "His name is Mars, and I am Sam. Nice to meet you," as he held out his hand.

"Whatever prompted you to name him Mars," April asked him.

"Well, when he was a pup he did some crazy things, like out of this world. That's how he got his name," Sam told her.

"What kind of things," April asked.

"Have you ever seen a dog swing from a ceiling light fan or lay upside down on stairs, or how about picking up a can of something with his teeth and drinking it all down. I mean all of it. He still does that and for the life of me I can't understand why he likes you," Sam said.

"Well, thanks," April replied.

"Oh, don't get me wrong. Hey, I am not looking for a girl, for nothing. I am not going to settle down until I am thirty, so forget it," Sam said.

"Good," April replied. "I am not interested in any man either. What I am looking for is a ride. West, if you are going that way."

"I am not. I am heading east. I just came out of the west. I am heading to Philadelphia, PA." Sam said.

"Oh," April replied. She was confused why she should go east when home was west, but this is where the Holy Ghost prompted her to go. "Sam, I need a ride to go home. Can you understand that. I can't pay right now. I know my family will pay you when they get there, but for now, I just want to go home."

For some unknown reason Sam's heart told him to take her. He never took riders, not ever, but for some reason he felt this was okay. "Well, I am all tanked up and ready to roll, if you are," he said to her. "Come on, Mars, saddle up," Sam said to his dog.

Mars jumped up the three steps easily and scrambled into his seat in the middle. "He is my co-pilot all of the time. He keeps me awake and farts to make me laugh," Sam said.

April crawled up into the passenger seat and when buckled in Sam started his rig and they headed out. Sam put sunglasses on Mars and the dog stayed still, seemingly loving them. "See. Crazy I tell you," Sam said. "So where are you from?" Sam asked April.

"I am from the west, near California," she told him. April did not want to share information, not just yet. She did not know him that well. It would take time, and this was going to be a three to four day haul. "What are you hauling and where to?" April asked.

"I am hauling beef to the east. I work for a company called D Farms. Have you heard of them?" he asked her.

April smiled until she had tears, her heart was happy. She did not show that to Sam. God is so great. And as she sat there she heard clearly, "Be still and know that I am." They drove in silence for a while when Sam said to April, "If you're tired you can sleep in the back. It's not too bad."

April thanked him and said, "I am okay for now. I will keep you awake," and Mars licked her entire face. They spoke off and on about the traffic, roads, weather, and Mars when Sam asked April, "So tell me about yourself."

April stiffened and said, "Well, I am from California, have parents there, a dog and a horse," she said.

"Well, how did you get out here in Wisconsin?" Sam asked her.

"I was on a trip to find artifacts in the mountain and got lost," she told him.

"I don't mean to be rude, but you have one hell of a wallop above your eye. Were you hit by a falling rock or something?"

"Yes, yes, that's what it was," April said feeling relieved.

"So did you find what you were looking for?" Sam pressed her.

"Oh, yes. I did and more."

"Did you go by yourself. I mean you're not a little kid or nothing. Are you a paleontologist or something?"

April yawned, and said, "Do you mind if we put on the radio for a little bit?"

"Oh, no, that's fine. I usually have it on. Good noise, you know."

Sam clicked on the radio and tuned into a country station, "Do you like country music?" he asked her.

"Nope, I love it," she said laughing. The two of them began to sing every now and then and they would laugh at each other or make comments. April liked Sam he was a jovial soul, kind and decent.

"So, Sam, I am not one to talk about politics or religion, but I am on a limb here. Do you go to church?" she asked him.

"I do when I can, but I am on the road a lot. But when I go, I am a Mormon. Do you know about Mormons?" he asked her.

This was too funny, too much to be coincidence.

"So, tell me what Mormons are," she asked him.

"Well, we believe in a lot of things, like we have what's called Articles of Faith and we have a book called the Book of Mormon that supports the Bible one hundred percent. We never want to take away what someone believes. We just hope to add to it, to offer more truth. I know that Jesus was real, that he died and rose again, and I believe he lives now. I believe in prophets today as they were two thousand years ago. If God loved them they had prophets, do you think he loves us less now? It works for me, I was not raised Mormon, but I found it, and it has saved me in every way."

April egged him on, "What is the Book of Mormon?"

"It is a history of a people who lived in the Americas and what happened to them. They were led by a prophet, Lehi, and his two sons who gave him a terrible time. But the one, Nephi, was a Godly man, and it tells about their struggles," Sam said to her.

"Why would anyone care about that?" April asked.

"Well, it's important because we have those same problems and struggles today. I mean look at the world. It's messed up. What is wrong is praised, and what is right people are afraid to do."

"And that is in the book," April asked.

"Well, not exactly. I mean it is, but it does not come out that way. I am not a missionary or anything like that. I do read the book, but not as much as I should. I am always driving, but I do the best I can. I love the Sunday School classes when I can go, they bring out things that I think about, you know?"

April kept on, "What are those article things?"

"Phew! Well, there are thirteen of them and I am not so good at saying them in a row, but it is something like this: 1. We believe in God the Eternal Father and in his son Jesus Christ and the Holy Ghost. 2. We believe in, and as he struggled, April chimed in to help him to finish to number 13.

"You little stinker. You knew all along," Sam said smiling ear to ear. "So you must be a Mormon. No?" he asked her.

"I am," April said. "I love the teachings and standards. They are difficult for many, but easy for me and the icing on the cake is the Holy Ghost," she said.

"Boy, I'll say. I have gotten in a jam or two. You know, with weather and so on, and I pray. He whispers to me, you know, in that small still voice and when you listen it's not so small or quiet, and it works," Sam said excitedly. "I am not a perfect person. I make mistakes. I can't memorize scriptures either, but I am a convert," he said.

"We are all converts, even those born in the church. We all must gain knowledge to find our own testimony," April told him.

"But, hey, man. I am so glad you are a Mormon. You get me then," he said to April. "I mean I can be weird like no swearing, no smoking, no alcohol, and you'll get me," and April laughed at him.

"Oh, man, we have been on the road six hours. Does it seem like six hours?" Sam asked her.

"No, it doesn't," she replied.

"There is a good truck stop up ahead. I think we should stop and go, and then get something to eat. I have diabetes and don't like to go too long without eating," Sam told her.

"I do not have any money," April said. "But when my parents come you will be repaid, so just keep track of it all. Okay?"

Sam pretty much ignored her. So she did not have money, and a lot of the girls he dated didn't. But she was all right, decent and funny, and a Mormon with good standards. That's pretty cool he thought.

They ate like ravenous birds, and when they had finished, April made sure to ask the cashier for a copy of their check.

Back in the truck, they let Mars out for about ten minutes then back inside and off they went again. This was repeated for the next two days.

Sam said, "I need some sleep. I can easily sleep for 6 or 7 hours." Then he rolled back to the sleeper cab and was out like a light with Mars sitting between the sleeper and the cab.

April petted Mars lovingly. "You watch over him and take good care of him. I will be right here to get some shut eye," she said to him. The dog laid down right there between them, looking from front to back from time to time. Mars knew his job and he did it well. These two were his responsibility, and no one was going to enter this cab.

Sam awoke and April was gone. "What the heck," he thought to himself. He stretched sleepily and came up front to exit the truck and he saw April standing beside his truck. "Thought you left us," he said to April.

"No. I just needed to stretch a bit," she said.

"Yep. I should do that too before we head out. Here take this and get us some snacks and something to drink," and he handed April a twenty dollar bill.

April went into the small stand and bought two bottles of water, two apples, two pears, and a pound of cherries. She paid the bill which was eighteen dollars.

"That's highway robbery," she said as she came outside with double receipts.

Sam was glad for her choices, being diabetic you have to be careful. They headed out again. As Sam was shifting gears, he turned and said to her, "We should be in the east by tomorrow morning, Kiddo. What do you say about that?"

"I am relieved. But before we get there, Sam, I need to talk to you. Really talk to you," she said. April leaned back and dozed off for a while. Her headaches were not as bad as when she was out in the weather. It was nice to have some of the comforts of her life back: she had someone to talk to, food, and a ride in a vehicle. April slept for about an hour.

Sam could not help but look at her from time to time. This girl has been through something bad. Her wrist was swollen, and she flinched going up and down the truck steps. Something was bothering her. The worst injury seemed to be her eye, it was enlarged, and there was an open spot above the brow area that would ooze some kind of fluid from time to time that April would wipe away. Sam did not believe this happened to her while finding rocks. It looked as if they were defensive wounds. He suspected this because of his brother's experience being a police officer.

But Sam said nothing. He did not want to offend her. She was really a pleasant person.

He hoped she would find what she was looking for when they reached the east. He doubted he would be repaid and that didn't matter. She was just a nice Mormon girl who had fallen on hard luck. At least, so it seemed.

As they cruised down the road April asked Sam how he came to join the Mormon Church.

"I had a friend that was a Latter-Day Saint in high school. I used to go with him to the Young Men's program, but some of those guys did not like me. You see, my parents divorced when I was little, and we had it hard for a while. In High School I was not the kid they sat with at lunchtime or invited to their homes. But my friend did, and we had great times. Then one day I asked him why he was friendly, and some others were so standoffish. He told me it was just a choice of who to follow and how."

"I understood what he was saying, and I asked why these guys were never told about their actions. He told me their parents would never see their children's failings. They loved them so much that they just thought they were all good. He said some of the girls got pregnant and had babies, but had little consequence came to them. He was not sure if it was because of their affluence or if they were close friends with the Bishop. In time it catches up with them. No one is above the law of the Lord. You either choose being good and your life is good, or you choose not being good and in time you suffer the consequences.

April sat there and wanted to offer other scenarios like what had happened to her. She wanted to explain about personal revelation and finding yourself through God's grace. But that would have to wait for their big talk.

They were rolling through the last part of Ohio now. Sam commented on how flat this state was, "It sure is a nice place though. I have a cousin who lives in Ohio on a small farm. The land is fertile, and he always has nice crops.

April did not have the heart to tell him about the farms that D Farms had. There was still time before they reached the end of the line, so she just kept up the small talk with Sam.

Sam had been engaged once when he was twenty. They were very young, and she was very close to her parents. Sam was spending every weekend with her parents and not his own mother. When he told his girlfriend that he was concerned about it, she got angry. Soon that disagreement was smoothed over.

Then one evening her mother came to his mother's home asking when Sam intended to marry her daughter. She was rude to Sam's mother and when he got home she told him, "Sooner or later your girlfriend will demand you make a choice, either her family or yours."

Sam said, "I didn't believe it."

Then the girl came to Sam's mother's home and started egging him on to find a place so they could be together.

They looked together for a while but most homes she liked were in the four hundred thousand dollar range and Sam could not afford that. Next his girlfriend pushed Sam into asking his mother for financing, to use her home as collateral. Sam knew his mother's home was paid off and so he asked her. But as soon as he did, he realized he was wrong to ask her.

A few days passed and, while visiting his girlfriend, she said that if Sam did not find a home for them and make a choice that it was over.

Her mother was nearby at the time and added, "Sam, you have to make a choice, our family or yours. Your mother has nothing to offer, so why not just stay with us."

Sam knew right away his mother had been right.

As they sat there waiting for his reply, he said, "You can bring back my sweatshirts and I'll exchange them for your clothes at my house. Then we'll call it even. Okay?" and he walked away.

Sam never did get his sweatshirts, and he took her clothes to the Salvation Army.

"I got the better deal. I am not about to play house with a spoiled girl," Sam said. "Almost, but not close enough. I am not going to settle down unless I find a girl who could love me and my family, because that is what it is all about. I could not imagine having children and them only knowing one set of grandparents. That would not be fair to my mother who put a lot of her life on hold to raise me. I am not like that. Besides having two grandmothers who are different enriches a child's life. Don't you agree?" he asked April.

"Yes. I do," she replied.

When the truck crossed over the Pennsylvania line, Sam let his air horn sound. April smiled and she knew that soon she would have to have a one-on-one talk with Sam. That moment came when they were crossing into Harrisburg, PA.

Sam pulled into a nice truck stop so they could eat. "What's the matter? Aren't you hungry?" he asked her.

"No, not really. Well, it's not that, but I need to talk to you, and soon," April said.

Sam wondered what was wrong. It was not what she said, but how she said it. "Okay. Let's eat and then we will talk," he told her.

They chose the buffet so they could have whatever they wanted. It was a very nice place, and they had an assortment of salads, vegetables, fruit, and condiments. "Wow, we hit the jackpot," he said jokingly to April. The buffet allowed them to take as much as they wanted, the servings were unlimited, and Sam ate until he was stuffed.

April also ate until she was full. After he ate Sam was looking very sleepy, "Why don't we go to the truck so you can sleep for a while?" April suggested. "After you wake up, we can talk in the truck."

"Okay. Man, am I ever sleepy," Sam replied. Sam slept for six hours when Mars woke him up with sloppy kisses. "Okay, Mars. Back off," Sam ordered the dog.

April was waking up in the passenger seat. She stretched her arms to the ceiling and grunted. "Oops," she said smiling.

Sam crawled into the driver's seat and said, "Okay. I am dying to hear what you have to tell me. So shoot."

April looked at Sam for a long time and then he took her hand to nudge her. "Come on," he said.

"Sam, I am not who you think I am. I need you to understand what I say and then never repeat this. Okay?"

"What are you a bank robber? a mass murderer? It can't be that bad. Spit it out."

April looked at Sam and held his hand, "My name is April Di Angelo. I am from California, and I co-own all the D Farms."

Sam was taken aback and looked at her. "Oh, yeah, you are her. What is going on?" he asked.

"I was kidnapped back in November from my school by two rogue cops, who beat me and hurt me in many ways. I murdered one to get away. I have left notes for my parents and am not sure if they know anything. And."

"Hold on. I know about this," he said excitedly. "How in the heck did you find me at the truck stop?"

April looked at him, "The Holy Ghost, that's how."

"No kidding, no freaking kidding. That's amazing" Sam said. "Where were you all this time? I mean you are splattered all over the television, internet, and radio. Your parents have to know. They were always one step behind you, then you disappeared over that mountain, and everyone thought you were lost," Sam told her.

"I was not lost. I was led by the Spirit, and I was always safe. But that is why I wanted a ride to California, but the Spirit told me to go with you, east," she said.

"I know why," Sam said looking at her. "Because in Philadelphia, PA, they have the best neurosurgeons in the world, and I think that eye of yours needs attention," he told her.

P. Costa

"Sam, I have lived most of my life without fear, of anything and now I have changed. I am afraid to walk into a hospital," she said.

"You? You afraid. That can't be right. You need to find the strength within and know you can do it," he told her. "Would you want a blessing? I mean I am not real good at it yet, but I am willing," he told her.

"Yes," she said. "That might be what I need to take away this stupid insidious fear I have inside me."

There in the truck, Sam had April turn sideways and he gave her a beautiful blessing that told her to not be afraid. Fear was from Satan, and she had successfully avoided him all of her life. Now was no different. You need to put on armor of strength around her, to walk with pride and humility, to continue what she started out to do, and finish with it. Knowing God is at her side always.

April thanked him.

Sam shook like crazy as he started the engine, and they headed out for Philadelphia, PA.

On route Sam turned on his radio and tuned it to a news station. He poked April when updated news about April Di Angelo came on.

April listened as it said that the authorities feared April had been lost on the mountain and would resume their search for her when the ground thawed in the middle of spring. April looked at Sam's calendar. It was April 8th, and in five more days it would be her birthday. She would be twenty-one.

116

She thought about that for a moment and then realized she might just see her parents after this long, long time without them: her mom and dad, her birth mom, Lena, her grandparents, cousins, and the man she hoped was still waiting for her. All of them, and she began to cry tears of joy.

At the Philadelphia Hospital

THEY PULLED INTO THE PARKING LOT OF THE HUGE METROPOLIS OF the Philadelphia Hospital. Sam left his truck running and waiting for April to make up her mind. "You are here your majesty," he joked with her.

April smiled looking at him and said, "I feel so sick to my stomach. I think it is my nerves."

"Do you want me to go in with you?" he asked her.

"No. I will go on my own. I have always been alone and so this is okay. I want you to know how much I appreciate your help, and you will be rewarded, believe me. If you no longer want to drive a truck and do something else, it's yours. I promise you that.

With that Sam leaned forward and kissed April on her forehead.

April hugged Mars, opened the truck latch, and stepped down on solid ground, slamming the truck door behind her. She began to walk towards the entry door of the hospital. Next she looked around to see Sam in his truck and he used his hands as if to shoo her, "Go on." Then she turned to go inside. The hospital doors opened automatically, and she walked in.

There was a reception area a woman was sitting at a front desk and asked April for her insurance card and I. D.

"I don't have any," April said.

"How old are you?" the woman asked.

"Twenty," April answered.

"Well, Dear, you must have your social security card, driver's license, or something on you," the woman said exasperated.

"No, Ma'am. I do not have any of those things, not with me," April answered.

"Then go and get them," the woman was now angry.

April apologized and left walking down the hallway. There she saw a sign that said "Chaplin," so she knocked on the door and heard, "Come in."

The Chaplin's office was brightly colored with all sorts of positive notes. There was a cross on the desk and behind it sat a plump woman dressed in a robe. She had gentleness in her eyes, and an aura of patience. "Come in. Come in," the Chaplin said. "How may I help you, Dear?" the woman asked. "Please sit down. Won't you?"

April said, "Ma'am. Thank you for inviting me in. I am sorely in need of someone who will listen to me. I need you to hear me out. Please be kind and listen until I am finished. I have nothing to prove what I say but myself. I am April Di Angelo who disappeared on November 9th from my college in Pittsburgh. I have been missing for over six months. I have been beaten, punched, kicked, stomped, and thrown. My eye socket is broken, my ribs are fractured, as is my wrist. I have had constant headaches and nausea for three months. I do not have any Identification, insurance cards, or driver's license like the front desk requires."

"Because of my ordeal, I cannot remember my own home telephone number, my Dad's, who is Sheriff, or his cell phone. This is the only one I know, and April wrote it down. I am not sure who this is, or why I retained this number. I am desperately in need of medical attention. Will you please help me. I beg of you."

The Chaplin got up and closed the door. She picked up her telephone and called security.

"Ma'am, I am telling you the truth," April said feeling very frightened.

"I know you are, Dear. I believe you. I am calling security to keep you safe, escort you to your room, and for anything you need," and she patted April's hand.

The alert sounded and in minutes security along with the hospital CEO was in that little room. The CEO apologized to April. He assured her that she would get the best of care, and he personally would call her family. He looked at security and the Chaplin and said, "We must keep this absolutely quiet. She does not need a circus. She needs rest."

Security helped April to stand and escorted her to a private room. There nurses scrambled to make a bed ready for April. They brought in an over-the-bed table, a cup with water, blankets, and explained how to use the bell and adjust her bed rails. Soon someone was there to take blood. Curiously, not one asked her for personal information, not even her name. It was all hush hush, top secret.

"May I please get washed or have a shower? Please?" April asked, and her wish was granted.

The CEO walked rapidly to his office and called the number April had written down in the Chaplin's office. His fingers shook as he pressed the numbers.

"Hello, May I help you?" the voice answered.

"Hello, this is Dwayne Hogan. I am the CEO of the Philadelphia Hospital. I was given this number by an April Di Angelo who recently walked into our hospital. Do you know her?"

Mr. Stevens almost jumped out of his chair. "Oh my God, oh my goodness. You found her! Glory be. She is found! Oh my, forgive me but this is such a welcomed shock. Yes. Yes, of course, I know her. April D and I worked together hand in hand developing the company called D Farms. April went missing in November. She was abducted, and," Mr. Stevens began to weep.

"Mr. Stevens, Hello?" Dwayne Hogan continued, "Sir, are you all right?"

"I am here. I am very sorry, but this is such wonderful news. Do her parents know yet?" he asked still shaken.

"No, Sir. I do not have their numbers. Would you be so kind as to give them to me?"

"I can, and I can also call them for you. They are personal friends of ours," he told the CEO.

"I had better call them. Since it is Saturday I am sure both her parents will be home."

"Thank you, Sir. Thank you again for calling me and healing us," Mr. Stevens said.

The CEO said, "Mr. Stevens before you go, I am asking you to keep this quiet. We do not want a zoo outside of our hospital. Understood, Sir?"

"Yes. Yes, I do, and I will keep this quiet. Thank you." and he was gone.

Miranda was in the kitchen mindlessly making dinner with the small TV on. Gordon had bought it for her last Christmas, and it proved quite handy for local news that would be on after the commercials played. Suddenly there was a news flash of breaking news: "April Di Angelo has been found!" the announcer said.

Miranda looked, froze, and then she screamed, "Gordon, Gordon, come here." At that same moment their telephone began to ring.

Gordon answered the telephone, "Hold on a minute please," he said. As he came down the stairs he heard his wife screaming for him to come into the kitchen, "Miranda please just wait, just a second," he yelled. "Hello? Yes, this is Gordon Di Angelo. You what? What did you just say?"

And Gordon began to weep. As he walked into the kitchen the breaking news was already on the television. "Yes, I see it on our television. Yes, it is. I see it. Thank you for calling. I do hope they keep her safe. Please I beg of you," and he hung up.

There on the television the news reporter was standing on the steps of the Philadelphia Hospital.

"Oh, dear God, she does not need this," Gordon said. He hugged his wife and they clung to each other crying. Remi was at a friend's house to go bowling and they were thankful, as this was huge news. It took several minutes for the Di Angelo's to compose themselves. Gordon called the folks where Remi was visiting, and asked if they might keep him over the weekend. Something had come up. They were more than happy. Remi was so well behaved and so good with their children.

Then Gordon made another telephone call while his wife called her parents in Mexico. Judge Du Val answered the telephone, "Do you have your television on?" Gordon asked him.

"No, what channel?"

"Six," Gordon said.

After ten seconds Gordon was weeping because he heard his friend openly crying. "This is so great. I told you she would make it."

There were several more calls made all over America, each one having the same reaction.

Miranda called Nora and Lena and they screamed and wept with Miranda. When they hung up they went to the living room to offer a prayer of thanks to God.

Miranda also called April's grandparents in Pennsylvania. It was Grandma who took the call. She seemed shocked, then hung up, and tapped Grandpa on his shoulder, "Come we go to church?" she said weeping.

Grandpa stood up and said, "What's wrong now?"

"Nothing is wrong. Everything is all right. She has been found."

Grandpa stood and openly wept. He was the first to be dressed and in the car. At church they lit candles and prayed prayers of thanks to God.

It was as if the earth had shaken off a terrible chill and was now content. Many, if not millions, prayed a prayer of thanks. This woman meant so very much to so many people. She had touched the lives of millions of people in her short lifetime, and not just in America. Those that knew her kept hope in their hearts. They would not give up, faith and prayers saved her and them.

Back in the hospital April was going through a battery of tests. It was determined her occipital orbit was indeed broken.

The most serious was the blood that had collected in her brain. That would have to be drained. There were other problems with the brain scan, but the doctors did not want to say anything until her parents arrived. Her wrist was fractured and five of her ribs on the left side were broken, several in two places. The makeshift brace did help keep them in place allowing her to walk with less pain, but there was no doubt about it, she had pain with every step. April lay in bed wishing her parents were here. She needed them more than ever.

Occasionally she would wipe the tears from her eyes as they rolled down her face and onto her pillow. Here she was lying on a hospital bed getting the care she needed, away from the danger, and she was crying. She never wanted to have gone through any of it. She would not have wished this on anyone. She knew it was a waste to wonder "why," because that was irreverent. It happened, and there was no going back. It was now up to her to deal with what was in front of her. She had the tools she needed at any time.

April knew she needed surgery to her head to stop the awful headaches. She knew her eye orbit would need attention and her wrist would need to be re-broken and cast. Her ribs were in a firm binding. After that, she felt in time she would be on her way again.

On Sunday afternoon there was a light knock on her hospital door and in walked her parents and Judge Du Val. She wanted to sit up, but Miranda was at her side and told her to lie still. They were here for her, kissing her face and cheeks. April reached for her hand and never let it go.

Her Dad came to her with tears in his eyes. He bent over her bed embracing his daughter and looking deeply into her eyes, "I am so glad you are back, Sweetie." He kissed her forehead and stepped back.

Then Judge Du Val came to her holding on to her other hand. "I never gave up on you, Kid. This is a remarkable day, and he kissed the back of her hand.

Her birth mother Nora and her sister Lena were there holding tissues, dapping their eyes. They both took April's other hand kissing it and holding it to their cheeks.

Soon police officers were in the room. April was fearful. Her Dad stood between her and the officers.

Agent Danny told her she had nothing to fear. They asked April what had happened. She was prepared to tell them, but first she asked her parents to leave the room. Miranda's eyes opened wide, and her Father was in disbelief.

"The only people that should be here are you, the Judge, my birth mother, and my aunt. I do not want my parents mulling over what I went through every time they look at me. I know these two women suffered at the hands of a man and they will understand. And you," as she looked at the Judge, "have heard awful stories. And, if my parents ask, you will be able to tell them a lesser version," April said to the Judge.

She recounted everything from the day her friend Sue and she rode the bicycles up to the day she stabbed Dan in his eye pegging him to the wall.

Agent Danny understood what had happened. He was just sorry he could not get 'in front of her' to stop the mayhem.

"I need to talk to you later, if you would stop in," April said.

Agent Danny agreed.

As her parents sat out in the hallway, they were confused and hurt that they were excluded. "We are her parents," Miranda said. "Why? Why is she doing this?"

Gordon was unhappy until he thought about some of the cases he had handled and how difficult it was for the parents to accept some details.

In one case a father rushed the court house and shot the perpetrator to death. Gordon began to explain to his wife the reasons he suspected April excused them. Miranda mulled it over and she reasoned it would be easier if she did not know. What had happened would not be there each time she looked at her daughter. Then she realized the wisdom of her daughter and how kind she was. Their memories would be only happy ones. She was humbled that her daughter was protecting them.

When the parents left the room, the two doctors wanted to discuss something important with April and those present. They said they urgently wanted her to have surgery, but there was a problem that prevented them. They looked at each other shuffling their feet and then said, "You are pregnant, four months. This is the reason we hesitated. It is likely any drug we use to put her to sleep will have adverse effects on the fetus. Then the doctor said, "Unless you want us to terminate the pregnancy when we are in surgery."

April was stunned. Ultimately this was her decision. The doctors walked out of the room allowing her parents to enter the room to discuss this together. They talked, the six of them, about the pros and cons. Only her birth mother sat with April holding her hand.

Then Gordon noticed his daughter wanting to speak but struggling. "April, honey, this is your decision, will you tell us what your thoughts are?"

"Mom, Dad, this is not this baby's fault. It had no part of the evil that happened to me. Granted this is from one of them, but babies are gifts from God. When I crossed that mountain one of the spirits touched my belly and said this is "warrior," so I believe we need to give this baby a chance."

Everyone was stunned but her birth mother.

They were all emotionally and physically exhausted. They had boarded the Twin Cessna the night before, slept little in the hospital lobby, and came up to her when they were allowed. They decided to head to the cafeteria and then get a hotel room near the hospital. Nora told them she would catch up with them soon.

As the two of them sat together Nora commented, "Your room is nice, and the nurses are really nice too," she said.

April shook Nora's hand from side to side and said, "You did not stay here to see the room," she said.

"No I didn't. I wanted to tell you something. When I was pregnant with you, your father took me to the doctor and wanted me to get a shot to get rid of the baby. He was fearful you would inherit tuberculosis like I was treated for. The doctor refused. He told your father that if he was man enough to make the baby, then he needed to be a man and support me to have it. I never prayed harder in my lifetime."

"You were born so beautiful and free from any disease. I had you and I have never been sorry, not ever. I can't help but believe God blessed you not to have tuberculosis. Some of the babies during my recovery did have the disease and their lives were terminated prior to full term. For years you were tested, and it was always negative. It was a miracle I tell you. So if you could be a miracle, why can't this little one be a miracle? I am with you on this one. If there are any health or mental problems, we will help you and all you need to do is ask. Don't feel ashamed or afraid to, that is what family is for, you know?"

"April, if anyone could help a child, you can. You know so many people and have so many contacts. You also have the finances to support them. But let me be clear, I believe in prayer. I know that through prayer anything is possible, and I do mean anything." Her birth mother leaned forward, hugged and kissed April, then left to join the others.

April sat there pondering about a baby. What would it be, a boy or girl? How would it grow up? What talents? What the baby might look like? We will make the best of it, and it will be the best. This child will have so many people in its life that it surely will be happy and well rounded. April lay there thinking when there was a knock on her door.

"We need you to sign the consent for surgery," the nurse said.

April scribbled down her name and they left.

Back in the doctor's lounge her doctors spoke with other doctors, and the CEO was also included. This was a huge surgery. One that they did not want April to go through and then have to repeat it over and over. There were many consults and other doctors were also called in. Through discussions and plans they felt confident all of April's problems could be resolved. The first was the blood in her cranium that was putting pressure on her brain causing headaches and blurred vision, then her occipital bone would be taken care of. Later her wrist would be attended to, and they felt Laser would correct her eyes. They shook hands and prepared to have April's surgery first thing in the morning. April's family was notified that evening.

That evening April was not allowed food. It was necessary for her to be fasting so she would not vomit and choke while she was being anesthetized.

Her family had contacted a Bishop who came with three other men to give April a blessing. This Bishop had extremely kind eyes, which were bright blue. He had silver and white hair. He shook April's hand and clasped his left on top. "I am honored to come give you this blessing, my dear. You have done so much good to the good people here in Philadelphia. You are much loved and respected," he said. The two others with him also shook her hand and thanked her.

The blessing was humbling. It told April to not have fear, that God was well aware of her needs. He had been with her throughout her journey and promised to be with her. He told her to heal, have faith, and give a little time and space. She would never again remember what she had endured. She was told that the warrior within her would be protected if she was faithful in raising him in God's way. If this little one would be steadfast in his teaching and training of the Gospel, he would be led to his calling in this life. He also told her on the day she knelt at the altar of the temple to be sealed to him for all time and eternity, she would have a clear witness to the truth of their union.

When April heard these words, tears fell freely. She knew keeping this baby was the right thing to do and she would one day find happiness. The blessing had much more to say, but April was so overcome she only retained part of the ending.

It was a good thing Lena had the presence of mind to write down everything the blessing had said. She would gave a legibly re-written copy to April the next morning before surgery.

Later that evening another visitor stopped by. It was Agent Danny. "Are you up for visitors?" he asked.

"Sure, come in," April said. "I have something important to tell you." Agent Danny pulled up a chair beside April's bed. "Do you remember I told you about the dog, cat, and raccoon?" she asked.

"Well, yes, sort of," he answered.

"If you contact Mr. Stevens at, and she gave him the number, he may have rescued the animals. The beagle goes to Larry, the cat and raccoon will go to Lena and Nora. I left them in a barn, the girl taking care of them will know where. And if you climb up to the top rafter in the barn there will be a metal cover over a briefcase. What you find inside that briefcase, you will find extremely valuable," she told him.

As Danny wrote down the information he tapped her leg and asked, "How about when you are better you go with me to this spot. I can take you on a trip and we can have dinner and get to know each other better. I feel as if I know you already, but if you are willing, I would love to," he said.

April just looked at him and told him the truth. "I am not pushing you off. You must understand how grateful I am that you were so thoughtful and considerate of my parents. I was in a relationship before I was abducted, and I am hopeful that we are still the same. I encourage you not to wait, go and find the brown briefcase. It holds the key to many others who were lost."

Danny stood up and thanked her. He was putting his chair back in its place, and was about to leave, when he turned and said, "Keep in touch. Okay?"

"I will, either my Dad or myself. You take care and good luck," she said.

That morning the CEO Dwayne Hogan parked his car and noticed people gathering in the hospital parking lot. He was curious as often they sponsored drives, but he did not recall having any this month. He went into his office and as he looked out of his window his mouth dropped open. He could see for miles. And what he saw were people walking, some pushing strollers, some pulling wagons, some driving and letting people off. It was starting. He tried to keep this quiet, but someone leaked information. April Di Angelo was splattered all over the television this morning. They showed the hospital and the front doors. This is what he feared might happen.

April was ready for surgery. She was in her green cap and tie gown on the gurney, Miranda, Gordon and her birth mom were with her. April asked about Larry.

"Oh, Honey. He knows. He took this real bad. It is planting season. He is so tied up on the farm and he wanted you to know nothing has changed. Those were his words to us. Wasn't it?" As Miranda looked at her husband, Gordon nodded.

April said nothing she had to focus on relaxing and getting well again. She took a deep breath and laid waiting. Soon she was being wheeled down the hallway to the operating room. The nurse beside her gurney was very kind. She tapped April shoulder and told her not to worry she was in good hands. Pushing through the operating room door, and inside were eight nurses who were all briefed on who this patient was, and not to say anything to her of her past.

She was a patient with no special treatment. April asked for that. The anesthesiologist was a man named Nat, short for Nathan. They all chatted and soon the anesthesiologist spoke to April "Can you tell me your name?" he asked her.

She did as she watched him draw up a drug from a bottle and inject it into her IV.

"Soon you will become sleepy. Can you count from 10 backwards?" he asked her.

April got to seven and could not remember anything anymore. She had nightmares during surgery. The staff had some difficulty keeping her still, which was critical. They quickly strapped her head, arms and legs more securely. She could no longer move anything but her fingers. And when she began to pull up on them, they taped those fingers down firmly. "Boy, oh boy, is she ever a fighter," one nurse said.

The surgeons came in and began. They cut a slit on her head exposing the bone on her occipital and found that bone was crushed. For that injury they knew they would need an insert. They continued along to the cortex and found the leakage and began working there. What should have been a two- to three-hour surgery, ended up to be six hours. They were all exhausted. The doctors came out of the OR and met the family. They said, "It all went well, longer than expected, but we found a sizable open crack in her skull. We sealed that leaking artery and extracted the blood. Her blood pressure has stabilized so we know the leak has stopped. We put an insert into the orbital area, and it should look much like she was before. We will know more when the stitches come out. Other than that, she will need her wrist set by an orthopedic doctor."

"Then we will let her ribs heal. She may, however, have some psychological problems. She literally fought us on the table while under heavy sedation. There are monsters in her past, and we suggest therapy." And then they left.

The small group sat down to digest what they were told. They were exhausted and grateful April was all right. She was on her way to the recovery room. April was not up out of recovery yet, so they decided to go to the hospital food court and have something to eat. On their way, they noticed the hospital entry was lined with many, if not hundreds of people. Some had flowers, and some had signs. It was amazing to see this outpouring of love towards their daughter April.

The three women walked towards the people outside, but stood just behind the doors. The people meant no harm. They were here to wish April well. The women were touched deeply by the gathering. They hurried to tell the men when they found them with the hospital CEO Dwayne Hogan who was expressing his frustration at the gathering crowds. He was not so sure this small party would be safe.

Miranda said, "They are not threatening. They are here with well wishes and prayers for April."

"Mrs. Di Angelo, may I remind you there are kooks in this world. It would only take one person to turn this into a terrible tragedy."

"You are right," she said. "But I believe when April is well enough she can address them from the balcony. If that is all right with you. They will disburse quietly when she asks them to."

Dwayne Hogan was a little taken aback. He was not used to patients or their relatives suggesting things to benefit his hospital. "Well, yes. I mean of course she can if she is able. These things can get out of hand you know."

That night was a difficult one for April. She was out of recovery and in her room with headaches, awful headaches. She tried to sit up, but they were worse than ever. The room was spinning, and she had dry heaves. She rang for the nurses who came quickly. They monitored her and put a call into the doctor for her. Luckily he was still on the floor and said he would be up to see April soon. The nurses soothed April by rubbing her back very slowly, and applying cool wash cloths to her forehead and cheeks, as her face was flushed red.

Soon the doctor came into the room. He used a small flashlight to look into April's eyes. He moved it from side to side. He then lifted her hand to look at her nails and then took his stethoscope to listen to her heart and lungs. As April leaned forward her body began lurching with dry heaves again. "Put her on D5, Lactated ringers, at 24, make sure she has a dose of dry antiemetics to combat those heaves. Use it rectally if she can tolerate it. Also draw up one lavender tube and check her blood sugar and have the lab call me with the results, stat."

135

"April, do you think you could tolerate some clear broth? I don't think you had much to eat in quite a while," he said as he looked at her thin body.

"If you want me to, Sir. I mean I really did eat a lot in the last four days. If I could just get rid of these headaches," she said as the nurses rolled April on her side.

"April, you need to understand that you had head surgery, and it is imperative that you rest. Do not rub your eye or brow, it has an implant. The headaches should subside soon and when they do, I want you to have some broth. Just broth and all the ice cubes you want. Okay?

"Okay, I will," April said softly. She was so tired. The lab was there and gone. April barely remembered them taking her blood. She was so tired and as she dozed off she saw Native Son. She was leading him out into a field, hopping on, and taking one of their rides on the side path trail. He snorted as he went, and she could feel his power beneath her. His neck muscles ripped with excitement. He was so powerful but gave at her lightest touch of the reins. At one point was the run and she let him out. Oh the thrill of having that kind of speed, her hair whipped behind her and her eyes teared at the wind. April could not help but laugh this was the most fun ever.

The nurses came in when they heard April laugh. It was obvious she was dreaming of having the time of her life. "Good for her," one nurse said. "That poor girl has been through hell and I for one am glad she can dream and laugh." The other nurses agreed.

The unit clerk looked up and said, "In the twenty-two years I have worked here this is the first famous person I have ever seen. How about you girls?"

"Well, some sort of famous, but not like her," one said. "She was such a go getter all her life, in the Olympics, and very athletic. I think she won the equestrian title when she was like twelve. I wish my daughter was half that motivated. I can't seem to keep her away from boys."

"You have to look at her parents and all she has. No average kid can do what she did," one said.

"The hell you say? That girl was homeless as a child fending for herself. I saw an interview about her in one of the magazines. They did a run down on her past, you know, and this girl came from nothing. She created the D Farms company driving her parents crazy. At the Olympics her parents brought along her birth mother, and I'm telling you that I cried like a baby."

"Oh, I remember that," the unit clerk said. "She really is something. How old is she again, twenty-one? Imagine that, twenty-one and she has practically ended hunger in America. She changed the entire welfare system. I think she should be governor. Can't do any worse than what sits there now," she said.

"Hey, Ruthie, she can't run for Governor of Pennsylvania, she is from California," and they all laughed.

"She can move," the unit clerk said, all gloomy.

April awoke early she sat in her bed, looked at her hands, pulled up her sheet and looked at her legs and feet when a nurse came in, "Boy you're up early, Sunshine! Let me check your vitals. How are you feeling?" she asked.

137

"With my hands" April teased.

"Oh you must be feeling better, are those headaches gone?" the nurse asked.

"Almost, just kind of a memory of a headache, does that make sense?" April asked.

"It does, let me see if we can give you another dose, I will be right back." She came back with two more nurses who rolled her on her side and inserted another antiemetic. "That should do it" she said, and they rolled her back.

They stood there looking at her. April felt confused and embarrassed and said, "What?"

"Well we were just talking about you out at our desk. How in the world did you turn out so well. I mean you make most of the choices in life on your own, and they were good choices. We struggle with our kids going across the street," she said.

April pointed to the ceiling with her finger.

"What? What does that mean?" one nurse asked.

"God. I answer to God. I can't think of a day that I have not prayed at least once, and sometimes ten or more times. When I drive or when I am alone. Prayer does not have to be formal. No one could teach me what I feel. I had to develop this on my own. I tested it and learned, and that became my faith, my testimony, and I would not trade that for anything in this world. My parents support me when I choose the good option. Ever since I was little I learned to make good choices. Listen, I am not a zealot. I love God, and I have felt his influence in my life. I know it. It is something I cannot deny because I know he knows."

The nurses looked at each other.

April said, "I know you all work and may not have off on a Sunday but teach them. Get them to church, take them to Sunday School, and learn the lessons from the Bible stories. The stories will give them courage when needed, and strength to draw upon. Your children are your best crop, the most important thing you will do in this life," April said.

"Well, looks like we are going to church, girls," one said.

April said, "If you can, carpool your kids, let others help you. Your family, your parents, a neighbor, they would love to help. I know they would."

"Oh, I can make it. I have gotten lazy, I guess, and you're right. I remember when I was in nursing school and when things were tough I used to think about the Children of Moses lost out there in that desert. The only way they could eat is if they depended on God for manna. At that is how I was, dependent on God for everything. I think you are on to something there girl."

"Don't let this day pass, write it down. Keep reminding yourself what is important. You found help drawing on Bible heroes would you deny your children the same chance you had?" April said.

"You're right. Now try to go back to sleep," the Nurse said.

"I can't. I am always up early," April told her. Then she asked, "May I walk for a little bit?"

"Hold on. Let us get one of the aides to walk with you."

A small girl came into the room, "Hi! I am Marcy, and I am to help you walk."

April slid sideways to get up and out of bed and felt a little woozy.

"Just sit for a few minutes to let your body adjust," Marcy said. The two then went walking the hallway, around and back, back and around about eleven times. "I won't need to go to the gym today," Marcy joked. They kept walking until the shift changed and a report had to be given. So April went back to her room and sat in the chair.

Soon there were vitals, fresh water, breakfast, and her entourage came to be with her again. "April how are you doing?" her mother asked.

"I am much better, no more headaches and the food is almost normal," she joked.

"The reason I ask is that there are many, many people outside. They have come to wish you well and pray for your healing. Do you think you could talk to them today?" Her mother asked.

"I will if the doctor says it's okay," and in walked the doctor.

"The doctor says it's okay and insists. They blocked the parking lot. I had to walk three blocks to get here," he said. After the exam he said he was happy with her progress so far, and would like her to say two more days, then he would make his assessment.

He ordered something in her IV to make her sleep. He knew she would be up early. That was in her nature and since there was no changing that, a little sleep aid in her IV would not hurt her. It would help. She needed to rest.

That afternoon some of the hospital janitors assembled a microphone and speakers near a balcony of the hospital. April walked out to it feeling strong, but she held onto her Dad for his support.

April took the mic. It was a sunny day in Pennsylvania, with very little wind on this Tuesday afternoon. She stepped out in a gown and a housecoat, and the crowd cheered and hollered. "Please. Please, how very good of you all to come. First, I want to thank you all for your kindness and prayers that have healed me. (The crowd cheered.) I want to thank all of the police men and women who have assisted in finding me, including private searchers and those with dogs. I also want to thank all of those who prayed for me and kept me safe. I never meant any harm to anyone, and I am sorry for what I have done."

"(The crowd yelled.) Don't be sorry. They deserved to die for what they did to you. Hang in there. Don't be sad, be strong."

"Secondly, I want to ask all of you to wait until I can come down. I want to meet you all, but please do not touch my face or forehead due to injuries and then go home in peace. I will be down in the lobby and come outside to greet you," and they all cheered.

"April, you can't do that," her Mother said.

"Sure I can, Mom, and I am going to meet them all."

And she did. April sat in a wheelchair for comfort, and they came. Adults, children, and babies, April greeted them all. They saw her bruises and realized all they said she had been through was true. Most squeezed her hand since they could not touch her face. It took almost four hours to have that crowd disburse, and sure enough the television crew was there to film it all. April thanked them all and asked that they go home and let the hospital take care of those who came for medical attention.

That night on the local television it showed her meeting the local people, and they said she was "beloved." That stuck April and she almost cried. She was on the verge when a nurse came in and snapped off the television.

"None of that. You don't want infection in that eye. Do you?" the nurse asked as she squeezed April's shoulder to give April strength. "You know you're strong. Keep your faith girl. You'll be all right. The folks on TV, they all love you. Feel the love girl, feel the love," and the nurse went out of the room.

The next day was April's birthday, she would be twenty-two.

The nurses all swore April's health rebounded. She looked refreshed and ready to go home.

The doctor said otherwise, "One more day."

So her family brought up a full-size sheet cake and they had a small party for her and the nurses on the floor.

As a nurse carried a couple of pieces of cake to the station, she said, "Those folks sure are generous souls. They include everybody."

Another came down the hall with an armload of spring flowers "These are for us. Aren't they beautiful?"

And that is how the Di Angelo's were known in that Philadelphia hospital. They had never known anyone as famous as April. And she was also humble, happy, and kind. So kind she included them in talking and prayers. In all it was a wonderful healing experience, exactly what April needed to heal.

Going Home, Finally

THE NEXT DAY, AFTER SIX DAYS IN THE HOSPITAL, APRIL DI ANGELO was heading home with her family. Scott had brought the new Cessna to the airstrip and waited. There were hugs and well wishes all around. Then she was gone, with her family on their new business plane heading home to California.

It was a good flight home. There was an air of happiness. They were all relaxed, relieved, and counted their blessings.

Gordon and Miranda had urgent news but that would have to wait. They were so grateful to have their daughter back that they just wanted a day or so with her at home as a family again before their next hurdle.

April dozed off on the flight home and her birth mother held on to her hand and watched her daughter. She was about to grow up real fast, she only hoped to protect her.

They landed about 2:00 p.m. in the afternoon. There was a car waiting to take them home. Nora and Lena kissed April and were whisked off to take them home while Gordon, his wife and daughter climbed into his truck to head home.

There was Ruby jumping up and down, not nearly as spry as she was when April last saw her. Soon Remi would be home from school. April walked into her home and began to cry. Her mother sat with her and rocked her daughter soothing her.

"Mom, I wanted to get away. I didn't know they were not real police, but then when I realized what was happening, it was too late." Next she remembered her friends. "Oh, Mom, I need to call Mr. Stevens. It is urgent." Just then, Dad walked into the room and said he would dial the number.

Mr. Stevens answered the phone and began to tear up realizing it was April on the other end. He did his best to compose himself as he wrote down information and instructions.

April apologized for not telling him sooner about where the raccoon, cat, and Happy were. She also asked that the girl who took care of them be rewarded. April told him detective Danny would need to find that barn. She did not go into detail. She also asked for Sam to be interviewed and she told Mr. Stevens why.

"Oh my. Oh, yes, I can take care of that. We sure have missed you and are so glad you are back. You are back to stay? No?" he asked her.

"Yes, for a while. It seems there are things I have to take care of. It's a lifelong process though. Isn't it?" April asked.

The next two days was a time of settling in, just like old times. Remi was an absolute delight, teasing her. And it seemed Ruby found a new soul mate which was fine with April. Ruby deserved someone who always came home to her.

That following weekend Miranda and her husband needed to speak to April. "Now we don't want you to get upset. Promise us!" her Father said. "While you were missing, an Arab made threats to us, televised, saying Native Son should lose his standing as he was not deserving. He kept repeating his horse, whatever its name was, should be champion of all time."

April laughed, "There is no such thing as champion of all time. Native Son out and out won the Triple Crown. That is history. No one can change that," she said.

"Well, he is trying. He has a big mouth. He never lets anyone finish their sentence. He shouts over them and cutting them off from what they are saying. It's a problem."

"So has anyone made a decision or are you just ignoring him?" April asked.

"No one has made any changes. We are not able to since you own three-quarters of the company. That's how it is. He spits venomously as he speaks denouncing you, April. He says that your disappearance was a ruse to keep you from his challenge."

April laughed. "It's not easy being the best or on top. There's always someone who wants your spot. Okay, how do I talk to him or what do I do?" April asked.

"No, no you do not want to talk with him. The Judge is handling him for now. You need to talk to the Judge and make your decision from there. To us he is a gnat who should be sprayed to get rid of him, but he is stirring up trouble everywhere he goes," Gordon said.

"Tomorrow," April said. "Tomorrow I will go and speak to my good buddy. If I am allowed to drive," she said looking around the room.

"Yes, I will let you drive the car if you drive slowly. We always trust you, April. You know that," her Mother said. "And April that Laser appointment is in two days."

That night ended with a blistering game of monopoly which April let Remi win. His eyes glistened with the joy of championship. He boasted like a rooster. It was all in fun.

Early the next morning, April took her Mother's keys and headed into town. She wanted ever so much to see the town again, all of the familiar sights and sounds. She had missed this, all of it and was so very, very grateful to be back. April knew that she had missed a ton of school. She wanted so badly to pass. She knew she had a lot to make up, and she had not seen Larry yet. She tucked that away for now as she parked the car and walked up the steps to the courthouse. Inside the courthouse Rusty was so happy to see her that she hugged her and forgot to screen her belongings. April continued down the hallway and was soon at the Judge's chambers.

She turned the knob and walked in, the room was empty, no Missy. So she walked back out into the courtroom and sat in the back. There was a whale of a case going on about a high speed chase out on the state highway and the man in front of Du Val was lying which exasperated the Judge. Finally the Judge threw the book at the man giving him thirty days in jail, a huge fine, and loss of his license for a year. April wanted to give Judge Du Val some distance, he was really upset.

April waited about five minutes and then walked to the chamber door and knocked. The door was opened by a police officer and April walked in. "Where is Missy?" she asked.

"Married and gone," the Judge wailed. April smiled at him, "So did you make good on your promise to your sweetheart?" she asked him.

He held up his right hand. There was a gold band on his finger. "We wanted you in our wedding, but you were gone," he said. "When is my next case?" he asked the policeman.

"11:00, Sir."

"Sit down and talk to me," he said to her.

"I am here to talk to you. I guess while I was gone someone was talking trash about me, my parents, and Native Son," she said.

"Yes, there is. He is an Arab, well to do, educated, and very wealthy with oil wells in Saudi Arabia. He claims your horse was not worthy to win," Du Val said.

"On what grounds does he make this accusation?" April asked.

"Nonsense grounds. He is all noise, but he has money and is buying people's attention and air time." he said.

"Well, what are we supposed to do about it?" she asked.

"Well, you were not here, and so, without your stamp of approval, we said nothing to him. But I made an outline for you because I had no doubt you would return to us," he said tearing up. "And Monte has been working with Native Son. Granted he is eight years old, but he is very spry and conditioned. Monte felt with a couple of months of training and conditioning he would be ready to race."

April was stunned! This was not fair to Native Son. He had earned his retirement, making a lot of winning beautiful babies who also were winners. "I don't know," April said. "I need to see the entire scope of what he said, what he is after. Then and only then can I weigh our options."

"I have saved many excerpts for you," the Judge said handing April several discs to watch. "These discs I recorded myself. I would like very much to stop him myself, but you know in America we are allowed to say whatever we want, weather it is true or not. He likes attention, and maybe we should give it to him. It's entirely up to you."

April leaned forward and hugged her long-time Uncle-like friend. "Can you all come out for dinner some night when we can discuss this after I view these?" she asked.

"Sure we can. That would be nice," and soon the bailiff came to get the Judge to sign some papers. April tucked the CDs into her purse and left.

April drove one hour to Larry's farm. She drove into the driveway and did not hear anyone or any engines running. The fields were planted, and the corn looked great. She got out and a German Shephard dog came out barking. "Come here," she coaxed the dog, and he came for attention and a good ear scratching. "Where is Larry?" she asked the dog and he turned to find his master who was welding in the shop below the garage.

April found him wearing a helmet with sparks flying from the arc welder. He did not see her or the dog. April waited until he was finished with that piece. He looked and flipped his helmet off and stepped forward to hold her. April was a bit surprised but was glad.

"Do you have some time to talk?" she asked him. "Yes. Yes of course I do. Let's go into the house where we can talk, and I can wash up a bit," he said. They went into the sprawling farmhouse that definitely looked like a man lived there. There was no woman's touch and no flowers. Although it was very clean, the house was drab, no colors, no pictures, not much but the furniture that he used.

"Did you have a sale or are you planning to?" April asked.

"I know this house looks plain, but it suits me. I am not inside much, and it functions for a guy like me. I can spruce it up, but right now I have no need to," and he smiled at April.

"You were not able to come to the hospital when I was found. But there were problems, are you aware of them?" she asked.

"No, I was told you were back, and I was so glad," and he teared up and his face became red. "I always believed you were alive and out there. I just had to be patient and pray," he said. As they sat together at the table Larry wanted to hold her, he felt news was coming that was difficult for her to tell.

He reached for her hand across the table, "It does not matter what happened, or what is going to happen, nothing has changed for me," he said.

April looked at him and suddenly became very emotional, "Larry, I am pregnant, and I don't have the heart to end this baby's life. It is not its fault. I believe this baby can be raised to be different, kind, and loving. But I wanted you to know. I would not deceive you in any way. I just can't end this life inside me," she said.

"Like I said, nothing has changed for me. I want you in my life, and sooner or later we will have children, so what does this matter?" he said and added "In time no one will remember anyway."

"Do you want to know what happened to me? I mean how this all happened?" She asked.

"No I don't. I know what happened was not good. I would never hurt you, April, not ever. It makes me sick to think someone hurt you, abused you, or wanted you dead. If you were with me, no one would ever hurt you again. I promise. I want a life partner. Someone with me every day, having a long life together raising a family, working, laughing, and enjoying life. Making our own memories," he said.

April was grateful to have found a man like this that no matter what, he would love her unconditionally. In the past weeks she pondered about the baby.

She felt in time, everyone would forget the conditions in which this child was conceived. If it was meant to be, this child would have a mother and a father, love all around from extended family, friends, and church members and that is what he was offering her. April stood and went to him, sat beside him and held on to him and they both had tears of joy.

It was clear to her that he meant what he was saying. He wanted her for his wife for now and eternity. He prayed and waited, and he was hopeful she would be his. "When?" he asked her.

"I don't know just yet," she replied. "Do you know about the Arab who is accusing me of cheating or whatever?" She asked.

"Yes, I know. Just ignore him or shut him down," he said to her.

"I am not sure what to do just yet. The Judge gave me CDs to watch and then I will have a small get together at home and we will decide. Would you like to be there too? I mean you are part of this as well, in a way."

"Yes, I will come. If I know when," he answered. They stayed together for a good half of a day. She helped him with a tractor he had been working on and they talked a lot. It was so easy to be with him. It was as if they had not been separated at all, and they took up right where they left off. April felt she belonged here with him, and when she went to leave he came to the car so say goodbye and he had tears. "I wish you were not going," he said.

"I am going home, and I will be back," she replied.

"You are home," he said, and he held her.

Driving home April cried. Her heart had been touched.

Never before did she have the conviction about any man as she did about Larry. She was grateful. She prayed a prayer of thanks as she drove home.

That evening April watched four of the CDs that the Judge had given her. They were ugly. The things the man said about her and Native Son were lies, and he spewed them easily, like a serpent.

April shuddered and she felt an urgency to pray. She asked her Father in Heaven to help her in this decision. It was wrong to allow someone to say things like this and not stop them. April did not want to retaliate in anger, but in righteousness to stop it. April knew that to react would be wrong. She wanted to do this right in God's eyes.

It was later that week when Miranda made a huge pot of her home made noodles, sauce, and sausage for dinner. Thirteen men and women came to their home: Du Val and his wife, Mr. Stevens and his son, Gordon and Miranda, Nora and Lena, Monte and his trusted helper Bryon, Larry and April, and Miranda's Father. This was the inner circle for the secret plans to be made.

The Judge was the one to start the meeting after Nora offered prayer. "He is challenging you for everything you own, and if we are to go forward, that means every farm in D Farms, including this home," he said. "He thinks we are stupid and will not require anything of him. I drafted a paper that says to the effect that we require the same of him: all the holding of this Shah to be on the line including his oil wells, the refineries, and his home. I have done research and he is very, very wealthy and has many oil wells.

We can secure them when the time comes, so the bottom line is this: Do you want to go ahead and challenge him?" he asked.

All eyes were on April. "I need to ask the one who will carry all this weight on his shoulders, after that I can let you know," she said.

Gordon said, "We will not have any insults hurled, no bad feelings whatsoever. We will comply with all he wants, for we know where God is. There will be no friction, no arguing, no insults or animosity. I would suggest that each of us here check ourselves to be free of judgments. If there is judging of anyone, it would be of yourselves," and that was the shortest meeting of all time in Di Angelo history.

Native Son Must Choose

APRIL SPENT A FEW DAYS WITH NATIVE SON. IT WAS EVIDENT HE had something weighing on his mind. That might sound crazy to some, but April knew her horse. Native Son was edgy, agitated, and flighty and that was not his nature.

After a full day of grooming him, April put her head against Native Son's to have a meeting. She watched his eyes communicate to her. "Okay, big guy, there is a big problem that is yours and mine. No one else can make this decision. Do you want to race the Arabian stallion belonging to the Arab man who is challenging you? You don't have to. We have a great life. We can ignore him, and . . ."

Just then, Native Son pushed her with his nose

"Let me finish. We have a great life, and nothing has to change. If he wants to spout lies, let him. We know better."

Again he pushed her, this time a little harder so that she had to take a step backwards.

"Are you telling me you want to accept this challenge, risking it all?"

The great horse's head went up and down as if saying "yes".

April sighed, "You do not have to prove anything you know. Those of us who love you will always love you no matter what. To us you are the supreme champion forever."

The horse stomped staring into April's eyes. April noticed a flash of light in his eyes. There was no doubt he not only wanted to accept the challenge, but Native Son was also feeling aggressive and willing to race with all his heart.

That evening April sat on the tailgate of her Dad's pickup truck watching the steers in the pasture as he checked the fence line. He returned with a smile and sat with her. "What's on your mind?" he said lightly slapping her knee.

"Well, Dad. I was almost dead for five months, and it comes down to a choice about living or dying, and I feel it is time to live, really live," she said.

"I think you should go for it," he said laughing and touching her leg.

"Dad, you could lose your home. Did you think about that?"

"Yes, I have. Both your mother and I have talked about this, and we want to lay it all on the line and accept the challenge from this liar. You know, April, there is nothing sweeter than living the life Jesus Christ laid out for us and showing the world we are not afraid. That we trust God in all ways. Besides, we will be all right no matter what happens. We always were and always will be. When you have the truth, life always seems better," he said. Then he patted April's tummy saying, "This little Bambino is coming into this world and might have a thing or two to say about this as well," as he smiled. Her Dad was wonderful, so supportive all her life, he was her rock.

"Dad," April said tearfully. "I saw you, you know, back then. I saw you and Mom praying on the living room floor in tears and I did not want to lose you. You two are the most important people in my life."

"Well you didn't lose us. You never will lose us. I know you believe in the Atonement of the Savior. I know you do. We were sealed in the temple, and we will never be lost, not ever," and he hugged his daughter tightly. "Well then, let's get a move on. We have a lot of work to do, getting things ready and in place. You better call Du Val when we get home. There will have to be a televised response to that guy.

When they got home April put the call in to the Judge, who gleefully rang up a local television station to came and interview April.

After the crew got there, they used a lot of makeup to hide the redness on her forehead since the surgery was not completely healed.

Once that three-minute, calmly stated interview hit the airwaves, it was carried by many stations. When the Arab saw it and became instantly angry. He denounced April by calling her nasty names and insulting her entire family.

April did not want to see his response, but that did not stop others from her circle from telling her about it. Remi became her number one bodyguard, both verbally and physically. He steered her away from those who would come to her to gossip, and he calmly shut them down when they did by simply saying, "Hope you have a wonderful day."

Preparations had been started before April was found. Native Son had been training, at first lightly, but now he was in full mode which explained his reasoning for wanting to race. Yes, it was true. Native Son was eight years old racing against a three year old, but experience and patience goes a long way in life, verses fear and force. April laughed because her horse knew what he was getting into and accepted the challenge with honor and courage.

Monte said Native Son trained longer than when he was three. His stamina was astounding.

The news reporters were soon out at the stables, wanting to know when the race would happen. The date was set for June 14th at a local track in California. It made no sense for D Farms to travel when they were not the ones accusing anyone.

And so it was, with consistent training, patience, and prayer, that they became ready - all of them, including the jockey, since April was not able to ride. Amazingly enough Native Son did not care, not this time. He would have raced without a rider. He was that determined, focused, and ready.

As the days wound down, April went to the barn daily. She was concerned about Native Son. She felt he knew and bore the responsibility of this race. But more than anything, she wanted him to race for the thrill and the fun of it. Sure there was a lot at stake, but to be truthful, no one was owned by those responsibilities. D Farms was like a well-oiled machine, people came and worked, they were clothed and fed, taken care of, shown love. They got their diplomas and went on to a job. It worked well, and it showed in all areas of people's lives associated with them.

April knew that D Farms would stand as an icon for the US, and no one would tear it apart. This became personal. No one had the right to attack her and her family by calling them liars. To lie and denounce one of the greatest racing horses of all time was an out and out insult.

The best response would be to remain calm and pray often and regularly. Live right and do their best, but not forget to laugh, love, and show respect to one another. April did her best to mentally communicate this to Native Son, but it was no use. He was too focused.

One day at the barn, April did not feel so well. She was nauseated and dizzy. While she was grooming Native Son she turned to hold onto the stall door. The horse knew something was wrong and he nudged his owner. April wanted to comfort him, but she could not. The stress she felt was overbearing and she began to cry, which was not her nature. She turned when the pain subsided, took her horse's halter in hand, and said, "I am all right. It is you I am concerned about, relax and enjoy this. You are older and wiser. You know the difference between being loved and cared for or not. You have seen horses whipped for no reason, and we never did that to you. I know you know that."

She again bent over with pain. "I want you to go out and race to your hearts content. I want you to shake off the time you spent here yearning to run. Do your best. That is all I could ever ask of you. Run and be happy."

The great muscular animal nudged her as if he understood and equally showed his concern for her.

That was the last time she saw Native Son until race day. It turned out that April had experienced early contractions and had to spend some time with the doctor at the hospital who warned her to stop stressing. April promised she would, but no one understood the weight of this race, as well as she, her family, and Native Son.

On the day of the race, the small track was fully decorated with banners, balloons, and some of the grandstand had been freshly painted. It was a nice transformation and had been needed.

Monte was relaxed and feeling confident. April asked to see Native Son and Monte asked her not to. "He is good. Let him be until race time," is all Monte said. April walked along side Larry to the front office of the grandstand. Her parents were there with Remi, Manny and Contessa. The two ladies could not come. They both had horrible colds and were unable to travel.

Gordon spoke, "Well here we are, together as family. I would like to take this time while it is still quiet to offer a prayer." He asked God for safety and good sportsmanship. Also to allow the horses to show their differences, and may God choose who is to be the winner.

Meanwhile in Arabia, men that had been handpicked by her friend, Sgt. Bob, were in position at the accusing Arab's home, as well as at all his family's oil wells, refineries, textile factories, and hotels.

Twenty-six retired military men who were armed and ready in the event of trouble. With one call or text from Mr. Stevens, the transfer would be complete, and so they waited.

April wore a white loose pantsuit with a separate top that was flowing in the breeze. She wore sandals, a gold belt around her waist, two gold arm bands, and a gold head band to hold her hair back. She could have passed for a desert princess.

April was nervous and Larry tapped her on her arm and leaned in to whisper to her. "Settle down, there is nothing you can do. Just let it happen," and he kissed her cheek. April flushed. She was not used to being fussed over like this.

The track was small. This was not a main attraction race and Monte, in particular, wanted to keep the crowd size minimal. But alas, already the cars were parked out on the highway and hundreds, if not thousands, of people were already along the track and grandstand. They stood under the bleachers, and anywhere they could to get another glimpse of Native Son. The reporters lined the track at the finish line. Cameras were set up along with over forty reporters. The entry where the horses came in had young boys sitting on the header and on the sides of the cement barriers. They were in trees, on lawns, they were everywhere. Seated at the Grandstand, April could not sit, she leaned over and kissed Larry on his cheek and said, "I'll be right back," and was gone walking to the stable as her family watched her leave.

At the stable, Native Son was already tacked up. His jockey, Joel Samanka, was a small Irish rider, well established and he was the one who contacted Monte. Native Son and Samanka had a good relationship. It was as if the horse understood this was a job for the two of them and they had to get it done.

April greeted Joel and he smiled and said, "It's going to be a great day. I can feel it in my bones."

April asked Monte for just two minutes with Native Son.

"Now listen, he is relaxed, and I don't want him getting jitters from you. Say your piece and let him work this out. He is ready and I don't want anything to interrupt his psyche."

April understood completely. She stood there looking at Native Son and said, "Look at how handsome you are," and the horse bobbed his head. "I want you to go out there and have the run of a life time and have fun. We are all so proud of you and love you so very much." She leaned forward and kissed his forehead and nose, patted his neck, then turned and walked away. April was choked up and began to cry and she did not want her horse to see or feel that.

April walked toward the grandstand again and many in the crowd began to cheer her name and call greetings of good luck to her.

As she walked she could see part of the other camp and their horse. He was a magnificent white stallion, strong and wild. His trainer had long lines on him as if they were afraid of the horse. They were saddling the horse and he reared up.

April saw them whip the animal to make him behave. April growled inside. This was no way to treat any animal. She stopped and watched this ugly show until the horse was saddled. The rider backed away each time the horse spun and each time the horse was whipped. Soon their rider was in the saddle. He was wild eyed and quickly rode out onto the track to load into the shoot.

The white stallion did not walk, he pranced on the track. His rider had trouble controlling the horse. It was such a contrast to see the white stallion compared to Native Son.

Native Son came out slow and methodically. He was not jumpy, nervous, or needing to show off. Native Son eyed his rival and as he walked to the loading chute, he noticed fresh whip marking that left open flesh on the white stallion.

Native Son walked calmly into the chute. It took almost ten minutes to load the stallion. The calamity of shouting and yelling would have frightened any animal. Once in the chute, it was less than two minutes before it would open, so April bowed her head to pray.

"Please let right prevail, Father. Protect Native Son who is out here to help his family, and bless the stallion to understand, and soften his heart. This is in your hands. Father. I trust you. I have always trusted you, Amen."

As April looked up the bell rang, the chute doors opened, and they were off. It was a fast pace. They were even with one another. The white stallion eyed Native Son, and Native Son looked, then looked away. He was not going to focus on anything but those whom he loved. On they went to the quarter turn, neck to neck. And then the white stallion's jockey began to not whip but beat the horse.

That is when Native Son made eye contact with the stallion and a telepathic message saying that his owner never allowed that. "If you were with us, you would be loved and taken care of, not like this."

On they went to the half turn and down the stretch. When the stick hit the stallion for the hundredth time, the horse bolted out of fear. The jockey hit the horse at his head, striking his eye. Native Son was shocked but surged forward passing the white stallion. The calculation paid off. As they came down the last quarter mile, Native Son was half a lead in front of the stallion.

The crowd was cheering so hard that you could not hear yourself think.

Native Son loved crowds. He loved the attention and he spurred himself harder.

Just then his jockey told him "Let it go, Pop," and he did with the last strength within him. Native Son pressed forward, his nose flaring, and his neck wet with sweat. He crossed the finish line one full length ahead of the white stallion.

The calls and text messages arrived in Arabia in less than one minute. There was no trouble. The Arab's holdings now belonged to D Farms. There were the right men in place to be assured of that.

Back on the track, the white stallion was breezing out on the track while Native Son was back at the winner's circle, waiting for his owner. As she approached her horse, Native Son reached his big head to April and lipped her cheek.

Everyone laughed. "No more races for you, big guy. You have impressed us all, including the world of nay sayer's."

Monte was all smiles with Byron at his side.

Oh No You Don't

IT WAS WONDERFUL UNTIL APRIL TURNED TO HER LEFT AND SAW the white stallion being beaten and whipped. April hoisted up her leggings and marched with purpose to the holding area where the white stallion was in danger. As she got close, she called to the men to stop it. Stop whipping the horse. She grabbed the end of the whip before it struck the horse again. April pulled on the whip quickly taking it from the striker's hand.

Next thing April knew she was being whipped. The small end of the whip tore skin from her cheek and April screamed.

The Arab laughed. He stepped forward to strike her again.

Then out of nowhere, came Native Son. He was rearing up on his hind legs striking at the Arab, knocking him down, and sending some of the men scattering like rats. The white stallion began to do the same thing. He turned to kick those who were inflicting pain on him. Native Son stood between April and the attackers. No one hurt his master, absolutely no one.

It was only minutes before the police arrived. April put her hand out to the white stallion coaxing him to come to her. Native Son stared at him, and mentally told the horse that he was now his brother. The horse walked to April and his nose touched Native Son's.

The newspaper men did not miss that photo. It traveled all across the United States.

April led the stallion to Monte, "He is yours now to train and work with. It may take some time to undo what they did," she said.

"He looks like an intelligent animal. I am sure he will come around," Monte said leading the white stallion away. He patted his neck speaking gently to him. The stallion was big-eyed and afraid, but trusted Monte and followed him like a puppy.

April watched them, Bryon leading Native Son and Monte leading the white stallion. Twenty minutes earlier the stallion was being whipped to follow or conform. Here he was following Monte with slack in his lead line.

Horses are not dumb. He knew who he could trust, and he knew he now had a gentle hand on him. April was happy that the horse would now be treated well. He would have a good home. The thought of what she gained and did not lose, never occurred to her until her Dad hugged her and told her. April of course was happy, but she made it clear that the mother of the Arab man was to retain her home. It was not right to punish her. She was not responsible for her son's mistakes or bad attitude.

After that, crowds began to leave, and the horses were taken away. April and her small entourage were making plans to go out to dinner. It was not late and would be nice to have an early supper. They went to a place in between their home and Larry's. It was an Italian restaurant. It was very fancy, and the people were courteous, helpful, and kind.

April nudged Larry, "We can come here every now and then." He winked at her with a smile. As they came out and stood by their cars, April wanted to go with Larry, and she held his hand.

Gordon said, "You may take my daughter home with you, but no monkey business. That is not until you make the commitment of marriage in the temple!"

Larry was all red-faced and told Gordon those were his intentions if he could get April to stay still for a week.

"Well, good luck with that too," Gordon said, and they all laughed.

April did go home with Larry. The two of them sat out on the porch on the wicker sofa and talked. It was a lovely summer evening. The sky was clear, the stars were out, and the moon was three quarters full shining down on them.

Larry stroked her hair and kissed her head with his arms around her. He then got up and brought out a quilt that his mother had made and covered April with it. They sat there just the two of them, talking, making plans until they both became quiet and fell asleep. Larry woke around 2 a.m. and carried sleeping April onto a bed that was downstairs beside the living room. That used to be their parlor. April slept and Larry went upstairs to his own bed and was out like a light.

They both awoke early. Their hair was a mess, and they laughed at each other. April offered to make breakfast and the two of them worked together in the kitchen.

They sat down together, then Larry walked out to get the newspaper. April thought, "You know this is nice. I could live like this. Some kids outside, one in a playpen or high chair." Yes, April was lost in her thoughts of what the future might bring.

And a compassionate loving Father in Heaven was in complete agreement with her, but not yet!

That evening, when April was still with Larry, they had planned to head back to take her home and get a bite to eat when the telephone rang. "It's for you," he said handing the telephone to April.

"Hello, April. Danny here. I got the brown suitcase. Do you know what is inside?" he asked.

"I do, but I only saw a corner of one of the photos. One day when I was their prisoner in the back seat of their car, the suitcase opened, and a corner of a photo stuck out. I saw a dead woman's head. I never looked inside at all the contents. It made me sick. I am sure in time I would have been one of those photos," April told him.

"You are so right! This was so instrumental in identifying over thirty-eight women who have gone missing over the years. The various counties and states never had a lead, and now because of you these families have closure. All of the departments are so thankful you saved these photos. It's a shame, but now we know what happened and we all thank you. I had to run the women who were taken in a computer. They were from all over the United States. After faxing and meeting with folks, we are going to have a press statement. I also know you don't want to be identified, so we are simply going to state their last victim escaped. That will preserve this case so families will know what happened to their loved ones. Is that okay with you?" he asked.

"It is. I don't want to appear on television anymore, unless I have to," she said.

Danny replied "We might briefly state you found them. That should be the end of it, and it is the truth April. If you had not saved this briefcase who knows what would have happened," he said. They both said goodbye and wished each other well.

Back on the porch Larry looked at her, "You don't want to know, believe me." That was all that was said. April and Larry went to his car to take her back home.

"Do you want a meal or a burger?" he asked her.

"I am hungry," was all April said. They stopped at a franchise country store and had a lovely dinner with salad, soup, and a potato. April was stuffed. Larry said he could have eaten more, but they left to go home.

After Larry took April home, her mother said Mr. Stevens had called wanting to speak to her. April said goodbye to Larry, but her mother had him sit down at their kitchen table to have some peach cobbler. She had just taken it out of the oven. April picked up the telephone and called Mr. Stevens.

"Hello, April. How are you? It was such a great day yesterday. No?" he asked.

"Yes, yes it was. I am very grateful," she replied.

"Indeed, indeed," he said. "April the Hawaii farm is doing fantastic, but the Alaska farm not so much. The worker there is unhappy. He realizes he is not going to be able to go outside after the winter starts. He is not prepared to be so secluded."

"May I come down and see you later today?" April asked.

"Sure. I will be here until 5:00 p.m. as usual, or we can meet at my home. I am sure my wife would enjoy seeing you."

April came back into the kitchen as Larry was finishing up, "This was good. Do you know how to make it?" he asked.

"I do, but I am sure if I called Mom she would gladly give me her secrets or bring some over. Right, Mom?" and Miranda hugged her daughter laughing.

"That's a long trip, an hour away. We might have to do something about that," her mother said.

Larry left soon after that.

April wanted to see how Nora and Lena were. She took the keys and was gone.

The ladies were at home, their flu was almost gone but they still had red noses and sneezed often. "Oh, we hope you don't get this, April." They kept their hankies over their mouths the entire time. April didn't worry about becoming sick. She loved these two women and never missed an opportunity to let them know. April left the ladies in good spirits and went to see Mr. Stevens.

He was in his office preparing to speak with her.

"Before we start," April handed Mr. Stevens the card from the Wisconsin library, "Please be in touch with her. I promised not to forget no matter the cost. We need to follow through on this," she said.

"I have the maps and all the information right here," he said. Spread out before them was a huge map that covered his entire work table. He showed April the building that housed three thousand steers all trucked in from other D Farms.

"The buildings were built in sections. The steers were not altogether. At most there were thirty in a pen. It required a person to walk the entire sprawling complex to feed them. The feed was in separate bins that moved it into the troughs. The hay was put out with a medium-sized loader. In all it was three hours of work in the morning and three hours of work in the evening. The water was never a problem. They were built in units. The cattle made enough heat to keep the building warm. Bedding was made up of ground corn stalks that were dispensed into the pens with a wide blower. It got so warm that they had to put pin holes in the roofing to avoid sweating and eventually rust. Everything was push button, automatic."

Cameras had been mounted so that April could view and see what was happening in each area. April asked why the man did not want the job after applying for it.

"I believe he was afraid to stay alone. That is not for everyone you know. Some people go stir crazy. They have to have someone to talk to," he said.

"I know that, and that is why we put in the computer system with skype. He could talk and be visual anytime he wanted," she said. April was miffed, "Do we have time to post the job again? I mean surely there is someone who wants to go. Even if there were two or three of them, they could work it out," she said.

"Well if there is, no one has come forward. The guy said a lot of negative things about the villagers, the equipment, and so on. He said no one could do what was asked of him," Mr. Stevens said.

"Oh, that's crap. I could do it. I am a pregnant woman and I know I could do it."

Going to Alaska

APRIL BEGAN TO REALIZE THIS MIGHT BE AN EXCELLENT WAY FOR her to finish her education. There would be no interruptions, and the computer would take her through the courses as fast or slow as she wanted. There were testing sites on line, and she began to realize this would be just what she needed.

Then she thought about Larry. This would indeed be another test for both of them. She wanted to talk to him before she made any decision. She was now twenty-two and wanted to settle down. But a few months would help them, she thought. She went home and at dinner discussed this with her parents.

"April, you are pregnant!" her mother said. "You will need to go to doctor visits every month."

"Mom, don't be silly. Many women do not go to the doctor every month, and many children are born at home. The exercise will be good for me, and I can complete my education with the time I will have there with no one to interrupt me. I am going to talk with Larry and ask if a few more months will matter," she said.

That is when Gordon spoke up. "I know Larry is a good man. He suffered when you were gone. I saw it with my own eyes. He may not say much, but he is committed to spending his life with you. Are you willing to take the risk that someone else might find his quiet way just what they want? I know the man wants to settle down, April. Don't make him wait for months on end."

"I know, Dad. I will talk with him tomorrow. I know this has to be done quickly. The man is waiting to get out of Alaska, and someone has to do that job." April left the table and sat on the couch. She fell asleep and felt the stress sluff off of her body. "It is so wonderful to let go," she thought to herself. As she dreamed, in her mind, she saw a few things to change in Alaska, minor changes, but necessary ones.

The next day was Sunday. They all went to church together. It had been such a long time since April attended where her parents went. Larry had decided to come and attend with them. He and April sat with Remi. The service was nice. After that they went home for dinner and April wanted to discuss the plans with Larry and her family.

As Larry listened he felt pain inside. He wanted to marry this woman and have her with him. But he also understood that she had goals she had not yet achieved.

"Do you think if you didn't go, we could do this together?" he asked her.

"But that wouldn't work. This way I will have the internet, and nothing else to do. I could go on line anytime, day or night and get it done sooner. I can work at my own pace." she said.

"How long will you be gone?" Larry asked her.

"I don't know, but we can talk to each other while I am there. There is Skype and we can set it up at your home and even here too. That way we can all stay in touch," April said.

Larry felt better. He knew that not hearing from her would bother him, and this would draw them closer, he thought.

So, in the next two days technicians added Skype at Larry's home. It was also put in the houses of her parents, the ladies, and Mr. Stevens. This allowed her to be in touch with them all.

The tenant was extracted eight days later as April said her goodbyes again. She was dropped off as the man was picked up. He went home on the same airplane that brought her and her luggage.

At the Alaska farm, April was shown the snowmobiles for her to use and an artic track vehicle in a separate garage. The complex was huge. She was shown all around. It was not one complex, but six. She was shown the machinery and how it worked. They showed her the loader which she was already familiar with having used one before at home.

April had one request. The small compartment she had was nice and had a door to exit. April asked that another small space be built next to that door, with another door, and another beyond that.

The workers were confused. Why would anyone waste space and put in another two small, enclosed areas with doors and nothing but tools or buckets giving her three doors to open and close before she reached her space? But it was done as she asked.

April thought her space was more than adequate. There was a nice comfortable bed with some additional blankets on the wall by the bed on wooden dowels. In the middle of the room was a nice heating stove that allowed a person to cook on top of it. To her left by the head of her bed was a desk with a long table. Hanging up high was a permanent screen allowing her parents to see her at all times. They requested this be recorded as well, and everything she did in her small space was recorded. Her television had an eight inch screen, and she was able to download shows or movies she liked if she wanted.

Her main focus was to study, study, and study. In the two compartments, April had wood stacked inside. There were three rows of wood, each twelve feet high and four feet deep. At each end were a few buckets, a broom and a shovel. No one needed to know what else was here, she had been warned to make a safe place, and she knew not to ignore warnings.

She did have a small sink and a toilet with an enclosed bottom that would need to be pumped out in the spring. Her shower was nothing more than a vat of warm water that was warmed by the stove. It circulated up a pipe and she would pull a chain to shower. The water was never much over one hundred degrees. April was assured she would never have scalded skin unless she ramped up the heat in the stove. Then the water would boil in the vat. April had to be mindful. She knew she could do this.

Before she left all the preparations had been made for her to continue her courses. She did have to test out at the end of the year. She tested out at school, and, for the life of her, she did not know how she passed. But she did. Now she knew she could finish and take her finals once she was back. April was feeling happier than she had in years.

April switched on the camera that allowed her to view pen by pen or each complex as a whole. She could see all around the buildings, at the garage, and the back doors. She turned on Skype and found a message from her mom. She knew Mom would have trouble with her being here all alone. After this past year, it was wonderful to get up, feed the animals, and come back for breakfast. Then go on line and get your lesson, take a test and so on.

She enjoyed walking around the perimeter of the building to see all the steers and it did not take long to know who was who. April felt it important to get exercise during the day. One of the nicest things about the buildings were there were strips of light colored roofing which allowed natural light in, and that was a perk for her.

Then the snow came. April was content. She made her own dinners, which were small and easy. Next she walked around and fed the stock twice a day, going from building to building. She studied every afternoon and night. She took a shower. It was only three to five minutes, but it was glorious warm/hot water. Then she put on her warm pajamas and went to bed.

Miranda was able to view April at any given moment. Sometimes when she could not sleep, she would turn on her viewer and see her daughter sleeping contently. Miranda could see April throughout her time there. Everything was recorded for training or for critiquing. It gave Miranda relief to see her daughter and know she was all right.

One morning keeping her routine, April decided to take out the Artic Track. She finished her morning chores and then left a typed, detailed message describing what she was going to do and where she was going. She headed to the garage and pulled the rope to hoist the thick heavy door. There it was black and white waiting for a trip in the snow. April stepped up, pulled the door open, and got in. She turned the key and the engine revved. One push on the visor would open the door in front of the Tracker.

As she pushed the button, April saw polar bears fifty feet or so in front of the complex. She gunned the engine and drove out, pressing the visor button to close the door.

The Artic Track did well on the snow, but it was not fast. It became interesting to see the polar bears could easily out run the machine. One bear decided to block the Track by stopping in front, and just sitting there. April tooted the horn which had little effect on the bear. Next she gunned the engine, and the bear still did not move. April quickly looked around and beeped the horn again. This time the bear took off running.

It was a nice drive. April did not see many problem spots, but for some uncanny reason the polar bears found a secluded spot close to base and that concerned her. One afternoon the sun was out, it was not snowing, and the temperature rose to almost forty degrees. April put on her snowsuit, snow shoes with grips, and slung her rifle over her shoulder. She wanted to investigate the area where the polar bears kept camp.

As she walked out, there were no bears in sight, but she knew that meant nothing. As she came nearer to the polar bears camp, she knew right away why they gathered there. The idiot that was here before she arrived had dumped the carcasses of steers that died. They attracted the carnivores. Terrific! Now they knew where the steers were. And when they were hungry, they'd want an automatic meal, and not hunt for it.

April had seen this time and time again. People lure deer or other animals, and in time the animals come to that spot rather than hunt or forage for themselves for survival. And when the food runs out, they die or turn on the provider. She had no way to remove the frozen carcasses. She would have to remain vigilant until the bears realized there were no more.

April walked around the camp when at the topside she noticed something dark in the snow. As she neared the dark spot, April realized it was a young female wolf pup caught in a steel trap. Her leg was broken, and she had chewed her own leg to get free. The young wolf lay weak and unresponsive. Even when April separated the steel teeth freeing the young wolf's leg, the pup did not move. April hoisted the wolf pup over her shoulder to take her back to camp. Maybe she could help it. April liked a project.

The walk was not far but became cumbersome for April. She had gained some weight and noticed her belly was beginning to become larger. The young wolf was not heavy, maybe eight pounds, but with her winter clothing, the rifle, and the pup it was a bit difficult. At camp April thought to put the pup in one of the enclosures next to her room.

She found something to use as a water dish and put her on fresh straw. On examining the dog, she had no fleas or open wounds just this leg and it was a mess.

She decided to put the pup in her room, so she could monitor her better. April pulled out her medical box and flushed the leg with a mixture of peroxide and water to clean out the wound. It was a jagged cut. This pup would forever have a scar. April only hoped she would be able to walk again. April dabbed on a medicated ointment and wrapped the pup's leg. She also put an IV in the wolf for additional medication and fluids. Then April pulled out one of her study guide books and sat on the floor. The wolf pup lay close by, and April mindlessly began to touch the wolf, petting it as she had Ruby, when April felt a rough tongue slide across her hand. April looked and the wolf pup had her eyes open watching April. Amazingly she was not afraid. "It's all right. You're going to be okay," and she kept reading and the pup slept.

When April had to go out to do her evening chores she put a harness type leash she hand made on the wolf pup to keep her safe. When she returned, the pup had pulled out her IV and was panting hard.

"What happened here?" April asked and the wolf pup growled. "Oh, hey. Hey. None of that," April told her. The pup tried to lunge at April but was too weak and her leg would not hold her. April put on thick gloves and reached for the pup. She sat beside it and pulled the wolf pup on her lap. April stroked her, talking to her all the while. She felt the pup relax and soon it slept. April reached for her book and read until the stove needed wood.

She carefully moved the pup, leaving her on the floor in the harness. April put four logs into the stove and said, "Okay. We need to find something for dinner. How about some rice and toast for you. My biscuits are not too shabby." So she set about getting water, adding rice and making a small batch of biscuits with the wolf watching her. "We need to but that IV back in you too, if you want to get better." April said looking at the pup.

Soon it was dinnertime and April carefully put some warm rice and biscuits mashed together for the pup with a tiny bit if milk. April went to the wolf and told her, "Now you be still. I am going to put this IV back in and you are going to eat your dinner." The pup stayed still, but she did not so much as smell her dinner. "That's an insult to my cooking," April said in a laughing tone. She sat by the pup and spoon fed her. The food fell out in small bits and the pup's head was weary. It took almost a half hour for April to get the food into the pup.

As her patient slept, April decided to take a shower and then have her meal. Next she logged on to type the day's events and then maybe Skype if anyone was on. No one was on. April looked at her clock, it was after 8:30 p.m. so she thought she would just go to bed. Tomorrow was another full day. April crawled into her bed and covered herself with blankets. The fire should easily hold until morning and she slept. During the night the wolf pup felt stronger. She chewed herself out of the harness and lay on the floor beside her alfa wolf's bed.

In the morning April's hand fell over the side of the bed and she felt something wet. She opened her eyes and saw the wolf pup standing beside her bed. "So you are coming to eat me?" April teased the pup.

The young wolf's ears came up at the sound of April's voice. Her eyes were soft, and she showed no aggression or fear.

"I am glad you are so young, and don't know any better. You are still dehydrated girly girl, so you need to increase your water intake," and she went to pet the wolf and the pup instinctively backed away. "Okay. I need to go, do you?" April asked.

So she let the wolf pup out of her room into the next and the pup limped to do her business while April in her own room did hers and dress.

April called to the pup, but the young wolf stood there staring at April. "Come here," as she made a kissy sound stooping over. Then April remembered her grandfather told her about alpha dogs, leaders. Young dogs obeyed them when they gave orders or ignored them. "Woof, come," April barked at the young wolf. The pup came in and sat where she had before. April was impressed. She knew in time the dog would warm up to her. She was too young to have been imprinted and retain it. "You need a name," April said looking at the pup. "How about Jade, or Jet? You don't have any green on you and Jet is easy to say. You are all black and you're going to be a fast girl, so Jet it is. Okay, Jet. I need to go and do the chores. You are not up to speed yet. I'd like you to stay here, but I have a feeling you won't. So I might have to carry you and put you down from time to time. Are you getting this?" April asked the pup.

Jet barked one bark.

April bent to lift Jet and she went limp in April's arms. Jet knew she was not able to walk well, and she knew she could trust April. From pen to pen April would set Jet down and the dog would balance on three wobbly legs, sometimes falling over. Throughout the feeding time Jet tolerated it well.

Back in their little space, Jet was showing signs of tiredness. April offered Jet fresh cold water which the dog lapped eagerly. "That's a good sign," April said re-attaching the pup's IV. Then April went to the outer area before the first door, there was a freezer hidden for safety. She pulled out two small steaks. In another bin were also vegetables and fruits that were dropped off every two weeks. April pulled out some carrots and cauliflower and put them in a pot of water on her stove. She let the steaks sit out up on the top shelf of her small refrigerator. Then she got out dry milk and mixed it with water so they would have milk for today.

"That's that. Now I need to study, but I'm tired and feel like taking a small nap. You want to nap with me?" she asked Jet, and the pup came to her bedside and lay down. The two companions took a much needed rest. When she awoke April put in two hours of study and took another test on line. Then she pulled out a book sitting in the only piece of furniture she had dragged north. A stuffed rocking chair from their front porch, her favorite chair, and read for another hour.

Again she dozed off and Jet moved to sit beside the chair as April slept. The wolf studied her face and smelled her hands. She was not her mother, but she was good.

When April awoke, there was a notice on her computer. It made a quiet ding dong sound. She stood up and looked. It was from Larry. She sat down and typed him a message, short and sweet. She also told him she had a girlfriend and promised she would post a picture soon. April stood and stretched her arms over her head and the pup watched her. With her hands back down she rubbed her tummy and felt something move inside. "Oh, wow! That was something," she said as she looked down and saw one baby on the floor and one inside her.

April checked the calendar in another week Billy would be flying in with fruit and vegetables, and maybe some bread or fresh milk. You never knew what she would have. April liked Billy a lot. She was a gruff soul, but she sure was an awesome pilot. She flew regular runs for companies, or to bring in hunters or take them back out. To many in the main lands and many people living in these parts she was a Godsend. She brought in fruit and vegetables, medicine for people and animals, and material or clothing. Billy was always on the lookout for good deals, and she liked to chaw the fat. Meaning she loved to talk, not too long just enough to learn the gossip and what was going on. April didn't

P. Costa

mind Billy. She spent most of her life in her airplane. She learned Billy had several planes, a bi wing, and a pontoon plane. Billy was teaching her son the ropes, but her son did not like flying. He would prefer to be ground crew, maintenance on the airplanes, and so on.

April kept a list for Billy. Sometimes she got it all, and other times April was lucky to have two of the items on her list, which changed her menu plans. It was no biggie. Out here you had to learn to make do with what you had. You could not be careful enough. One slip and you might not recover. April knew her parents were not happy about this trip, but what other choice did she have. She was the CEO of D Farms. The buck stopped with her.

Her mother kept saying, "Hire someone, April. If you paid more, you could get someone." Miranda did not understand, not just anyone would do. Even on the other farms, some people are not cut out for farming. Some could do it for a day or a week, but then they were gone. Farming is work, hard work, with long hours. What April was doing right now was nothing like what farmers in the states were doing. Her job was to push buttons. It was the isolation that the other guy could not handle, but the work was easy.

Back home, farmers made hay in the hottest weather. The old saying goes, "Make hay while the sun shines," and that's no joke. Things like sweat, being tired, and having cut hands are only a quarter of the job. April remembered stacking hay in the eve of the barn hoping the bees would leave her alone. The temperature in the barn was easily over one hundred thirty degrees, but the hay had to be stacked and put away.

182

Winter was much the same. She had great admiration for the farmers in the North. It was tough to feed animals with frozen hands and fingers as they learned to suck on a nipple. She remembered her toes feeling numb and wishing to get out of the cold winds, as well as wading through the snow. She watched a calf die because it was too cold. That is the life of a farmer. They are not tough. They are tender. They do care. But if they cried at every loss, they would not be able to stick in there and do their job.

Farmers do not receive the credit they deserve. How often did April see cars toot their horns for a tractor to get out of their way. Were they aware that that's how the farmer puts food on their table. Or when they pour a glass of milk, do they think about where it came from? To April there was no greater, honorable job on this earth.

Farming is close to nature. To see the animals being born is a miracle, as well as a new lamb suckling at its protective mother. A calf being licked dry by its mother. And a hen clucking in the yard as her baby chicks scratch dirt all around her. When she calls them they all hide under her wings. Feisty little mothers who would give up their lives and fight to the death to protect their babies.

April remembered one day while riding Native Son along an old creek bed, some rude folks had thrown trash from their cars as they drove. Over the years that trash landed on the bank and some in the water. On this particular day a small duckling had caught it's beak in a plastic wrapper. The mother duck did all she could and kept biting that wrapper until her baby was free. Another time April watched a baby duckling disappear in the water as the others swam behind their mother. The mother duck was aware of what happened, and she swam in a circle and dived down. She circled again and again, diving over and over until the little duck surfaced. The mother duck dislodged her baby's foot from the mouth of a snapping turtle.

April loved the many different animals she had over the years, including the steers. She used to laugh when they were put out to pasture. They would run and kick their legs in the air holler out "Bauh." It must have felt so good to them.

To learn about animals, their specific care and needs; to be responsible for their care, even if there were other things she wanted to do; that is what April believed made her responsible in life. That is the kind of life she hoped for her baby and all of her children. To learn that this great big world is not just about you. There are many people and animals in this world, that if given to you for their care is a huge responsibility.

Kindness matters to all, animals and people. Animals are not to be abused. They do have feelings, or they would not yelp in pain when abused. Kindness costs nothing, it can be given liberally, and you will be the benefactor.

April made her list for Billy while the pup was snoring. "Puppy food, if she can get it," and then she left to do the evening chores. It went well and she was back in about two hours, give or take. The puppy was yawning. She was just waking up, so she let her out while she made dinner. Just something light tonight. Tomorrow was Sunday and she never did more than she had to on Sundays. She loved to tune in to TV from the dish on the hillside and watch the church service. She enjoyed hearing the talks and singing with them. It kept her from feeling so isolated.

April cooked some noodles and put peppers and onions on top of them with a small amount of oil and a biscuit. Jet was going to have some noodles and a biscuit with some milk. For dessert there was peanut butter on no-salt crackers with a scant bit of chocolate. She felt spoiled.

That is how her days went. Chores every morning for two to three hours, depending on whether the steers needed bedding or not. Then breakfast for her and Jet.

The afternoons were either spent studying or testing, and often the two of them would go outside for a jaunt.

Each day April crossed off the days on her calendar with a marker. Each month April weighed herself on a scale and measured her stomach girth and kept track. April did keep her doctor's appointments every other month if the weather was not too severe. When the snow and bitter cold set in, she stayed inside and only went out if she had to. And then every other weekend, weather permitting, April loved to see Billy and it was like Christmas.

Taking care of Jet was more like a pleasure than a job. She was turning out to be so friendly and dependable. Jet was a fast learner. She would guard steers or turn them if needed with April motioning with her hands. Jet watched carefully knowing what to do. Jet did not have a limp, but often would run on three legs. It was more of habit than because of pain. The leg never hindered Jet in any way and no longer looked mangled. The scarring was minimal thanks to April's diligent care. Jet turned into a dependable watch dog. She heard noises April could not. Jet also was protective of April. No one came near April.

On one of the Billy days, April took the snowmobile down to the landing site with Jet on the back behind her sporting a pair of sunglasses.

Billy laughed when she saw the wolf. Jet didn't mind Billy.

"I can't stay long. The winds are moving in. I think a nasty storm is on its way, a Northeastern." April was going to help load the boxes on the sled behind the snowmobile when Billy stopped her. "Some of these are heavy," she said.

April knew that everybody was aware she was expecting. She was not upset because they were just trying to help her.

"Okay. I am off. You take care and batten down the hatches. If it's not tied down, it's going to blow away. "Oh, and before I forget, there was a large group of whites heading this way." April thanked Billy and soon she was barreling off in the sky.

Billy was right, April just got her supplies put away and was backing in the snowmobile when the winds hit. They almost knocked her over. April hung onto the bar that had been installed for storms to help her get inside.

"Where was Jet?" April thought. The dog was smart. Jet had hunkered down and was crawling on her belly to get inside.

They ate a nice dinner that night and made rounds after chores to be sure everything was secure. The building shuddered like someone was shaking it, but the building stood strong. April was very glad D Farms built this complex. They were familiar with the requirements and steel beams, not wood, were used as supports. They were pounded into the ground and cemented.

April's small space was fairly quiet. There was no reception for internet or TV because of the storm, so the two of them just sat it out. No one would have guessed the great conversations you can have with your pup like April did during the storm. Jet was a wolf, but she wasn't. She was part of April. Jet could anticipate April's moves and thoughts. At chore time Jet knew the routine, but if a problem arose Jet was right on it.

That night the two companions slept for the longest they ever had. The stove was warm they were cozy and safe, so they slept. That storm raged for three days.

On the third day, April received some messages on the CB in her room. The mainland was intact, but many of the homes along the river banks were taken out. April prayed no one was missing or dead. Alaska can be brutal. That afternoon the winds diminished, and the sun came out. Only every so often did the wind blow snow around in swirls.

April wanted to go out to see how things were around the encampment. She opened the garage area were the snow tracker was and headed out with her companion riding shotgun.

April did not make it out more than five feet when she heard a thud on the roof of the tracker. It was a polar bear, a mean and hungry one. They were on the roof of the garage for warmth and were waiting for a way to get in. April went forward, and the bear slid down onto the hood of the tracker. The bear roared at the two inside. They had a good look inside a polar bear's mouth and teeth. Jet began to bark. "Shh" April said to her. April gunned the tracker, closing the garage door behind her.

As they drove around the upside of the complex, she could see that there had to be forty or more bears. And April had enough. She slammed on the brake and the polar bear on the hood slid off. Then she continued forward in 4 x 4 low. She felt the tracker rock from side to side as she drove over the bear. Next she pulled out her rifle and stood up. She opened the hatch leaning out and took out three of the most aggressive bears. It turned into a feeding frenzy.

April did not want to stay there. She sat down and pushed the tracker forward. The tracker handled well up the slope and to the top of the hill. The sun almost blinded April so she fished out her sunglasses and continued on. April drove all around the complex and when she came back around the bears were there waiting for her.

She sat in the tracker idling when all at once she felt like the machine was rocking. April looked to her rear view mirror and saw five bears pushing on the tracker almost lifting it off the snow. April reached for her rifle when she felt another thud on the roof. A bear was pounding on the roof to get to her. April unlocked the clip and shot two shots, hitting the bear twice.

Then April realized the tracker was being pushed over sideways. Once it was lying on its side, April had to pull herself up and close the latch. She also knew she was a good two hundred yards from safety. There was no way she could run, so she tried the CB radio. She put out a call for help, explaining what happened. Some calls came back and said they could not make it. One said they would be out by nightfall and to stay where she was. April knew that was not a good idea.

She looked at her companion and asked, "Can we keep them off of us?" Jet barked and nuzzled her companion. April looked out the side mirror and saw nothing. There was no noise on top of the garage and obvious movement.

Slowly she opened her cab door which was high in the air. She looked around and saw nothing. April knew the bears would not go far. She stepped out onto the track and listened. She slowly and quietly made her way down with Jet following her. Once out on the snow, April made a direct line to the door. It did not take long before they heard the bears growl, as if to say, "There she goes. Let's get her."

April was in good shape, but the snow was deep, and she struggled to move as fast as she could. How she wished she had her snowshoes. April found twisting from side to side helped maneuver the snow out of the way, making room for her to move forward. The bears were faster, and April turned in time to see they were now twenty feet behind her. She picked up the rifle and sighted in one after another. But they kept coming. Jet was barking while a polar bear stood over her. The dog was stealthy and fast.

April was able to take out three more bears and move closer to the compound. She was eight feet from camp when a big mama bear on the roof barred her way. With all her might and anger, April screamed at the bear, "Then come and get me." The bear howled back at April, but in a minute she and Jet were safely in their compound. There was a small window in the door that April was able to see through. Those bears were trying to get in by digging at a spot at one side wall. She would have to brace that wall better.

Once inside, April took off her outer clothing and went into the steer area. On the rafters were pieces of metal and lumber that April would need to fortify that wall. She climbed up the ladder and pulled down one piece at a time. Each piece she had to drag through a pen while Jet kept the animals away from her and from escaping from the open pen. When all the boards and metal were in place, April ordered Jet to stay so the steers would not be curious and tear the wall down. April returned with a drill and lock screws. It took April almost three hours, but now the steers did not avoid that area. They had avoided that area before and April knew why. That should hold the bears and they can go and find their own food. They did before we came here she thought.

That was enough excitement for one day. She hated to ask for assistance, but she needed to tow the tracker, so she swallowed her pride and called on the CB. There were listeners who told her that they would come tomorrow. April told them they needed someone to stand watch with guns. April did not want anyone getting hurt.

April was able to Skype with her parents that night and the ladies too. They were able to see Jet who was growing like a weed and her mother wanted to see her tummy. "Oh, Mom! Really! It's kind of embarrassing." But being a good sport and loving her mother she did.

"Oh, April, the little bun is growing. I am so excited. I have crocheted a blanket and some hats."

April was happy. Only a short while ago her mother was giving up and it was because of her. So, if this made her mom happy, then so be it. April would not have anything without her parents.

April was able to Skype with Larry. She heard Happy in the background. "Has she taken over?" April asked him.

"Well, not everything, but pretty much me. She goes everywhere with me including inside the tractor cab and on the road. She won't have it any other way."

"Is there room for me?" April asked.

"It's doubtful. She's put on some weight and takes up a lot of room," Larry joked.

April laughed. They wanted to stay on longer, but they both knew they had to get up early. After the important "I Love you," they hung up.

Days turned into weeks, and weeks turned into months. April realized she had been here in Alaska four months already and was now seven months pregnant. She was showing a good sized belly. The work was not difficult, but she did not climb anymore. April walked laps during the afternoons to keep limber and to help with childbirth. She had passed the veterinary classes and kept up with her reading. She felt confident that she would pass the exam. She read and kept up and walked a lot.

Who Is Coming In Here?

ONE EVENING WHILE THEY WERE GETTING READY FOR BED, APRIL saw Jet's ears go up. She was listening to something. Jet walked to the door and looked at April.

"What wrong Jet?"

Jet kept her eye on the door, then April heard it too. Someone was in the compound, not just someone but several of them. April reached to the backside of her bed and pulled on black pants, a black long-sleeved shirt, and a black masked beanie. Only her eyes showed. As she slipped on thin gloves, April put a gun in her leg holster and cautioned Jet to be quiet. No barking by putting her fingers to her lips.

Outside of the three doors April and Jet stood still listening when they heard noises. It sounded like they were after the steers, to take them. Jet walked silently while April tried to do the same. They got very close to the four men in this operation. April was uncertain what to do, but she knew it would be best to get one at a time. Without any signal from April, Jet went into action.

"Hey, how did a wolf get in here? Go and get it," one yelled.

Jet came in April's direction along the pathway out of sight of the other men. April hit the man looking for Jet in the head with a shovel and knocking him out. She tied his hands and feet and gagged his mouth.

Then the three men were moving cattle into another pen with some other steers which was a very bad idea. It did not take long for the steers to push and shove each other. Some tried to get on top of each other.

Jet went into the pen silently. She kept moving the steers so they would run into the men. One man was knocked down and trampled by several steers. "My legs. I think one is broken" the man whined.

Jet backed off and came to April and lay down. The man was hurt. His other two companions drug him to the outside of the pen and hollered for their friend that April had tied up.

"You go and find him," the one said to the other. That man pulled out a pistol and began to look for his friend.

April did not want Jet shot. She was not concerned about herself. She was a steady shooter. The man was walking as if he were pursuing a criminal. As he came down the alleyway, Jet pawed April's leg and disappeared. Jet crossed right in front of the man who was not suspecting that.

He turned and fired, missing Jet. Next he felt a huge smack on his head, and he was out.

April pulled that man to another area close by and bound and gagged him too.

"One to go," April thought. She was beside a huge wall of bales in the alleyway. They lined the entire wall from one end to the other and April felt if she could get up higher she could take this man out. April lifted her leg onto the top of the first bale and stepped up. "Uh, this is not going to work," she thought to herself. She felt if she could wedge her way into the side of a bale, she would not be seen. April waited and watched, the last man standing was frustrated and getting angry.

"Shit! Where the hell are those two guys?

The other man was hurt badly. His leg was broken, and he cried with pain.

"Oh shut up will you? I have enough to think about. I need to get those two so we can load up and get out," he said.

Now with April in the bales, she knew she could not get out fast enough to stop that man. Again, it was Jet who ran full force, sprang, and knocked that man to the ground. Jet quickly reversed her run. She grabbed the man's dropped gun in her mouth and ran away.

The man ran after her and at the turn he found someone in black with a pistol at his forehead and a wolf behind him growling. April tied him up similar to the others and had Jet help her drag the injured man.

Leaving him lay in the alleyway. She tied his arms to the bales. Then she walked to her "office" and used the CB to call for help.

Within an hour, the sheriff and his men showed up on their snowmobiles. There were about a dozen of them in all. April welcomed them in at the main entrance of the compound. One deputy had taken the keys from the track truck and trailer. They were all talking about these men. This group of men had been rustling animals: cattle, sheep, or anything they could get their hands on. They traveled out of Alaska to Michigan and sold them at auctions. On the seat of the truck were sales slips from several states. They had been pretty slick, and the sheriff asked April how she was able to get them. April told the men it was the wolf. She was a keen hunter. And the men laughed.

The sheriff knew April. He knew she had been in Ops in the military. She was a tough girl, even more so doing this job out in the middle of nowhere. Isolation could really wear a person down, make them crazy, but she was keen enough to handle four rustlers.

This would make for good stories for weeks. They teased April and she offered all of them some blueberry tea. Within the hour they left with their prisoners in tow. The track truck and trailer would have to wait. April told them that was okay. She understood. Just send her a message the day before to let her know when they were coming.

April was exhausted. Being pregnant was tiring. Her tummy was bigger. Her weight was now 132 pounds. She had gained 13 pounds in seven months. April knew she had to be careful. She made a mental note to walk more in the compound and eat more meat and vegetables, but no more biscuits. Jet could have all she wanted.

The seventh month soon slipped into the eighth. The weather patterns were inconsistent. One day it would snow and be bitter for two or three days. Then the sun would break and be such a beautiful day. On one such day, April was walking with her skis. She had been using them for the last three months. Getting out felt great. She followed a trail she had found. It was great exercise, and she was able to really move on the snow. Jet had to run often to catch up with her.

On this particular day, April was up on a rim and was able to see the water. Then a Bald Eagle swooped into the water and came back up carrying a fish. There was no doubt about it Alaska was beautiful. There were pristine forests, the fish were abundant, the people were friendly, and she loved it. April longed to go home to be with her family, but for the remaining days of her life she would look back on Alaska as a special time in her life.

She was independent and strong and was not afraid of anything. These memories were hers forever.

April was concerned. She was beginning to have back pain. And sometimes when walking she had to stop because the pain would reach into her back and legs and twist, almost taking her breath away. Now it was time to leave before anything bad happened. April so dearly wanted to take Jet with her. She was willing to pay any fine or demand made by the Alaskan government. Jet was not wild nor would she survive in the wild. Jet was now April's. They had bonded and April would take her home.

Near the end of the eighth month, April made a request to Mr. Stevens who was keenly aware that she was still there and needed to leave.

There was another person who seemed interested in taking over the Alaskan compound. He was twenty-four and no longer interested in college. He yearned for adventure in his life. He continued with D Farms, wanting to do something more. That evening Mr. Stevens put a call into the young man. Who said he wanted a few days to think about it and then when Mr. Stevens called he would have an answer.

"Two days. That is all the time I will give you. The person there has been at that compound for nine months and it is critical they leave for health reasons," Mr. Stevens said.

By the end of the eighth month, April felt like a beached whale. Even Jet was concerned about her. April knew that she had to get the chores done, but it took her so much longer.

Her weight was now 135 pounds. She had gained another two pounds in one month for a total of fifteen so far. April was drinking more than eating. Doing all she could not to put on so much weight to help with an easier delivery. April also knew the baby was dropping and she was having trouble with pressure on her bladder. Into the ninth month, April wished she had help. She was tired a lot. She did get the work done, but it was a chore to climb or bend.

Jet never jumped up on her and seemed to understand. One evening after a shower Jet licked April's belly. She never did that before. It made April think Jet knew more of what was going on than she realized, and she was right.

April never reached full gestation. She was six days from her due date, and she had back pain constantly. She found herself holding her back while walking. April made a call into the hospital, and they assured her that she was not yet ready.

"Not ready. How do they know. They are not here. A baby comes when a baby is ready, not when you are ready," she said out loud. She felt like giving up.

April began to cry and could not understand why since this was out of character. She could not remember the last time she cried. Maybe when she was six or ten, the time Dobbins was sick. Oh, yeah. When Hugh pulled the stunt with that girl. That really hurt. There was no reason whatsoever that she should be sad or sitting here crying. April reasoned it must be due to hormones.

April put in another call. This time she reached a nurse who listened.

"Oh, honey, you need to get in here right away," she said.

April looked at her watch. It was almost 3:00 p.m. It would be dark soon. "I don't know if I can make it on the snowmobile," she said.

"Oh, honey, don't you even try that. Can you get someone to bring you in?" the nurse asked. Then while she was standing there April got a stabbing pain unlike any she had before. "Hello, April. Are you there?" the nurse asked. Next the nurse heard something fall, something big, and then the line went dead. Instinctively the nurse put out an emergency call to get April to the hospital ASAP!

April woke to Jet growling and feeling wet. Her water had broken and there was blood on the floor. "Oh, God, please help me. Send me help, Father. Please."

Someone was knocking hard on the door and April could not get up.

"Come in," she tried to holler. It seemed like hours, and then April heard voices around her. It was the sheriff. He was reassuring April that she was going to be all right. He had teams of dogs outside that would take her as fast as lightening to the hospital. He said other things April could not take in or retain.

They hoisted April onto a transport gurney and lifted her up to carry her out with Jet following beside her. "That wolf is going too," the sheriff said. "That is her baby, and she will not leave her side."

Soon April was on a bed on the dog sled. The dogs were barking and ready to go. There were two teams of sled dogs pulling.

April thought about the compound. No one would be there, and she asked the person behind her on the sled in a whispered voice.

It was a woman who answered her. "Don't worry, honey. My son is there, and he is real good with animals. He knows what to do. He used to come when the other man was here. Don't you worry about a thing. Just relax and enjoy the ride. My boys will have you at the hospital soon."

Jet was not about to leave April. She sat clinging on the footboard near April's feet. "It's a good thing she is short so that dog can fit on there," one woman said to another.

"Well she is not short. She is just right. If anyone is a shrimp, it's me!" April's driver said and laughed.

And they were off. The snow sprayed along the sides of the dog sled bed and to April it was so beautiful. She could look up and see the black night sky with the bright dots of stars. It was almost magical. The ride was not bumpy at all. The sled glided over the snow.

The dogs concentrated on their run. They only barked every now and then, and April felt herself being rocked to sleep. If only that back pain would stop. On and on they went. The drivers had no conversations, they just drove.

At one point April had pain and she cried out. The woman driver with her said, "Here, honey, take this into your mouth and chew on it."

April did. The stick had a mild taste, but in a few minutes her pain subsided.

"Works every time," the woman said. "Mush boys, mush. Keep it going." There was no way for April to know what time it was or how long she was on the dog sled. The ride was comfortable, and they were flying over the snow.

Then they were stopped. April felt herself being lifted up and put on a helicopter. Next she felt Jet lay her head on April's chest. The door closed and she heard the whirr of the chopper blades. She put her arm over Jet to comfort her. She imagined the sound waves would bother her ears. Jet did not look in distress. In fact she looked a whole lot better than April.

That ride was a short one. Soon people were unloading April again and carrying her into a hospital. "We were told the dog stays with her." one of the men said.

"Oh, yea. I don't think so. At least not in the delivery room," the nurse said. April was rushed into a room, blood drawn, prepped, and taken into the operating room. The man tried unsuccessfully to put Jet into a room, but Jet would out maneuver him, and she kept a vigil at the OR door.

"So long as you don't go inside," the man said. Jet lay down by the side of the doors waiting for her master to return.

Delivery was fast. April was already fully dilated. The baby crowned and was out in less than twenty minutes. He weighed 8 pounds and 7 ounces and was 19 inches long. He was pure white with a small impish face. and had many of April's features: her ears, her nose, and her chin. No hair, just some wisps of blonde over his bald head.

April counted his fingers and toes. She held him and was so full of love. If ever anyone had told her she would fall in love with a short, fat, bald guy, she would have laughed at them. Here he was and his mother was in love with this little guy.

April prayed and thanked God for his infinite wisdom for her to keep this little boy alive. April was tired so they cleaned her up and put her into a room.

There were no other deliveries that week and she was their only patient. April was alone in a room. Jet found her and stayed by her side. Soon they brought the baby to April and Jet stood on her hind feet to meet her new master. Jet smelled him and looked at April.

"He's yours, Jet. You can train him all you like." The dog licked April's hand and lay back down.

"You know, we don't usually allow dogs in here, but that is more than an average dog. I'd swear it's human," one man said.

Big News to Share

APRIL ASKED IF SOMEONE WOULD PLEASE CALL HER PARENTS. THERE was no telephone in April's room. One nurse brought a telephone to April. "Hold on a minute," the nurse said covering the mouth piece. "It's your mom," and handed April the telephone.

"Hello, Mom. How are you?" April asked.

"I am fine. Are you at a friend's house for dinner, April? I don't see you on the monitor," her mother asked.

"No, Mom. I am not there. Is Dad nearby?" April asked smiling.

"Yes, he is here. Gordon, come to the phone. April wants to speak with you," Miranda said.

"Hello, April. How are you?" Dad asked.

"Dad, please put the phone on speaker. Can you do that?" April asked.

"Sure I can, sweetie, just a minute," he said, and April heard a click. "Okay, it's on," Gordon said.

"Well, Mom and Dad, I am calling you from a hospital in Alaska. It is March 14th, and you are now grandparents of a healthy baby boy," April said beginning to cry. All she heard was screaming, laughter, and her mother crying. "How big is he, April?" her mother asked. April told her.

"Oh, April, can we come? Can we come to Alaska and be with our grandson?" Her mother tearfully asked.

"Sure you can, Mom. And tell the ladies, too, and Larry, and Du Val, and tell Mr. Steven. He has to get someone out here soon. Mom and Dad, I love you so much and I am so thankful for you both. I can't thank you enough for all your support all my life and especially through those awful days. I know I owe you so much and I love you for it" April said crying. The nurse in the hall had to turn away because she began to cry too.

Her dad was on the telephone asking for a supervisor, so April called for someone to take the telephone. From what she could determine they were giving her dad the name and directions of the hospital. They told them they were welcome. The hospital had a small holding area or empty rooms they could sleep in since there were no hotels nearby.

April was elated and so very tired. She encouraged her baby to nurse and then she handed him to the nurse who put him in a bassinet beside April's bed.

April slept for what seemed like days. She needed some help to go to the bathroom the next morning and then she went back to sleep again. At lunchtime April was feeling somewhat human as they brought a tray of food for her. It had roast turkey, yams, green beans, a roll, milk, hot tea, and some kind of sweet roll she did not want. She would eat for the baby, but not for herself. She put on too much weight she thought.

Soon her doctor was in the room. She was a small and feisty woman. "So you had this baby when I could not be here," she teased April. "You did well. That baby decided to come in a snowstorm. They could not use snowmobiles because the snow was coming down that fast. You are very lucky," she said.

April did not know about all of that. She wanted to be sure to compensate those who had helped her and jotted down that information for Mr. Stevens to take care of.

By 2:00 that afternoon her visitors came. Yes, they all came: her mom and dad, Larry, Lena and Nora, and Du Val and his lovely wife. They brought in flowers and gifts. They were all so happy and chatty, all except Larry who just stood by April's side.

"Who is this?" Gordon asked.

"That would be Jet! She is my shadow, and where I go, she goes," April said.

"Is that the puppy you raised, April? She sure got big and filled out nicely," her Dad said.

"Don't reach for her Dad. She is very protective, and I am not sure if"

"You mean like this?" And there was Dad stroking Jet's head and ears like she had known him all her life.

"Well, she is very smart too," April said smiling.

Larry took her hand and kissed it. "Are you feeling all right?" he asked.

"I am. I really am okay after all this," April said.

Just then the sheriff came in to check on April. "I just wanted to see how you were. You certainly tolerated that dog sled ride in. You did fantastic. Elaine, your driver, said anytime you want to go, she would gladly take you," and he laughed.

That is when April told the sheriff she wanted everyone's name that had helped her, including the boy who was left behind to take care of the compound of steers.

"Don't you worry about that," he said. "They don't expect anything."

April said. "I know it, but that would not be right, not by me. I am thankful and show my gratitude when I can. So please, will you help me thank them in the right way."

"Well, I know for a fact that Elaine has fallen on hard times, but she was one of the first who volunteered to come out in the storm to get you," the Sheriff said.

"So knowing that, since they helped me, surely I can help them back," April said.

"Okay then. I will do what I can," the Sheriff said and waved goodbye to all as he left.

"April, you came to the hospital on a dog sled?" her mother asked.

"I did. There were two teams. It was amazing. We flew over the snow," April said.

Nora told April that because of how he came into this world, this boy would be an animal lover too. That was a fact in their tribe.

Larry just said, "Oh boy, with her loving animals, my farm will likely be a zoo." And they all laughed.

April wanted them to hold the baby and the nurses brought him in. "April did you name him yet?" Nora asked.

"No, I have not. I thought since Larry was going to be his Poppa, he should have that honor."

Larry stood there becoming emotional. His face reddened, and he almost had tears in his eyes when the baby was put in his arms.

"What will you name him, Larry?" they asked.

Larry did not answer. He was studying the baby's face and eyes. The little baby stared back at his daddy. Larry looked at April and asked her, "What names do you like?"

"I don't know. I can't think. I am just glad he is here safely," and she held onto his tiny hand. The baby began to fuss. "I think it's lunch time for him," April said, and Larry handed the baby to April. The four women watched in awe as their daughter, niece and dear friend who they watched grow up, was now holding a baby of her own. They soon left to let the baby nurse and give April some privacy.

Larry remained behind leaning over the side of the bed watching the tiny baby nurse. All the while the baby's eyes were on him. Soon one tiny hand was reaching for Larry's face.

"I think he likes you Poppa," April said to Larry.

Larry was in awe. He wished his parents, who were no longer living, could have met this little one. He was sure both of them, his mother in particular, would have enjoyed this. "So when are you coming home, April?" Larry asked April rubbing her neck to soothe her.

"As soon as I can get out of here. Mr. Stevens has someone at the encampment to help out until a replacement comes. There is no reason for me to stay."

Larry said," April we need to go to the temple and seal this little one to us. Don't you agree?" Larry said. "I think it's time."

April agreed, she had done everything she could to help out and now it was her time. Her stay in the hospital was three days. It was just long enough for a quiet stay from the weather, yet long enough for all of them to go home together.

During their time in Alaska, her family made the most of shopping and eating at the local shops and cuisine. Many knew about April and her family. They were all curious about her baby adventure. Some asked about D Farms and how to get involved. Some wanted their children to have a chance to earn an education. Du Val was very helpful giving them the information they needed. Her family was treated very well by the town folks. Indeed they fit right in.

On the day of release, April was dressing, and her mom and the two ladies came in to help her. There were her bags and baby items, and the men had already retrieved her luggage and things from the small space she lived in at the compound.

April never had much, but she hoped they had gotten all of her personal things, especially for school. Her father assured her they did. They had help, the guy working there had boxed up everything that was there. The only things left were the small TV, the CB radio, and the large computer. The surveillance tapes of April were collected and the monitor dismantled since it was no longer needed.

Going Home at Last

APRIL WAS READY TO GO HOME BUT A LITTLE UNEASY. THERE HAD never been a real plan in her life. Things just happened and she dealt with them.

Now she was a Mother, and she could see her life at home, raising children with Larry and that's it. It did not sit right with her. April never was much of a sit down, stay-at-home kind of person. She had an A-type personality. She liked to be on the go. Her mother was keenly aware of her daughter's change in mood, and she hugged her. "It's going to be all right. We are all here to help you. You know that," she said.

As they stood at the front desk to be signed out, the nurse gave them a bombshell. "You need to sign your baby's name for state records before you leave," she said.

The group looked at each other when Gordon asked Larry, "Larry, we are not going far until you come up with a name."

"I don't know," Larry said looking at April. "Do you like . . ." and he whispered in her ear.

"I do. That's nice and no nick name," she said.

Larry reached over and wrote Ian Gordon on the paper.

"Are you going to tell us?" the others asked.

Larry turned and said, "Ian Gordon. His name will be Ian, pronounced as Ean." The group said the baby's name over and over and they all smiled and said they all liked it very much. Gordon was deeply touched.

That is when Du Val's wife leaned close to April and said, "Our baby is due in June maybe these two will be playmates."

April was so happy, her face flushed, while her friend put her finger to her lips to indicate that it was a secret.

They all took a ride with the gracious hospital janitor who took anyone where they wanted to go in the snow. He was experienced having been born and raised in Alaska. He took April and her family to the airport.

They boarded with Scott waiting on the steps to take the baby from April so she could board easier. Scott took the little one in his arms and snuggled him "We are all going home, little guy," he said as he carried the baby up the steps to April. April was trying to put the baby in a car seat and Larry stepped in to help her. Larry sat on the seat next to April and little Ian sat facing them in a seat with a blanket partially over him.

It was a nice flight, sunny and no wind. "Someone's watching over us," Scott said. They landed by 4:00 in the evening. They got in their cars to go home. April and Larry would go home to her parents and then she would sit down and talk with him about their life plans. April agreed that she wanted to be with Larry, but part of her did not want to sit at home every day. She was the CEO of D Farms and wanted to oversee things and travel if there were problems. The two of them had a lot to think about and work out before they went to the temple together.

The following week Larry had April, Ian and her parents at his home for a meal and a meeting. There they discussed temple wedding plans. They knew they had to meet with the bishop first and Ian would come along to be sealed to them.

Then April had to take her finals, with Larry's help. When she went in she was nervous. When she came out she was confident and relaxed. She felt good and was sure she had passed.

"I guess I will have to refer to you as doctor from now on," and they both laughed. April loved this man so much. He was always helping her. These were her finals, but he was here with her. They made each other a priority.

April spoke to Larry and asked if he would consider moving. Larry was stiff, but as April spoke he began to see the benefit of moving closer to her family. He needed time and the possibility of seeing where they would go verses what he had now. He liked farming period! That is what he wanted to do. But being an hour away from her family, who wanted to help raise Ian, Larry knew that one hour was too far away. He went with Gordon to scout land and they decided that the abandoned farm that April had used to raise steers would work well. That farm had 386 acres, most of it tillable with a borderline of trees. It had a pond and two good size areas of woods for wild animals and fallen trees that could be used for firewood or stacked for small animals to nest in or for protection from predators. After a meeting with Tilly who was now in control of the farm, it was settled.

The temple trip was planned. A small group went to the temple. They were all family. Little Ian was so good, he did not cry at all. When April knelt at the alter and joined Larry's hand in hers, she knew without a doubt this was the man God had chosen for her as her life's companion. She felt it throughout her whole body. It was a powerful feeling in her chest and April could not hold back her tears. Larry was a sweet man, kind and humble. He too had those same feelings, and both of them wept at the altar. The officiator who presided over their marriage was also touched.

He too felt what they felt. The ceremony was small and endearing. Their words were spoken with firm commitment.

April looked into her husband's eyes and thanked her Father in Heaven for his love and for watching over her. Right then and there April knew her place was to be beside her husband. But only so long as he was obeying God and doing right. They would work it out together. April knew her heart. She would not, could not obey him, even though she loved him, if he chose to do wrong. A marriage had the wife submitting to her husband because he is the head of the household. But April added, so long as he runs his home with God as the head of the home.

After their sealing, a temple worker brought in baby Ian. He was almost a month old, and his dark eyes would dart about the room focusing on everything. After Ian was sealed to his parents, the three of them walked out with their family and friends who were all witnesses.

The old farmhouse took on a new persona. It had a face lift inside and out. April insisted she wanted a fireplace, but Larry did not. He did not want to cut, split and drag wood into the house. Miranda agreed completely with Larry. Wood had bugs and dirt that little children got into. A compromise was reached when the plumber suggested putting in a tubular system with water inside. Using that as the fireplace grate, the fireplace would heat the home, but the heat would not go up the chimney, only the smoke would. April was thrilled. She also took the time to gather rocks and she herself made a beautiful mantel for the fireplace. When friends visited, they all commented on how nice and beautiful the fireplace was. When they would ask who did the work, Larry proudly said his wife did.

They kept the original wood work in the farmhouse while adding some modern touches. April was able to make six bedrooms where there had only been three. She finished the attic by making it into a long spacious bedroom with three twin beds and shelving. The beds were all painted in primary colors. On the walls hung photos of horses, April during her Olympic days, and Larry on his tractor.

The kitchen was spacious. So Larry finished the table that was in the kitchen at his old home including all eight of the chairs. They really came out beautifully.

The two of them worked diligently on their home. It took almost a year for it to come together, and Ian had such fun with boxes, tape and anything he could get into. Ian was walking by the age of five and a half months.

April kept her job as CEO of D Farms. When there was a problem, she would go and assess the situation. Then she would make plans to correct the problem and implement the changes. It was common for her to fly once or twice a week, always taking Ian with her. Usually they would be home that same day in the evening, but once in a while the next day depending on the weather or the problem.

Larry learned to enjoy flying too. They went as a family to visit Miranda's parents on her mother's side and to her grandparents on her father's side. "It's a vacation," April would say. They were all happy to see April and her husband. And, of course, little Ian who was as fearless as his mother. They would laugh and dote on Ian. He was such a loving child. Yes, they saw their aging grandparents once a month. Taking turns, that was something both of them felt strongly about, especially since Larry's family were all gone. He knew the importance of family in his life, and he missed them. It would be wrong to have family and not see them. He was not in a job that prevented them from traveling and they had the finances to go, so there was no excuse.

On one such trip April crossed paths with an associate from another farm cooperative named Frank. He asked her how the cattle raising went in Alaska. April candidly told him and outlined her work chores.

He was very interested and asked April if she would mind coming to a seminar he wanted to plan sometime later that year. He would be in touch.

April said they could talk and discuss plans at that time.

A month passed and one evening as April and Larry were on their porch watching Ian play with kittens, her cell phone rang. It was the associate she had met earlier. Frank asked April if she would be willing to do a presentation of what it was like in Alaska. He said that some in the cooperative did not believe what D farms did could be done.

April said anytime any one of them wanted to go to their facility in Alaska, they were welcome.

Frank pressed her asking if in November April would be willing to come and explain what had been done in Alaska. Everything from the beginning including the construction, what was put in, how it went, any problems, and so on.

April sat looking at Larry and he said, "Go ahead."

So it was arranged for April to make a presentation and be in Washington in November. It was the week of Thanksgiving which meant she would not be able to make a big dinner for the family and April was disappointed.

Going to Washington

April made an outline later that week. She called Mr. Stevens, who was more than helpful. She had diagrams, the work schedule, and how the entire process came about. There were even photos with the compound's various building stages. And she remembered what she did while tending the farm, and some of the problems she had encountered. She also recalled Miranda had those 24-hour tapes as well. April would have to sort through them to see what they should or should not see.

April was not concerned. She knew with Ian turning two, he was beginning to become very active. And she would need some help from her parents to watch Ian while she was away.

April did show her family what her ideas were, and they said they were good. They suggested ideas and had questions that might come up at the presentation. When the time came, April felt confident and ready.

The week before the presentation April felt odd, not herself. She asked Larry if they could go to the temple together, just the two of them. She would ask her parents to watch Ian. They loved to have him anyway.

They went and there they found a deeper peace in their feelings towards each other and recommitted their marriage vows.

April was amazed that they were married only a year and a half ago. She and Larry were so much alike it was uncanny. Often they made the same comments and sometimes she could complete his sentences. April was happy and content. She loved her husband so much because he loved her, and he never put restrictions on her. She could come and go so long as she told him. Good communication is important in any relationship, marriage, or business.

April knew in her heart Larry would never cheat on her and she would never so much as look at another man the way she did at Larry. He was her one and only, and he felt the same way about her. They made a pact to have a date every week. Even if that meant just a ride together or going to the mill or library. It did not matter, so long as they had time just for each other.

They knew so long as they prayed and kept this pattern they would be all right. They would be blessed throughout their lifetimes.

The night before her trip April clung to her husband. Larry was tired and just wanted to sleep but he put his arm around his wife and held her. That was what April wanted, to have him as close to her as possible. They slept and at 7:00 a.m. their telephone rang. April answered the call sleepily.

"Hey, it's Scott. I am at the terminal. Where are you?"

April jumped out of bed and dressed in a flash. Larry awoke and he tried to help her. "Just get Ian to my parents," she asked kissing him and running down the stairs. She had her two bags, one with clothing and the other with the presentation including slides, tapes, and photos. She knew she could do her hair and redress on the plane. As she drove, the stress melted when she met Scott.

She was a half hour behind schedule, which she knew Scott could make up flying. "So how does having a kid agree with you?" Scott teased.

April threw her sock at Scott. "It was not the baby, it was us. We were tired. We cleaned the back lot by taking out fallen branches then mowing it. Larry used the bush hog, and I had the trimmer and push mower to get close around the trees. With that we made a nice area for picnicking or if we wanted to put a pony there or maybe two or three steers," April said.

"Now don't go starting that again," Scott said. "You have an uncanny way of sneaking in steers to raise at home," and they looked at each other.

April said, "No, I am not doing that. But it would be nice for Ian to like calves and he must like ponies."

April was dressed except for her shoes. She stretched out and relaxed, but then had to sit up suddenly because she felt nauseous. She looked around and found some unused cups and spit in one. She did not feel well. April went into the tiny bathroom to the medicine closet and found some chewable Tums and Pepto Bismol to hopefully quiet her tummy.

April asked Scott how far out they were, and he said he could have her there early. The sky was so clear above the clouds and as he promised they arrived at Washington International two hours ahead of her presentation. "Do you need help carrying something?" Scott asked.

"No, but you are welcome to come along. They are having a full meal and desserts. I think you could eat well and then scout the city if you like," April said.

"No. I have seen enough of this city. I can go with you and help you set up. After that I will eat and take a nap. I will let you know where I am, and you can come and get me. How does that sound?" Scott said.

"I have a better idea," April told him, and she tossed him a small black triangular thing.

"What's this? he asked.

"It is a reminder. You set the time and either you wake up or I can press my button like this." And when she did, Scott's triangle went off in a series of beeps.

"Oh, it can be an alarm clock or a come and find me button," Scott said.

"Exactly," April agreed with him smiling.

They made their way from the cab to the building which had many, many steps. Scott had April's bags as they went up the stairs outside the building.

"Goodness! There are a lot of steps. There are so many that the builders had to put landings every twenty steps," she said.

As they approached the front doors they noticed security guards at the entryways. April had to show identification as did Scott. They had to check April's name to make sure who she was and what she was doing there.

"Please. I apologize, Mrs. Di Angelo," the guard said noticing April's wedding ring. "You have the main presentation. Come follow me and I will show you where you can set up. There are people waiting to help you."

April and Scott followed the guard and found themselves on a huge stage. When they went backstage a woman saw April and greeted her with an embrace. "I am so glad to meet you. I am Pat."

They quickly went to a table where April opened her suitcase showing Pat the photos from the compound from start to finish.

She handed Pat a CD with the edited film Miranda wanted of April. The CD was not a movie, it was all photos.

"These are great," Pat said. "I will have a video player set up for you and also a still projector to show your photos on the large screen. The CD will advance with you pressing a button. I can show you when it is all set up," Pat said.

Pat was like a buzzing bee. She went here, then there. And since she knew everyone, she ordered them to get this or connect that. She was a one-woman army and April admired her for her skills.

When the set up was complete, Pat showed April how everything worked. "Awesome, now do you want to speak for me too?" April asked Pat laughing.

"I know you all too well. You will do fine," Pat told her hugging her. April liked Pat immensely. It is not easy finding people who love their work so much, and who are happy and uplifting like Pat.

The people who paid to come to this presentation began arriving in the dining room. The meal was buffet style. The tables were all set up with a huge life-like ice sculpture of a steer. April and Scott walked all around it. They both thought it was amazing. The two chose a table close to the stage steps near the back. As they sat at the table and began looking around, Frank came up to them.

"Hey, I am so glad to see you," he said shaking April's hand. We have over 280 individuals or cooperation companies who are interested or skeptical to hear your presentation, he said laughing. "Are you ready?"

"Yes, I am," April said. "As ready as I can be."

Soon the waiters came out in an army-like procession with the food, and it smelled delicious. Scott leaned over and thanked April for this "date" and they both laughed. Next came the announcements, the invocation, and the food. They encouraged people to go up by tables, one table at a time.

Who should go next? April and Scott did not wait. They got their food and sat down. Scott's plates were overloaded.

"Two? You had to take two?" April asked him.

"It's okay," Scott said. "I told them it was for you." April punched him lightly on the arm.

April had an upset stomach, so she reached again for those Tums. "I am so glad you had these on board," and she showed Scott the tablets.

"Oh, sure I keep them handy," and he pulled out a packet from his jacket pocket. "I travel in some interesting places and some of the food does not always agree with me, so I keep these handy," he said.

April was not nervous, but she was okay. She did not feel sick now and hoped she would not have a repeat on stage. So she got up to walk around and quickly went to the bathroom.

Walking to her table, April heard someone on stage talking, so she stood by Scott just waiting for her name to be announced. "And with us tonight is someone who did do the impossible. Successfully building and raising steers in a remote corner of the world. May I introduce to you the delightful and lovely April Di Angelo."

April went up the stage steps. She walked with confidence. She talked awhile and showed the photos on the overhead screen of the complex buildings. They had questions from time to time about materials, how long permits required, and so on. Then April popped in the CD to show what life was like in the remote area of Alaska, the real deal.

The first photo was when April arrived. The second was of the various pens of steers showing the automatic feeders, bunkers, and auto bedding. April showed photos of hay against the walls, the interior, and roof.

April had not been aware that the track had a camera. When she discovered the camera, she decided to use some of those photos in the presentation. She showed photos of the neighbors, the polar bears, with some of the damage they did. Next was a photo of the bear with the big mouth from that day on the track.

She included pictures of the beautiful scenery, of her wolf pup, and of the equipment she had at hand. Some were photos of the long days, with her sitting on the rocker studying with one leg up in her pajamas. And one picture showing April beside a CB radio and computer. One of her head and shoulder, showing her back only, all wet in the shower. She had all the amenities of home. The men whistled and April quickly changed the photo.

There was a series of 228 photos on the CD. Seventy-five were for questions and answers the rest were set to music and rotated from one to another. The sound was turned way down for another round of questions from the audience.

"Are you saying you were there through storms all alone for over seven months?"

"Yes, I am, and many can do it. It is not frightening if you have something to do. I had studying and courses to take when weather permitted," she said.

The man shook his head and said, "That is a lot like being put in isolation. It's not for everybody."

April agreed. She told them the pup was a great distraction to her and kept her busy.

"If you had had a partner there, he would have kept you busy," and he laughed.

April did not approve of that type of humor. It bordered on vulgarity. "Are there any other questions?" April asked.

One man stood up and April felt a bit flustered.

"Did you finish your studies and test out yet, and if so what is next for the famous April D?" The men in the room looked at the speaker who turned out to be Hugh Marshall.

April composed herself. This was unexpected. "Yes I did finish. I knew at home there would be many distractions and up there I could concentrate. I did the test and passed. Those close to me teasingly call me *doctor*," April said.

Many of the men raised their glasses to her and one man stood up. "I want to salute you young lady. Not many men, let alone women, could do what you did. I spent several years in Alaska when I was a younger man, and it is a harsh place. If you are not careful you could end up dead. And if you are not taken, this old heart would love to take a wild, beautiful woman with an untamable soul such as yours," and the crowd began to whistle, pound their table tops, and cheer. He stood there waiting for an answer.

"I thank you for your kindness, but you are wrong. I am not wild or untamable. I have found the man for me, and I am spoken for in heart, body, and soul," April said

The man sat down. There were hushed voices all around the room. "If there are no further questions. I am going to turn the time back to Frank, our host for this evening," April said handing the microphone to Frank.

Frank quickly came to her on the stage, taking the mic.

April walked to the stage steps holding the rail and then walked down. She looked for Scott when someone caught her wrist.

"Hey! I thought we could talk," Hugh Marshall said.

April was not interested. She was not angry. She was indifferent. "I am looking for someone. Will you excuse me, please?" April said, walking away to the veranda far away from Hugh.

Out on the veranda was the man who almost proposed to April during the presentation. She graciously took his hand and kissed the back of it.

"Oh, Darlin'. You have stirred my soul. The man who has captured you, truly is a lucky man," he said to her. As the man and some others with him spoke to April about the frightening things she had experienced at the compound, they were interrupted. Again Hugh came to her taking her by the wrist saying, "If you excuse us for a bit, I need to ask April a few questions. You can have her back when I am through with her."

April was not happy. He did not own her. April reached into her pocket and pressed the alarm and hoped Scott would find her quickly.

At the far end of the veranda Hugh positioned April at the rail and stood directly in front of her. "So I never heard from you. Why is that?" Hugh asked.

"Hugh, I was busy," was all April said.

"You were too busy to think about me? April, you know I was the first man you ever loved and that never will change," he took April's hand and held it to his face.

"Hugh, don't do that," April pulled away. "You belong to someone and so do I," she said.

Hugh said, "I don't belong to anyone. I do what I want, when I want." His eyes bore down on April, and he touched her face.

April brushed his hand away from her face and there at last, like her hero, was Scott standing beside Hugh.

"Excuse me, but she is with me," Scott said whisking April away to his side. Hugh was tall and broad, but Scott towered over him. Scott led April away very quickly inside where there were people.

"So, are you hungry?" Scott asked April.

All April said was, "The nerve of that guy. I am so glad you came for me Scott. I was beginning to worry."

Soon Mr. Marshall met up with April and thanked her for her presentation. He asked about her parents and April encouraged him to call them. "So where are you living now?" Mr. Marshall asked.

April told Mr. Marshall she was married over a year and a half living on the old farm near her parents.

Mr. Marshall nodded as if understanding. "I'll do that. I'll have Elaine call when we get back."

"Are you still raising Angus?" April asked him.

"We are. Hugh has come back to us you know. He is out of the service now because of the boy and its nice having a partner. Hugh always did like the animals and raising steers and it's nice to think maybe my grandson might too someday," Mr. Marshall said.

"I am very happy for you" April said.

"Are you married now to a good man?" Mr. Marshall asked her.

"Yes. Yes, I am," April answered.

"It's none of my business to say so, but I don't know if you were aware that Hugh got married after that Sandra girl, and that one did not work out either. I don't know what's wrong with the women today," he said. "You and Hugh would have been a good pair. You both liked many of the same things, and well, Oh hell. There is no point to say anything more. Is there?" he said.

April stepped forward and touched Mr. Marshall. "Yes. We might have been, but life changes things, circumstances, and lives. I chose to move on, and I have found happiness. I do hope you are happy for me."

"Oh, I am," he said.

"Maybe this is not the right time for Hugh. I mean I did not find my husband, he found me when I was not looking," April told him.

"Yeah, I have heard about things like that happening. You know it was not like that for me and Elaine. I knew her from high school, and I said that's it. We were married and happy ever since."

Now April understood who Hugh was really alike, not Elaine at all.

"I want to reassure you that when it is going to happen, it will. He needs to trust the Lord and it will all work out," April said. Then she wished him luck and said, "goodbye."

She and Scott got her things from the stage. Before leaving, April hugged Pat and encouraged her to come for a visit. Then they caught a cab and were in the Cessna in no time.

April and Scott were waiting on the taxiway when April got that nauseated feeling again. "It must have been the banana peppers," she said.

Scott looked at her and said, "You know, you have that glow about you. You know like in motherhood. Are you sure you are not pregnant?"

"Awe, no. Not me. I have just been having trouble with some foods lately," and no more was said.

Number Two On The Way

APRIL BEGAN TO WONDER ABOUT WHAT SCOTT SAID AND FOR kicks and giggles she bought an early detection pregnancy kit at the local drugstore.

She came home, did the test, and almost cried. Scott was right! April was pregnant. She was so happy and wanted to find Larry, but he was nowhere in sight. She decided to surprise him by making a cake with baby shoes on top.

Next April called her parents and asked them to come for dinner and to bring the ladies. April baked a meatloaf, au gratin potatoes, green beans, and carrots. She kept the cake in a side room. The cake had turned out so cute. She had used a small pattern for baby shoes, cut cake to make the mold, and then iced them in blue.

They all came for dinner. It was a really nice time. Ian was now in a booster seat like a big boy and the six of them sat around the table enjoying the meal. "Is anyone ready for cake for dessert?" April asked.

"Sure bring it on," both Dad and Larry said laughing.

Her mom and the ladies quickly cleaned off the table and set out small dessert plates and forks. April went into the side room and had to compose herself. She lifted the cardboard supporting the cake and walked out placing the cake on the table.

At first no one said anything, then her mother said, "April. April, is this for real?"

April began to tear up and next they all knew.

Larry stood up and hugged his wife and he began to cry.

"If you are crying now, wait fifteen years," her dad joked, and her mother hit him. They were all so happy for her.

"April is it a boy or a girl?" Nora asked.

"I don't know. I was feeling sick in the mornings and decided to check with an early pregnancy test, and it was positive," she said.

"April, you have to go to the doctor," her mother said.

"Mom, I will. I just wanted to tell all of you at one time. I promise I will go." It was a lovely evening they played with Ian for a while and had an impromptu Family Home Evening.

That night in bed Larry held April with her back to his chest. Then he quickly took his hand away from her tummy.

April pulled his hand back. "It's okay. You can touch my belly, and in time you will feel the baby kick," she told him.

April turned over to face him and Larry said, "April, you have made me so happy. I love you so much. You support me. You help me in every way. I was not sure if I would ever meet someone or ever have children," as tears fell from his eyes.

"It's okay. You're pretty nice yourself, you know," she said. "Honey, you were what I was looking for and didn't know it. You have completed my life. You helped me find a higher level of happiness that I hoped for, but wondered if I would ever have. So, the both of us are blessed," and she kissed her husband.

The days blended from day to day, week to week, and month to month. They were a busy family with jobs, visiting, keeping a home, and going to church. April was going to celebrate her 23rd birthday and would be a mother again very soon. That Saturday the 13th, at her birthday picnic, April began to have contractions, and a well-planned and organized birthday party turned into chaos within minutes.

It could have easily been in a comedy show. Someone ran to the bedroom for her bags and put them on the porch. Then Larry ran up to the bedroom, but her bags were missing.

Her dad pulled his truck up to the porch while the ladies ran around putting food away while Miranda stood there trying to direct everyone.

Finally April got Larry and asked her dad to bring the bags. She also asked the ladies to follow them to the hospital. Forty-five minutes later a healthy 7 pound 9 ounce, 20 inch, baby boy was born and lay on April's lap.

Within ten minutes the nurses allowed her family into the room.

Ian peeked at his little brother and asked his mother what was wrong with him.

Everyone laughed and told Ian that is what he looked like when he was born. But Ian was having none of that. He insisted he was never that little.

April asked someone to bring Ian to her. "This is your baby brother. Can you understand that?" April asked Ian.

The boy shook his head "yes".

"You are now the big brother and that bring with it a lot of responsibility," she told him.

His eyes grew big.

"Now, since God has chosen you as the older, bigger, and stronger brother, your job will be to watch over him, and to help take care of him. One day the two of you will be almost the same," April said.

"Almostest da same?" Ian asked.

"Yes. One day you and your tiny little brother will be best friends, play together, and do many things together with Mom and Dad. Would you like that?"

Ian looked at the tiny baby, and he shook his head "yes". He leaned over and kissed his brother on his forehead.

"She is such a good Mom," Nora said.

"She sure is, and she has you to thank for that," Miranda said.

"No, it is both of us. I had the baby, and you had the very young girl," and the women hugged each other.

"Let's not make the same mistake as we did in Alaska. You two come up with a name," Gordon said.

That evening Larry asked if anyone could help watch Ian. The ladies answered first, so they had dibs. Ian happily went along with them.

Larry wanted to stay with April as long as he could.

"I am all right, Poppa," April said to him.

Larry leaned back in the recliner and slept.

April's nurse came into the room and checked her vitals and her bottom. She was doing well, so the nurse let both of them sleep. The nurse did come back to bring a blanket for Larry.

For the first time in a long time they both slept. April had a tough pregnancy. She was sick a lot and Larry was relieved her delivery was quick. April was not on any medications. She felt good and slept soundly until around 11:00 p.m. when nurses woke her for vitals again.

At that point Larry kissed his wife and left to go home.

April knew he would sleep well at home with Ian at the ladies' house. He was such an active boy. "Just wait until we have the baby home with Ian," April thought to herself and it made her smile.

As she slept, April entered a deeper sleep than she had in months. She dreamed about the trip to the mountain. In her dream she vividly saw the faces much clearer than she had at the time. The one Native American in particular kept speaking to her, rejoicing with her. And the name of "Benhali" kept coming to her over and over. April woke up saying the name.

A nurse was in her room, "Are you all right, sweetie?" she asked April. "I heard you talking and came to see if you were all right. You kept saying a strange name," her nurse said.

"Could you please write down the name you heard me say?" April asked.

The nurse did and April decided that would be the name of their son, Ben. Not Benjamin. Just Ben as in Ben Hali, Hali could be his middle name. This would honor the warrior who had come to her in her dream. She did not know the significance of the dream, but in time she would know.

In the morning the doctor visited April and told her that if she felt well enough and if her labs were good, she could go home on Sunday. April longed to go home to sleep in her bed and be in her own surroundings with those she loved.

On Sunday Larry arrived with Ian to pick up his wife and new son Ben. You could not have found a happier man on the face of the earth. The nurses were so touched by Larry's careful way with April and the baby. The sight of that warmed their hearts.

April came home and her sweet husband hired a woman to help her around the clock. Tilly was more than anxious to come, whether she was paid or not. And Tilly was awesome with the baby and Ian.

Tilly took the initiative and made dinner, cleaned, and did laundry. Often when April went about to see what needed to be done, Tilly was already there finishing the job.

April said to Tilly, "I am so blessed you have come, Tilly. I don't know what I will do without you." But within a few weeks April was strong enough to handle her home and children on her own.

She had almost completely taken over the job as CEO and working with Mr. Stevens and his son. His son was all grown and in his second year of college majoring in business. Soon he would take over his father's position. It made perfect sense. He had been there all through the growth of D Farms. He knew everyone and learned from his father.

April made it very clear to Mr. Stevens that if he ever retired, his son would take the helm. But should he ever want to feel welcome and needed by D Farms his service was always welcome.

As the days moved toward the fall months, April wanted to go on a trip somewhere. The baby was almost 6 months old and walking. Ian was almost three. So, Miranda put a bug in Larry's ear to take his wife on a cruise.

Larry was uncertain where to go and asked for help to surprise April without April knowing what her preference would be. St. Thomas with white beaches and warm breezes that was April's choice.

Larry asked Miranda if she would help him book the cruise. It would be just him and April, and Miranda was delighted to. She even took April shopping for needed items.

April felt she could buy clothing there, since it was not as warm here.

They left on the first of November for a two-week vacation cruise. April's parents, the ladies and the Du Val's all helped with Ian and Ben, who were well behaved and quiet. The ladies in particular enjoyed the boys. It gave them opportunities to go for ice cream or to the park. They boys had a vacation just like their parents.

While they were relaxing at a dinner table one evening, a couple approached their table and introduced themselves. April thought the girl looked familiar but was not sure until their conversation began.

The girl, who was now grown and married, was one of the girls in the swimming competition at the Olympics with April.

April stood to hug the girl and they all caught up on the past few years.

"So would you be interested in going one more time to help us out?" the girl asked April. "I am still involved but our U.S. team is looking for a captain of the swim team."

April almost choked. "Me?" April asked. "Oh, you can't be serious. I just had my second child six months ago. It would take me forever to get into Olympic shape and I don't know if my time would be good enough," April told her.

The women spoke with April about the team and told her the Olympics would be in Brazil that year. She handed April a card and said, "If you are interested call me. You can try out in the spring or even as late as early fall. If you make it, you're in," and she left.

April held the card and turned it over in her hand.

"Would you like to do it?" Larry asked her.

"I don't know. I'm getting kind of old for the Olympics. Don't you think? I don't know if I would make the team or, well, I don't know," April said.

Larry touched April's hand and said, "You won't know until you try. I can manage the boys and we always have help. You know that."

April laughed out loud, "I would be gone a lot, you know, in the water in the morning, afternoon, and evening. I am far behind those who are trying out. I don't know."

"All I am saying is that you have a blank page. Do what you want. The boys and I will support you. You know that. And Mr. Stevens is still at the helm. If you are going to do it, now is the time," Larry told her.

April took the card with her to her room and tucked it into her suitcase. For now that would have to wait. These two weeks were for her and her husband. It was a wonderful time. They ate and danced. They rode horses and surfed. They took out a boat, paddled a canoe, deep sea dived, snorkeled, played volleyball, and went treasure hunting.

It was on the treasure hunt that proved to be their closest moment. When they stood looking at the judge who was counting up their items and waiting for the results, Larry leaned over to pull his wife to him. Then he whispered in her ear, "You are my treasure. I have already won."

Her Dad told them, when he picked them up at the airport, that Mother had made dinner for them. Also that the ladies would bring the boys home since they were excited to see them. When they got home, their house had been cleaned and the meal was waiting.

They were all there together. April and Larry gave them gifts they had purchased in St. Thomas. At the dinner table April announced what had transpired that evening while they were at dinner concerning the Olympics. April barely finished when Larry said he thought it was a good idea and he thought she should do it.

Her guests looked stunned, but they also were supportive of Larry's decision.

Later that week the ladies stopped by for a visit. April was on the telephone with the local YMCA to see if she could pay to swim at their pool. She had secured a coach and right now was on hold for what seemed like eternity. She put the phone on speaker while chatting with the ladies.

That's when Nora handed April a letter from her brothers. It was a lengthy letter.

When the woman came back on the phone to quote a price, she said she apologized. She was unfamiliar with who April was. Her boss said April was welcome to live there if she chose at no charge.

Then April sat down to read the letter. It said that both brothers had taken jobs offered by D Farms.

John was an over-the-road truck driver four days a week and then home for three. He was now married and had three children.

Tim was also working for D Farms. He, however, wanted more of an education. He was in the animal husbandry class, compliments of a D Farms program. He was to graduate later this year. Tim was also married but had no children yet. That is not until December.

It was a nice letter, and April was so pleased they wrote to their Mother. It was a reconnection for them all.

April encouraged the ladies to stay a little while if they could when April heard Ben cry to get up from his nap. Ian came out to report about his brother. The ladies were all smiles. It was true that the boys could turn frowns upside down where the ladies were concerned. They did not have a favorite. They spoiled the boys equally.

They also were there for a second reason. They wanted to let April know they had cut back on their cleaning jobs and could take care of the boys two days a week if needed. Especially because of her upcoming training and all. April was deeply touched and very thankful.

Preparing for the Olympics Again!

THAT FOLLOWING WEEK, APRIL'S SCHEDULE CHANGED SOMEWHAT, she was up by 5, put a clean diaper on Ben. Then she gave him his bottle as she held him on her lap while going over the day's itinerary. Larry was up soon after her.

April would lay out dinner or put it together in a crock pot or casserole. Next she grabbed her packed bag, kissed her husband, and was out the door to the Y.

April would swim for three hours and then go to Mr. Stevens's office to discuss what was needed for D Farms. If she had to travel, she would leave his office, stop at home to pick up the boys, and meet Scott at the airport.

She would make her arrangements wherever she was going to swim, often using the Y's daycare. If they stayed overnight, she paid for daycare while she put in another three hours in the pool. If she went home, she would drop the boys with Dad, and swim for three hours.

April made sure she was home in the evenings no later than six. She wanted to have dinner with her family, and she often was the leader for Family Home Evenings.

Her coach knew April was putting forth a huge effort, but it was not enough. She kept telling April to do more. So April then got up at 4 a.m. and lifted weights for an hour every morning. For all she was doing, she was not tired. In fact, she had more energy.

Larry was concerned that April was putting in too much time and wearing herself down. But in all, he had no complaints. The house was clean. The laundry was done, and sometimes he folded it. The boys were doing well. They were happy and obedient little boys.

Larry and April both had to give huge credit to their family. Both her mom and dad helped, and the Ladies never ever said no. They were all so helpful with the boys. And as far as spoiling them, that was not true. They showered them with love.

April knew she had to do more for her coach, and as always she prayed. She had a goal and was more than willing to do whatever it took. She applied herself just as she did when she was in the military. April contacted a trainer, who was a miracle worker. Doug was a professional trainer. He took some swimming time from April and had her running, lifting weights, and dancing. He wanted her to be limber in the pool. As the months went on, April was becoming stronger and stronger.

Finally she pleased her coach who saw improved time with the building of muscles and endurance. April kept up this schedule for seven months straight. Into the eighth month, her coach said it was time to go to the swim meet for the final selection.

April was not the same person she was when she did this the first time. She swam her best, but her time was not the fastest. Even so, the coaches loved her. She had leadership skills that would be useful with this handful of girls. April was happy with her time and relaxed. She flew home to tell her family

She re-met the team later that month. They worked together for another four months. April kept her trainer, and he helped many on the swim team. They did workouts as a team. April's coach was happy. Now that April had relaxed, she began to blossom. She would walk into the Olympic venue and be remembered. The crowds would cheer her, and she excelled.

April's trips home became fewer. Now she called more, and Ian would run to the telephone when asked, "Where is your mommy?"

April knew this would not last forever and it would be her last Olympics. She felt a little crazy for taking up this challenge, but part of her was glad she did. April met many of the people from her past Olympics. They were all good friends. Many were surprised to learn April was the Mother of two boys. They were glued to the television and radio when April had disappeared, and during the race they cheered for her. April was touched. It meant so much when people believed in you and showed they cared.

April's training in the pool was much shorter than for the rest of the team. She had almost missed the cut off. But from her past experience, April knew what to do, and her trainer deserved much of the credit. April dared not think of home. She hoped that when they went to Brazil, her family would come to support her. That is what she told her mom before the team flew to Brazil. And Miranda said they would.

It was winter here in America, and Larry was caught up with his work. Even if there was more to do, they would get help. Miranda stressed to Larry how important it was for him and the boys to be there, and he never hesitated.

Many in the community supported April. Someone made the boys matching red, white, and blue outfits that Miranda and the ladies thought were darling.

Passports secured, bags packed, and the Di Angelos were on their way. Larry and the boys, April's parents, and the ladies all came, and they all helped out with each other to keep things smooth and calm.

On the day of the swim meet, April was looking for her family. Before they walked to the swim arena, April gathered all the girls together. She told them to fold their arms for prayer. After a lengthy prayer, April wanted the girls to all hug each other, because what they did or did not do in the water would be shared by all. As they walked to the pool they all felt confident and calm.

The door opened and the girls went to their lockers. They kept to themselves, but if anyone was in contact with another swimmer, they were to be friendly and kind. April drilled this into their young minds because this was important. They changed into their country's colored swimsuits, with their team sweatsuits over the top. Some played music to calm them. April had to admit she began to feel the stress build inside her.

When the announcer called them, they assembled in a line and walked into a room of noise. As soon as they entered, the crowd of people began to clap, holler, whistle, and scream. As each girl was introduced, she raised her arm.

When it was April's turn, she raised her arm, and the crowd went crazy. April scanned the crowd, to her right and half way up she saw Larry and her boys. What got her attention was how cute the boys were. They were dressed alike in red, white, and blue outfits, and they looked adorable. They wore hats that resembled sailor's complete with red, white, and blue tassels that hung down. April waved and was smiling from ear to ear.

The television crews panned the audience and stopped with her boys and family, including Manny and Contessa. And the crowd whistled.

Then it was time to go to work. This would show if the last ten months of training paid off.

The girls took off their sweatsuits laying them on chairs and put their towels on top. They each limbered up their arms and then they lined up. There were two team and two individual swimming meets. April was in all four events as were two others from her team.

The two individual team events were 500 and 1000 meter swim meets. In the first event, April placed second out of a group of 14 swimmers. It was a good feeling to get in and push. The second meet would not happen until later.

Next, was the team swim events. April was Captain and the last swimmer since she was the strongest.

The gun shot signaled they were off, and the girls swam very well. When the next to last swimmer came in, they were four tenths off. April knew she had to push hard and make no mistakes. "Make it count!" as her coach said thousands of times to her. April watched for her teammate to touch the wall, then April was off her pedestal leaping as far as she could. She was doing the butterfly and that was followed by freestyle. Freestyle was April's favorite. As she hit the wall and turned, April got as much distance as she could. Then she surfaced and began to swim as perfectly as possible. In her mind she had the tune of a song with a fast beat. She cut the water and on her first turn the time meter came out for the people to see. April was close to breaking her own record. She did not know that. She just knew she had to swim as fast, as straight, and as hard as she could. April touched the wall eight tenths ahead of her old time and made a new world record. The crowd cheered. People with USA banners shook them and whistled. April waited for the time to be posted, and, when it appeared on the scoreboard, she put her head back in the water and laughed.

The announcers were ecstatic. The cameras panned to April's family. Little Ian was jumping up and down. Miranda was holding a rail screaming with the ladies. Gordon and Larry had a time holding onto the boys. Manny and his wife were crying.

When April was out of the water and dried off, a reporter caught up with her to interview her. He showed April her family's reactions during and after the race. She watched it on the reporter's screen. She laughed and then cried to see her sons rooting for her. They had a brief exchange of conversation and then the reporters were gone.

April would return tomorrow for the last of two races, one with the team, and one individual.

That evening April and her family went out to dinner. It brought back many memories of her previous Olympics. Some of the people were still involved with training or coaching. But there were many new faces as well. At dinner, the boys did not eat well. They were too busy looking around at all the people in different colored clothing.

That was fine because April knew the boys had good food packed and waiting for them back at the hotel. It was a nice time at dinner. April looked around the table at her family and knew she had been blessed. Dinner ended too soon. They all separated, April went to join her team and her family went to their hotel.

April knew that consistency was good, so before bed she got the girls all suited up for a good hour run. The girls relished the idea. On the run, they got to see much of the area's unique birds and terrain. They came back feeling rested and not stiff or sore. They all were in bed asleep by 8:00 p.m. sharp.

To April these girls, although teens, were like her children. She handled squabbles and hurt feelings, encouraged them to eat and drink, and for them to do their best. The girls often turned to April with questions or problems, and they talked it over. It was nice having a stable person like their mom with them. So it worked both ways for April and the girls.

The next morning the girls were in the gym, working out, stretching, and trying to keep their minds on the job. Already some had jitters. April told the girls when one starts to feel uneasy that feeling will go to another and another. Just silently pray or hug someone and those negative feelings will go away. Then they paused for prayers. As one finished praying, the next one began. After a minute of silence, April finished with her prayer for success, safety, for them to learn, and to have fun.

Soon they were back in the pool area. It was much like the day before. However April had also told the girls second place was not good enough. If they stayed consistent in the water and just did their best, they would be in first. The girls trusted April and believed her. They soon found themselves on the podium for the team event. The gun signaled the start. They girls all did well, much better than the previous day. For this team event, April did push being the last swimmer, but not nearly like she had yesterday. They took first place and the girls' eyes danced with joy.

Then it was April's last race. There were two swimmers who aimed to beat her in the race. April knew she had to take her own advice and more. Next she was on the podium and the gun went off. April leaped. This was the longest race, and she knew she had to have enough energy to finish.

She kept pace to be a length ahead of the fastest swimmers. The news anchors were not sure April would have the stamina to maintain this pace and then increase it at the end. It was good April did not hear that. All she heard was a song in her head that had a good drum beat. Her swimming was in tune with that song.

At the halfway point, April kicked it up a notch. She was now two lengths in front of the leaders and was going strong the entire time.

April kept this pace until they were two minutes out. She trained that way. When she had two more minutes, she would push with all she had, that is exactly what she did. The crowd noise was not audible to her. She just did what she had been trained to do. April began to surge forward. The strongest swimmer was two lanes from her. She tried to catch April, but it was too late. April swam with every bit of energy she had. On her last turn, April flipped and pushed like she was being chased. As she came down the stretch and touched the wall, she looked to her right and saw no swimmers were there. That is how April knew she had won the race.

She did not care so much about the time. It was not close. She knew that. April rested in the water and could hear the crowds. There were reporters already standing by. She knew they wanted to interview her. But for just a moment she wanted to stay, to feel the aura of her last Olympic race. It was over now.

April knew she was too old at twenty-four to keep going and she smiled. "Old at twenty-four. Imagine that!" But April was done. She no longer wanted to be in the limelight or be famous. It was time to be a mom, wife, daughter, and granddaughter.

April pulled herself out of the water, up the steps, and greeted the reporters. It was an emotional time. Her last race. She would never do this or be with these people again. April knew she was in top physical condition, but in time this would change too.

That was the way of life and April wanted to embrace it all. Each phase of her life. Not everyone gets the chance to become old and April wanted to enjoy it all. As she went to leave to go to the lockers, her family joined her.

Many of the spectators lingered. They knew that this was the end of April's career in Olympic competition. She was a great athlete with a good sense of judgement. She would be missed.

Some came to greet her and hug her. They thanked her for her faithfulness in representing the USA, being a great role model, and said they would always remember her.

April knew what they said was sweet, but in time they would forget. We all forget. It was all right. April firmly believed that even with her framed medals in and photos, she too would forget. That is why she felt compelled to race while she still could. If she had waited, she would not have been able.

This is also true in life. If you wait to do something and keep putting it off, most likely what you hoped to do will never happen.

Of course there are seasons in life. When you are young you are busy, then some have children or careers they pursue. All too soon comes retirement. Which is a time to reflect and pick a new career or choose what comes next.

April thought about what she would do after the Olympics. She knew that she had a job with D Farms, and she also wanted more children. That would keep her quite busy.

April had a goal of finding her family's history. She wanted to go back as far as she could, and now was the time before something happened to the ladies who had the knowledge she needed. April also wanted to record both sides of the family. She knew they were now up in years. So these next few years April wanted to travel to visit family in order to preserve their history. If not, it would be gone.

The closing ceremony was nice and became even more emotional for April having served in the military for four-and-a-half years. The American flag was even more significant to her. As they sang, tears fell freely down April's face. She tried to sing but was too choked up. Those on the platform reached over to congratulate each other and then it was all over. April walked over to her family and was ready and focused on going home.

They all went to the venue to gather April's things, and then to the hotel room to get ready to leave. They had to wait at the airport and the boys were amazed by the elevators which they had never seen before. Many of the nearby people laughed at them. The boys would run back and forth and say excuse me when then came to people. The boy's parents watched them like hawks. Next they noticed that overhead their flight was ready and the ten of them headed to the gateway together. Dad and Gordon were carrying the boys.

They took a commercial flight to the US and once they touched down Scott would shuttle them home.

On board a round of applause met them. April had been through this before. As she walked to her seat, most of the passengers stood to shake her hand or hug her. April could not hold back her tears. These folks meant to thank her and wish her well in life. Although she was smiling, her tears ran freely.

April sat in her seat holding Ben with Ian in the middle and Larry sitting in the aisle seat. Manny sat with the ladies, and Contessa with Gordon and Miranda. The flight was good, no problems, and zero turbulence. For the first time April did not have ear pain and having to chew gum, but Ian did. Ben slept for four hours on April's lap. He was so cute dressed in the red, white, and blue outfit made for him. His cap was darling. April wanted to thank the neighbor back home who made these for her boys.

Touch down was great, and, as in the past, the Captain of the airplane asked for the passengers to allow April and her family to exit first. Again the passengers clapped and hollered out, "Thank you. You will always be remembered, and good luck," and things like that. As they came down the ramp, again there were people there, and a crew from a local television station. April stopped to give a brief interview as she held a now restless Ben. Ben tried every which way to take the microphone and chew on it. Then Dad came to the rescue. He was standing nearby holding Ben to allow April to finish. There were many fans standing nearby that shook April's hand. One of them April did not notice, but it was Scott. April laughed and Scott said, "Let's get out of here," and they all did.

The new Cessna was there to take them home. It was a smooth flight. The ladies slept as did Gordon and Larry. The boys played quietly on the floor with their cars and trucks. Touch down in their home town and April gathered up the boys' toys and carried Ben while Ian held onto her hand. April was in the car before Larry, and they drove home silently. It had been a long day. No more getting up early for swimming or training, but April did want to keep the trainer, even if he came in the afternoon two or three days a week. It would be good for her.

That would be a discussion for another day.

Once in their home, Happy and Jet were their constant companions. They did not leave them for days on end. Jet usually accompanied April when she traveled for work, but that stopped when she was in training. It sure would be good to have Jet back with her again. Back to reality was good. Every day April got up she did not need to tend to the boys, they would come down on their own. If she was lucky, her husband would join her, she loved mornings when they had that time all to themselves.

Next the boys came down, they all had breakfast together, then went upstairs to shower and change. Sometimes the boys went to April's parents, sometimes to the ladies, and sometimes they stayed with her.

After that was sorted out, April always stopped at the office and took care of business. If she was home, she picked up what she needed for dinner that day or did errands. She knew the ladies were not home on Tuesdays, Thursdays, or Fridays so on those alternate days we went to her mother's. April encouraged Ian to ride the ponies and he did, but Ian chose his Grand-pop to take him out riding. Gordon was careful and slow almost methodical.

Ian had to ask "Am I holding the reins right? Like this?" Ben on the other hand was just the opposite. He would literally crash his body into things, and never cry. He had no fear of the ponies, not even a healthy dose, so April had to keep an eye on him. Miranda did too. Eventually she made a small harness for Ben as he moved faster than his grandma. That harness was a good idea. It kept Ben out of trouble and from getting hurt.

The boys grew up with animals. Happy and Jet were their constant companions and there were kittens in the barn. They each had their own pony, and the calves were in the pasture. If only they could keep Ben from going into the calves. He'd always come out with calf poop on his pants.

Yes, it was a good life, a fun life. And then the following Fall, Manny was stricken with a heart attack and almost died. Contessa hovered over her husband and cried often. April took a month off to go down with her Mother to help in any way they could.

Manny, however, wanted April to sit with him. And while she sat there, she recorded the stories he told her. He mentioned family names, how they were connected, and what they did in life.

Manny was so proud of April because she wanted to do the family history. No one in his family had the idea to preserve it. Manny never said it, but he was partial to this one, his wild horse trainer. She was such a good Mother too. He could hardly believe it, but here she was and if he had not had children he would have sworn she was with child again. She had that look. One day as they sat together Manny asked her. "You getting belly again," as he scrutinized her tummy.

April said, "Maybe. I am not sure yet?"

"Oh you be careful, not too many. You know, bad for your health," Manny said.

April replied, "I am not concerned. I am in good health, and I love children. I want 21 of them."

Manny's eyes almost bugged out. "Twenty-one? You kid me, no?" April sat there laughing. "Oh, my girl. You scare me sometimes," he said.

While April was there with him, she felt that old familiar nausea. She could not believe it Manny was right. It was almost every other year that she had children. Not that she did want children, but not every other year. She and Larry would have to take precautions.

That May April was in the hospital and delivered twin girls. They were named Sam for Samantha who weighed in at 6 pounds and 4 ounces, and Rae who weighed 5 pounds and 11 ounces. Each was 19 inches long. Larry was not thrilled about the names, after all they were girls. But in time he took to them and liked them. They had four-and-a-half years of marriage and four children all born on the fourteenth of any given month: Ian on March 14th, Ben on April 14th, and the girls on May 14th, so Miranda sewed a calendar for April. She put a button in each of the children's birthdays so it could be seen at a glance.

Grand-pop in particular was overjoyed with the girls, he doted on their ever whim.

Throughout the next six months April and Larry were home bound. At the beginning of the New Year, they made another trip. This time to see Grandpa and his wife in the East. They felt this trip was long overdue. When they returned, their grandparents came back with them for a three-month stay. Grand-pop wanted to play with the boys all the time, and Grandma just giggled at them.

Out of courtesy Gordon took the elder couple to the Catholic Church where they claimed their membership. Gordon was there to pick them up at 7:40 sharp and they were in their seats well in time for the 8:00 service. He and Miranda were there to pick them up at 10:10, missing their classes. Gordon did not mind at all. He and his wife enjoyed this couple.

When the couple would speak their own language neither Gordon nor Miranda could make out what they were talking about. They were cooperative, kind, and quiet.

Gordon reflected back to when April was young, and this man had a heart of a lion. He came on a long trip to find his lost granddaughter. Yes, everyone was glad they had come and stayed. They had no pets to look after except the chickens, and the neighbor had agreed to take care of them in exchange for their eggs.

April and Larry went out of their way to include the elderly couple in everything. They went to the horse farm, and to a Mennonite farm that grew produce only. Grandma loved this farm and spent many days there picking produce and fruit. Larry took Grandpa fishing at a local lake. He caught trout and was very pleased with himself. Those nights they had baked trout and fresh vegetables for dinner.

The girls at two and a half loved to hang on their grandparents. They knew they did not have to eat what they did not like with them. At first neither Larry nor April were aware of this, but Larry whispered to April, "Let it go." So she did, but she made sure their snacks were healthy during the day. The evenings were the best, with all four adults sitting on the porch watching the animals or the pond, and a cup of warm spearmint tea on their laps.

April took her grandmother to a second-hand clothing shop. Inside the shop there were very expensive clothes that were for sale for a fraction of the cost. They had blouses, skirts, dresses, women's slacks, purses, and scarves. At first Grandma was hesitant. In time she moved through the racks of clothing and began to lay the ones she liked on the counter.

Soon she realized how much she had and kept saying, "Too much," which made April laugh. April enjoyed this woman and saw much of herself in her, determined, loved to laugh, loved her husband, and more.

Those three months were filled with things to do like boating, going to the race track, and spending time on picnics with the kids. Scott took them out flying to see the mountains and Grandpa got very excited when he saw the mountain goats. Grandpa was NOT allowed to work. They all kept them busy and at the end of those three months it was a bittersweet goodbye. Grandma said she needed to go home to rest, but as April and the others hugged her, Grandma had tears in her eyes. Scott flew them home and had them taken right to their front door step by a hired driver. When they got home and rested, they talked about the time they had spent with the Di Angelo's. Many visited or stopped them on the street to ask how their vacation was and no matter where they were in the grocery store or on the street they both told them.

Back home, life settled down. The kids were growing fast. The following year Ian was entering pre-school. Ben was 4½ and the girls were 3. April and Larry sat down and spoke about how to be careful.

April needed to stay in good health. The babies took a lot out of her. Larry encouraged her to ride four times a week and go swimming either here at home or away three times a week. He helped make healthy dinners for the family when he was able.

The year that Ben, age 5. went into pre-school was April's fourth delivery. Trent came into this world on September 14th, weighing 9 pounds and 2 ounces, and was 21 inches long. Trent was not a quiet baby. He was always trying his parents from the time he could walk.

Then two years later Tyler was born on June 14th, weighing 8 pounds and 14 ounces. Their house was full, four boys and two girls. April's friends thought she was crazy to have a big family "these days." To April and Larry they had created a home they loved. They still traveled together, visiting their elderly grandparents. It was wonderful when the kids were all home, and the ladies were there with Gordon and Miranda. Anyone who came was welcome and never did anyone leave without taking something with them. Sometimes April wanted to hand them a child.

Yes, time marched on and everyone was happy, until the evening when the telephone rang late one evening. Larry said he would get it and when he did he was very quiet.

April stood beside him and whispered, "Who is it?"

Larry did not say anything, but his eyes gave it away. Something bad had happened. He handed April the telephone. Her beloved Grandfather was in the hospital asking to see her. It was a cousin who had called at the request of April's Grandmother. April stood there, she felt she had to go, but what about the kids?

Larry picked up the phone and called Scott. "Scott, I am sorry to call you this late, but if you can fly us out yet tonight, we would be very grateful."

"I can be there in fifteen minutes. See you then," Scott said.

Larry called Gordon and Miranda and told them what had happened. They were over in five minutes. They kissed April as they came in and April and Larry headed out.

Scott knew April was tense since she was not her jovial self and she looked frozen.

"I don't mean to pick on you like I usually do, but that look on your face is bad news. It would sure help if you were your usual self. That is what they are expecting," Scott said.

April realized Scott was right. She would have to suck it up and hold it in. This was NOT about her.

They arrived at a small strip and took a taxi that was waiting for them. April and Larry got in and were whisked to the hospital ten minutes away. April knew the kids were sleeping and this was going to be a long night. On route to the hospital she dialed Mr. Stevens to keep him abreast of what was happening. He told her not to worry about anything he and his son would take care of any problems that arose.

The cab pulled up in front of the hospital, the two exited, and then entered the hospital. They had to ask what floor his grandfather was on, and they hurried, got in the elevator to the third floor. As they walked into the hallway, they saw a room overflowing with people. That had to be the room. April hesitated. She did not know all these people and did not want to take over the room. Her brothers were there, and they both came out into the hallway and told her "Get in there. He is asking for you." As April entered the room she could not see her grandfather because of all the people in the room.

"Excuse me, please," she said over and over. "Pardon me," and then her eyes met his.

With his hand Grandpa motioned for her to come to him and he padded the bed for her to sit down beside him. He had an oxygen cannula in his nose, and two IVs in each of his arms. It was evident this did not look good. "It's okay," he said to her, and she broke down.

"I am so sorry. I do not mean to cry. It's just . . ." and her grandmother rubbed her back.

"What happened? You seemed so well at our home?" she asked.

"My heart, it's giving out," he said.

April was confused, his heart was never an issue. It was his stomach.

"He had a heart attack," Grandma said.

April looked at her grandfather who's skin looked grey. She turned her head and asked to be excused. She wanted to ask the nurses what was going on. Who his doctor was and could he be transferred.

The nurses would not answer her or cooperate, which frustrated April even more. "I am asking for his doctor's name. Is that a secret?" she asked.

She said, "It's not, but not a privilege for you," the nurse said.

"What is your name?" April asked, and the nurse covered her name tag with her hand and walked away.

Her brothers met her in the hallway. "April, there is nothing you can do. They are just trying to stabilize him. He is too weak to go anywhere. His doctor is all right, not the best, but they are just stabilizing him."

April said, "That's fine," but she told them what the nurse said.

"They have some really nasty nurses here, lazy, and mouthy," they said.

April sat in the hallway crying.

Again she was summoned to her grandfather She sat beside him holding his hand and he said, "Of all you who come to my home and eat at my table, this is the one I wanted."

April loved this man, but also felt bad as she knew the people in this room were good people. They lived here and saw her grandfather on a day-to-day basis.

It was almost 10:00 p.m. when the people began to leave. "You go too," Grandma said to her.

"I have nowhere to go. You go and rest," April told her. "I will stay and keep him company and watch over him."

Grandpa was sleeping, so April pulled her chair close to his bed and laid her head on the mattress as she held onto his hand.

His hands were big and strong. April turned his hand over and thought about all the things these hands had accomplished. He was a bull fighter as a young man, earning enough money to come to America with is bride. His hands had held babies and his wife, worked hard on the farm with animals and in the fields. He carried 100-pound milk cans and lifted them up on the truck. He had pushed her many times on the swing up into the tree boughs. His hands picked flowers and baby calves up out of the field. His hands gathered chicks to their mother hen. These hands held him as he leaned over the casket of a son and daughter. His hands held hammers, nails, saws, ladders, and they showed him there was no job he could not do. April saw the purple age spots and realized Grandpa was older than he lived. Grandpa loved adventure and traveling. He was never afraid to do anything or go anywhere.

April felt like she had failed him. There were great doctors she knew that she felt could have done more for him. She turned his hand back with the palm down and kissed it. Grandpa opened his eyes. He could only whisper, "it's okay. Don't worry."

April knew that he believed in the Savior Jesus Christ. She knew he attended church as often as he could. He had lived a lifetime of being a good man. He had little if any regrets and she was afraid he would let go.

"Grandpa, I know you can hear me. I am staying right here with you tonight to watch over you. So you rest. If you get enough rest, we can get stronger, and get out of here." April felt Grandpa's gentle hand touching her hair.

"I want to go home," he whispered.

April's heart sank. There was nothing she could do. Out of respect she said, "Whatever you want, Grandpa. I am going to miss you like a lost soul. Forgive me for saying that, but this is your choice and I respect it."

Grandpa breathed slowly and steadily all night long and April was beside him each minute asking God in prayer that his will be done. In the morning after vital checks, April showed Grandpa

259

photos of the girls and boys on her cell phone. Grandpa looked and began to tear up. "I am going to watch over them," he said.

April kissed his cheek and forehead. "Oh, Grandpa, my heart is breaking. I miss you already and will pray for you every day."

Grandpa just put his head back on the pillow to rest and soon his wife came in chatting away about what was going on in the neighborhood, the church, and newspaper.

Larry came in with the brothers and realized from the look on April's face it would not be long. Larry went into the room and thanked Grandpa for his love and support for April.

Grandpa smiled, "You take good care of my girl. I am counting on it."

Larry said he would and touched Grandpa's hand and left the room.

April went in as did her brothers. Grandma was dabbing at her eyes. "His son never came in," the one said. That did not matter to April. Those who loved him were here. The boys did not stay long, they could not take it.

April sat on one side of Grandpa's bed with her Grandma on the other side. They would look at him and sometimes make a comment and he would smile. April kept her eyes on the telemetry and lines hooked up to him.

Then as lunch time approached, Grandpa opened his eyes and said something. Grandma looked behind her and said, "No, he is not here."

April asked what he said.

"He was saying his brother was here."

April knew the end was soon. "Grandpa, who is here? Who do you see?" April asked. Grandpa was smiling and he pointed to the blank wall. "Tell me what he is saying," April asked her grandmother.

"He says his father is here with his brother. They are here for him," as she dabbed her eyes. Then Grandpa closed his eyes, breathed his last breath, and was gone.

The two women sat there in disbelief and then April said, "Goodbye, Grandpa. We will see you on the other side." And that was it.

The nurses came in. The time of death was recorded. They covered Grandpa, but not before the two women kissed him for the last time.

April swore that she felt him at her side, touching her arm. Soon they left the room to allow the orderlies to do their job of tagging Grandpa and taking him to the morgue until the funeral home could come and take him.

April and Larry called her parents and asked how the kids were doing. "We are selling them to the gypsies," her dad said. April understood. Ian and Ben were solid, but the girls were, "my way or the highway." Trent was a handful that made Tyler turn out so quiet.

April sought out her grandmother to take her home. The two of them entered the home and the presence of Grandpa was so thick they both sat down and cried together. Slowly throughout the day they gathered information to put in the paper for his obituary.

April found two photographs: one of him as a young man, and the other with them three months earlier.

Her grandmother liked the photos and felt with both he was easily recognizable by friends near and far.

The funeral was five days later. The director was wonderful. He was very respectful and kind. Grandpa was buried near his children, up on a hillside so he could watch over them. There was one plot left which was for his wife.

After the funeral April and Larry took Grandma back to her home. Several other people came along. As Grandma sat at the kitchen table, April and Larry sat with her and said. "There is no reason for you to stay here. We would like you to come and stay with us. We promise you will never be lonely and when your time comes we will make sure you lie beside your husband."

Grandma just sat and shook her head, "I not bother you. I be okay." She blew her nose and others there tried to have her see how much better her life would be to go than to stay. She was having none of it. Within a week she had decided to sell her home and move into a small apartment on street level downtown.

April and Larry were back home two days after the funeral. Ian and Ben came home from school getting off the bus at their grandparents' lane and walked home. It was not more than two hundred yards. They always came home this way to say "Hello" to the Grandparents, take what Miranda had to give to them, or go to their mother. The boys were so happy to see their parents, they ran to them hugging them. The girls clung to Larry's legs while Trent kept his distance and Tyler came running in from the yard. April was concerned about Trent he was an angry little bugger, and she was determined to work more with him.

Two months later Trent and April had just come back from a Mom and Son ride when the telephone rang. April answered the phone in the barn. "Hello?" she asked.

"April, I have decided to come and stay with you and your family. If that is all right?" the small quiet voice said.

April knew this was her grandmother in the East. "Good. When can you come?" April asked her.

"I have to make sale here and get rid of some things and then I have small things to bring, I want to keep if that's all right" the old woman said.

"Sure. Sure it is. I can come and help you if you need help," April told her.

"No. I am okay, but how will I get my things to where you are?" she asked.

"I can help you with that. Don't worry," April said. "When you are ready, call me. I can fly down and we can load up what you have, and you come with us. We are so happy and excited you are coming," April told her.

April and Larry had often spoken about the small building that was used as a summer home on this property. It stood not even twenty feet from the main house. How easy it would be to turn it into a small cozy home for someone. Larry met April and she told him about the telephone call. Larry walked to the phone and called a carpenter that had helped them in the past. The carpenter said he could start it tomorrow since a job he had fell through because the people changed their minds.

When the carpenter came, he looked at the foundation, the inside, and roof. He estimated he could have this done in two weeks. That evening April thought about some ideas she had for the little house, and she wrote them down. The carpenter came. He did start and finish the tiny summer home in three weeks with the ideas April had. It would be perfect for Grandma. She would be with them during the day and when she wanted to be alone she would have her own space.

Grandma could make telephone calls, watch television, work on her needlepoint, or take a nap in the privacy of her own home.

They were happy, Grandma had buried her grievances with Nora, and the ladies often took the elderly woman with them on outings. One of Grandma's favorite things was to picnic in the park. She loved to watch children on the playground or enjoy the many musical events there. Out of respect, April went with her to the Catholic Church every other Sunday. It was not right for her to go alone. In time the two women became close, more than April ever thought possible.

Manny and Contessa visited more. Miranda, Gordon, and the ladies all became closer doing things together as a family. The kids were delighted. They always had someone to pay attention to them, to kiss a boo-boo, or tie their shoes. April had a mind for detail. She noticed all the good that was around them and was so very thankful.

Two years of blessing them with her humor and kind ways, Grandma was in April's home watching television with the girls who were now five wanting to play a game Grandma taught them. Grandma would cut their apples into slices, and they would share them. Grandma would say, "One for you, one for you and three for me," and they would giggle.

This day they could not wake Grandma up as they tugged at her arm. April became alarmed and came to see what happened. Grandma was not breathing. Her hands were cold. She had passed away while playing with the girls. What a wonderful way to go.

Grandma was never alone. She had been kept happy and content until she passed.

Within minutes Larry came in as April took the girls outside. Larry called the mortician and explained she was to be shipped and then buried beside her husband. The next day April and Larry went to pick out a casket while her parents watched the four children. The girls did not understand why Grandma did not wake up and were so very sad.

The arrangements were made, Grandma would have a viewing at "home" and would be buried beside her companion of sixty-five years. April and her entire family flew in to be at the viewing and funeral. Everyone commented on how good Grandmother looked.

"They took good care of her," they said.

The children were all well behaved including Trent who was intrigued by the funny speaking people. After the viewing and burial, April had made arrangements for a luncheon at the local hotel. It was a nice meal giving everyone a chance to talk and eat before going home.

One woman came to April and said. "I know you do not know me, but I am your cousin. I wanted to thank you for taking her and giving her a good life. She was happy. I know that because she called me often and we spoke about what she was doing. She said she was so very busy with the children, going on picnics, taking rides in the boat, and visiting. I remember thinking, she never speaks about work, she never mentioned sweeping the floor, or dusting, or doing her own laundry, or grocery shopping, or cooking because you did all that for her. She truly had a good life with you. Here she would have been alone and fend for herself. We are all busy with jobs, so I wanted to thank you."

April was touched and hugged the woman. "I am ashamed that I am your cousin and do not know you," April replied.

"It's okay. I have cousins on the other side of the world I do not see either," the woman said. "I just wanted to thank you and tell you all of us feel this way."

That evening they all went back home to California. The monument stone would be put on later when the ground was settled. The insurance policy covered the funeral, casket, burial, and stone. April paid for the luncheon and any other expenses.

What was left in Grandma's bank account, April divided equally for her brothers. They could use it. April and her family did not need it. She did, however, keep the jewelry. It was not a lot, but there were two granddaughters that might want it someday. She doubted she would ever wear any. It took a while for the children to settle down. The girls, in particular, because they spent the most time with Grandma who adored the girls.

That fall Ian was now 11, Ben was 9, the girls Sam and Rae were 6, and Trent was 5 and Tyler 3 they were all growing up so fast. Gordon loved to have Ian and Ben come and help him do odd jobs and it was good for the boys. Sometimes Sam and Rae would go and help their grandma work in the house. Some days they would vacuum the rugs or dust and other days bake.

Gordon also took a hand in Trent. He felt, for some reason, this boy was struggling to be heard or noticed, which was silly because April and Larry were good to all of the kids. Trent acted out. Gordon took him with him often, to fields, or riding four wheelers. Over the years Trent developed a deep loving relationship with his Grandpa. As the years passed, it was obvious Trent was a hunter. He loved hunting, especially archery and was good at it.

Tyler developed a love for the land like his Dad. Both Ben and Tyler loved farming, driving tractors, and being with the guys.

Sam and Rea were very different although twins. Sam was a tomboy and Rea liked being all girl. They never dressed alike and had different interests and hobbies. Sam liked field hockey and was very athletic. Rea liked riding horses, but she loved clothes and was particular about getting dirty.

April wondered what happened that Rae was so different. The girls were close though. No one could step in between their relationship. They rarely argued and if you found one the other was close nearby. They supported each other in their own individual pursuits.

Life was good. For many years April flew around the country making improvements in D Farms Inc. Now Mr. Steven's son was in charge of the office. From time to time if he had a question his father graciously came in and helped him.

April was content. She and her husband took vacations with their family twice a year. They visited most every state in the US, went to the beaches, the forests, they hiked, zip lined, canoes, kayaked, swam, ran, bicycled, boated, rode jet skis, and hover craft. As a family they were busy enjoying all life had to offer.

Often her parents came along or the ladies, but as the years went by April noticed Lena, Nora, and her mother would often lag behind. Mother would often be tired and need to rest so the three of them would rest together.

April understood why her birth mother would have trouble, as she had no ribs on the left side of her body and no left lung. But her mom was always active, as was Lena. April suggested the three of them go for a checkup. Miranda put her off, but Lena and Nora did go. Nora and Lena were anemic. Their doctor wanted them to find sources of iron that would not bind them up. So, iron-rich foods were best. In a short time their color was better, and they had more energy. However they were both in their sixties now and would be slowing down.

Finally Miranda went to the doctor at April's constant urging. He wanted to do a test on her carotid arteries. When he called for her to come back in for her test results, April went with her. The doctor showed them both the occlusion in Miranda's arteries. And Miranda asked what could be done. He explained there is a procedure where the arteries could be "cleaned out," but Miranda refused.

"I will be more careful and eat better," she said.

The doctor tried to explain that the damage was done. No amount of careful eating would clean this out, but Miranda refused. April wondered why her mother was being so stubborn. On the ride home Miranda explained that a friend of theirs had this surgery and it did not turn out so good.

April encouraged her Mother to go to another doctor for a second opinion, so they did. A month later this doctor told Miranda if she took a prescription, it would benefit her greatly. So for Miranda it was the lesser of two evils. She got the prescription, which was very expensive, and took it faithfully every day.

April's lane that connected to the road where her parents live was a familiar path. She had walked it every day as a child. When she used the four-wheeler she had calves at this farm. It was not far. They had lined the road with split-rail fencing and April had planted flowers at each of the posts giving the fence a lovely country look.

Gordon was about to retire. He was nearing 65 and April planned a retirement party right on their property. There was a lovely area she and her husband kept open with trees for shade and plenty of room to walk around. Over six hundred invitations had been sent out, out of the five hundred and sixty who wanted to come.

April made sure the printer put "if you know of someone who knows Gordon that did NOT get an invitation, be sure to let them know they are welcome."

The food was ordered, as well as all the tables and chairs. April wondered how she would keep this a secret. It was decided they would not set up until that morning. The caterer could set up. The food would come in after Dad was there. They would use the little house to put food in or for a kitchen if needed.

Dad did not have a clue. He was busy trying to figure out how his retirement would play out. So one morning April had the two boys, Ian and Ben, ask their grandfather to take them for a haircut. Gordon loved his grandchildren and spending time with them. Next the boys asked him to take them to the trophy shop, then to drive past the theatre to see what movies were in. All to buy time. That way people could be dropped off and their cars driven away.

Larry and friends drove up over the hill to the next farm. They all sat and visited until they saw Gordon. The decorations were simple, table covers and all plastic dinnerware and flatware. There were lights strung in the trees. She and Larry had put the lights up two days earlier and almost had a divorce while doing it. As the large group of people waited, April knew soon the boys would be home. They texted her to say they would be there in a half hour. People were still coming in late.

Then in the distance April could hear her father and mother walking down the lane to the house. Her mother did not know about the party either. They chatted with the boys. As they walked to the back porch, April slipped her arm inside her father's, and they walked to the clearing as they heard "Surprise!"

Gordon froze in his tracks while Ben and Ian pulled up the large banner that they made across the lane that read "Happy Retirement Grandpa." Gordon was all smiles. He went to join the crowd of people.

Miranda was full of questions, "How in the world did April pull this off without me knowing."

April smiled.

The party went on long into the night. April had to leave to put the youngest to bed then came back. There was a man there to see her, who had just happened by. Rupert Manning, the man she had met so long ago when she was on the airplane heading into Florida for her frogman training.

"Hello, how are you?" April asked the man.

"I am doing all right. I did not know there was a party going on or I would not have stopped," he said.

"Oh, don't be silly. Come and have something to eat. There is a ton of food," April told him. April walked with the man, and she introduced him to her father.

Then she led him to a table with several other people sitting there and she said she would be back soon and left.

Rupert Manning loved parties, and he loved to drink alcohol. He was surprised there was none. "Say, anything hard to drink here?" he asked.

"There is some horse urine in the stalls," Ben told him running away laughing. Let it up to a 9- and 6-year-olds for pranks.

April rejoined him offering him a large glass of sweet, iced tea picked from her fields.

"Ahh," he said "Just like my grandmother used to make. Say, I need to talk to you about a proposition," he said to April.

"Excuse me?" April said.

"Oh no. Don't take it like that," Rupert backtracked. "Do you remember what I told you I did for a living?" he asked.

April did not, she only remembered him talking to her on the plane. She may have been nervous or not paying attention and she apologized.

"Well, I am a numbers person. You know, fact finding. And, well, I represent a large party of folks that are interested in you running for Governor."

April laughed out loud, "Are you kidding me? Me, run for Governor of California?" she laughed again.

"No. No, do not dismiss this. I am telling you the truth. I am not here to waste my time or yours," and he handed April a card. April was flattered but in no way was she interested. She insisted Rupert make himself at home, fill a plate, and enjoy himself. There were games to play, horseshoes, shuffle board, a rousing game of volleyball, and when that was over a game of softball. Unless he liked tag, the kids played that all the time, and she left him.

Rupert got a plate and mingled with the crowd. Later April saw him sizing up a horseshoe to pitch it just right in the horseshoe game.

Finally April found Larry and the two of them sat down. They had some time before gifts were opened, which April asked them NOT to bring, but some did anyway. April kissed her husband and sat holding his hand.

Larry had a plate of food that he was eating and soon they were joined by Scott and Susan.

"Very nice party. Good job," he said.

April sat there and remembered the card in her pocket. She fished it out and handed it to Larry.

"What's this?" he asked.

Then Scott picked it up and looked at April. "Do you know who this is?" he asked her. "This man is a numbers man. He can tell you who will win an election. He does tons of ground work with people to make odds in his favor. Where did you get this card?" he asked.

"From him," and April pointed to Rupert.

Scott looked at her quizzically and asked, "About?"

"He asked me if I would run for Governor of California," April told them.

Scott's face turned to solid attention and said, "You should. You'd be good, April. You know finances. You have employed thousands of people. You know business, and I say go for it."

April looked at Larry who was too busy eating and then they had Tyler come over with messy pants. "I have a job," April said hoisting Tyler up to go and change him.

The night went beautifully. April and Larry had a small surprise for her parents. April sang while Larry played the mandolin. Gordon was impressed, as was April. She learned Larry had many hidden talents. He could play the mandolin, a trumpet, and a guitar when begged. He would say he was not that good, but the truth is, he was very good when he practiced.

Yes, it was a lovely evening. The kids were in bed long before the party was over. Only Ian and Ben were allowed to stay up until 9:30. Ian was now twelve and Ben ten. They adored their grandparents.

That night April helped put the food away and encouraged many of the folks who were there to take what they could. April loaded up the ladies, putting platefuls in a cooler for them to take home. Warm ups were great on days when they worked.

Later as April sat on the side of her bed weary with tiredness, her husband joined her pulling her over to him. "Did you have a nice time tonight, dear?" he asked her.

"Yes, I did. I think Dad and Mom had the nicest time, but it was good for all of us. You know?"

Larry agreed and soon the two lovebirds were nestled in their bed and sound asleep.

The next morning Rupert Manning was knocking on their door and Ben ran to answer it. "Come on in," Ben said.

Rupert stood at the door waiting for April. April told him to come in and have some breakfast.

"Oh, mercy, no. I am still full from last night. Say that was one swell party. I wish my wife had been along with me. Say I was wondering if you had any chance at all to think about what we spoke about last night? I know you may have been up late and all but maybe?" he said imploring her looking hopeful.

"No, I did not give it much thought at all. You see I love my life. I am President of D Farms, and I travel all across the country to take care of problems or make improvements. I hire and fire people. I create jobs and move people around. I also plan parties for holidays, and retirements." April smiled, "and my children are young and need me" she said.

"How old are your children?" Rupert asked.

"Ian is twelve, Ben is ten, the girls Sam and Rae are seven, Trent the terrible is five, and Tyler is two," April told him.

"My, my. You have a big family. They are all good children and that brings votes, my dear," he said. "How about I contact you later this year. We have two years really, and maybe by then you might change your mind," he said to her.

"Do they offer free babysitting?" April teasingly asked.

"Yes. Oh, yes. They do," Rupert seriously said. "I will be in touch. It was good of you to treat me so well last night, and I really enjoyed myself," he said.

April told him, "You feel welcome to stop in anytime."

"Again, if you get fed up and want to make a difference, which I think you can. I know you like people. I saw that last night and you are good with them. Handling them you know. You handled me," and he laughed. "Just keep it on the back burner of your mind. Here is my card," and he handed her a second card. "You were Mayor of this town, weren't you?" he asked her.

"Well, I still am. No one wants the job. Truthfully, I don't mind," April told him.

"Yes, you are the material we are looking for in a candidate. There will be others, but I'd vote for you, hands down!" he said to April. They said goodbye and he was gone.

"Thank goodness," April said with a sigh, happy for the solitude of her family. Larry took the card and tucked it into his wallet. April had a bad habit of throwing things away and regretting it later.

That winter April and Larry decided to treat her parents, the ladies, and all the kids by taking them to an island to be pampered and treated like kings and queens. It was difficult since the ladies still cleaned businesses that depended on them. Dad was now retired, but he and Mom had doctor appointments to keep. So April did her homework and spoke to the owners of the businesses to explain why the ladies needed two weeks off. They understood completely and agreed to allow substitute cleaners. They said they wanted the ladies back. They were thorough, did a very good job, and everyone liked them. April then rescheduled her parents' appointments without their knowledge. She stressed that the offices should not call her parents. They would keep the new appointments and she told them why.

It was a go. On December 22nd they would all be leaving on a flight to St. Thomas, and they could see other islands as well. The hotel was booked two months in advance. April and Larry were so excited to tell them.

For Thanksgiving the ladies insisted that they prepare dinner. April knew this was a big undertaking for them. She also thought that Judge Du Val, his wife, and kids would love to come as well. With such a large group, April decided to help them.

They started by cleaning out space in the dining room and the parlor which were only separated by a door. This would allow enough space for everyone.

Next the food was purchased. April told the ladies to buy the turkey, and she would pay for whatever else was needed. It was a lot of fun shopping with them. They were so comical together.

April told them she would make the mashed potatoes and yams ahead of time and bring them to their home to bake. The mashed potatoes was actually a potato filling recipe that was given to her long ago and one that everyone liked. She also baked a ham. There were cookies, nut rolls, sweet rolls, and desserts of all kinds.

At Thanksgiving they were all aware that this would be April and Larry's Christmas meal because they were going to the islands. What they did not know was that they were all going.

After the meal, the Judge and his family went home. They were stuffed and needed a nap.

When everything was cleaned up and the dishwasher was loaded, it was gift-giving time. After all, they would be gone over Christmas.

Lena and Nora handed April and Larry a book. It was all about April's family history complete with photos.

April was astounded. She paged through the book making comments like, "This is so wonderful."

They said, "Turn the book over and upside down," and there was Larry's family history. "It was easy to find. They never moved away."

Larry was deeply touched. There also were some tin type photos from the 1700s. What an awesome gift.

Meanwhile the boys had opened some of their gifts. They had squirt guns and darts.

The girls opened a box that had material and instructions on how to make pot holders. They both liked it a lot.

Trent got a bow and arrow set from Grandpa who was showing him how to hold it and aim. "We will go outside later and give this a try," he told Trent.

Tyler was eating paper. So April swiped it from his mouth, and he began to cry. She got him a small hard biscuit to chew on. "He is teething," April told them.

Gordon handed the ladies an envelope. Lena opened it. Nora and Lena looked inside. Then they looked at Gordon and Miranda and jumped up to thank them. Inside the envelope was the mortgage to their house. It was now theirs, free and clear.

Next Larry stood up and handed the ladies, Gordon, and Miranda envelopes and waited . . .

Soon there was screaming and crying. "Oh my, we have always wanted to go, but never thought we'd get there," the ladies said.

Miranda had tears in her eyes and stood to hug her children. "You are both my children and I love you both so much," she said.

Gordon could only hug April and shake Larry's hand with teary eyes.

They were all so happy. And before they could say more, April explained about the changes she made to enable them to go without any worries.

"This is so wonderful, April and Larry. Thank you so very much," Lena said as the ladies got up to kiss April and her husband. "He still gets red when I kiss him," Lena said laughing.

That trip was so much fun. "The best Christmas present ever," they all said. The kids were entertained. They always had someone helping them. And April and Larry enjoyed seeing the four older adults play like kids. They laughed, danced, swam, and played with each other. It was all so wonderful to see them worry free. They never thought about not doing something, they just jumped in and did it.

On the flight home, they all slept. Getting back to a routine was a little hard for the ladies. Every time someone asked them where they had gone, they told them in detail.

For April she was relaxed and ready to return. Every day April went to the office and was home by noon. If she had time in the morning before the office opened, she swam for an hour or two.

On Mondays they had Family Home Evening with the kids or whoever was at their home. Tuesdays there were music lessons for the children who played string instruments. Thursdays were for music lessons for the children who played brass or blowing instruments, like flute and trumpet. Wednesdays were "pick your meal" days. Everyone took a turn on Monday and would write down what they wanted to eat on Wednesday. April didn't mind since they asked for things she usually made anyway. On Fridays April often took them to roller skate or bowl. For a special event they would go to the observatory to see the stars. She found a ton of things to do nearby. Saturdays were for errands, shopping, and preparing a large meal, so April would not have to cook on Sunday. On Sundays they always went to church. April was a teacher in primary school. She had Tyler in her class, and she loved it.

Often when April sat reading her scriptures to prepare a lesson, her mind went back to her grandparents, which saddened her. She was not ashamed to cry and admitted she missed them, especially her grandfather. He was a man she would always think about and miss dearly.

That is why she made a greater effort to spend time with the ladies, her parents, and Miranda's parents. They were getting up in age. Each of them was now well into their 60s. Her older children helped them with chores. And they loved the four of them as much as April did. If they could get out of chores at home to go and help any one of them, they would go.

April was so thankful for all that she had. She remembered where she came from and had so much to be thankful for.

Several more years passed.

Suddenly, without any warning, Nora called April. She was very upset. Lena had passed away in her sleep.

The arrangements were made. And April spoke with her husband about having Nora move into the little house near them. Loneliness is a curse, and Nora could die sooner from missing her sister.

Larry agreed, but it took a bit of convincing before Nora agreed. Once she had settled in, she liked being there very much. There were no memories of her sister associated with any room.

April took Lena's death hard. She knew it was only a matter of time before Nora was gone and then her parents. She felt like she could not breathe.

Larry took April to the temple and in the Celestial Room where the two of them talked and cried together. They believed families were forever, the design of Heavenly Father was to be born, live, and die. Because of the Savior's atoning sacrifice they would all rise again and in the temples they were sealed as a family. They would not be lost, not one.

"I know this to be true," April said. "It's just that I will miss them terribly."

Larry embraced his wife holding her near. He knew what she said was true.

April was a good daughter and a wonderful wife.

Larry also knew that if he passed before April, it might kill her. He also knew that he did not want to live without her.

The following spring the twins helped Nora plant flowers around the cottage and put some in window boxes. Nora liked to watch the birds come, especially the hummingbirds. April came out and watched them. Nora was now using a cane to walk most anywhere. She was often short of breath.

One day, a car came up their driveway. It was not your typical run of the mill, every day car. The car was a long black limousine that parked near their house.

April looked and asked, "May I help you?" and out stepped a man wearing a business suit.

He looked around and began to walk up the steps toward April with his stogie in his mouth and the smoke swirling around him. Then he was met by a growling Jet with her teeth bared.

"May I help you?" April asked again.

The man looked at her and began to smile. He removed his stogie, and said, "I am Arnold Canes. I am the head organizer of the Republican Party. I was sent out here by Rupert Manning. You know him I believe?"

April said she did, but she also warned the man that her dog did not like him, and he should stay down on the steps.

The man looked at April closely. She was a small woman, with an athletic build, and meant what she said.

"If you want to talk, I can come out. Just wait a minute and let me get my shoes," she said. April went inside and closed the door. She called Larry on the walkie talkie and asked him to come down to the house ASAP.

Larry came down from the field in his tractor, parked, and got off. He met April in the driveway in front of the man's limo.

"Hello," the man said offering his hand to Larry while still clenching the stogie in his teeth.

"How about you get rid of that if you want to talk to us?" Larry told him.

Arnold Canes eyed Larry, then he squeezed the fire out of the stogie, and put it in his pocket. "It's a nasty habit I know, but I like it. It's not for everyone. I know that. Sorry if I offended you."

They sat down and Arnold Canes outlined a strategy to April and Larry concerning the upcoming election.

The primary is in the spring and the election in the fall. Larry put his hand over April's, and she looked at him. April felt her heart begin to beat faster and her forehead was sweaty.

Mr. Canes noticed this and told April there is nothing to be afraid of. Your past is squeaky clean, and you have an excellent record with D Farms. I know you could win.

April was still unsure. Her parents were aging, and the kids still needed her. Ian was now fourteen, Ben twelve, the girls nine, Trent eight, and Tyler six. Yes, they were all in school, but they still needed her. When they called, "Mom, are you there?" She wanted to be there.

Mr. Canes told her she would it was a commitment of six years, and the children would have bodyguards and nannies,

"No!" April adamantly shouted, making Mr. Canes' head jerk back. "I am their Mother, and I take care of them." April nodded towards Larry. "We do."

"Oh, that is completely understandable and all right," Mr. Canes said to her. "So will you run?"

April looked at Larry. "If you want to do it, go ahead. I will still farm and help with the kids, and your parents will have to go along with you." April nodded. From there the project ballooned. By spring her picture was on banners, yard signs, and buttons.

Running for Governor

"STRONG FAMILY VALUES", "HONEST", "INTEGRITY", AND "VOTE TO April D," these were some of things used in her ads. Also mentioned was how she created jobs. And there were testimonials from people who supported her and who dealt with her.

Then, of course, there were smear campaigns that brought up the fact that April had murdered a man. They left out the honest details because the truth would not help their cause. Naturally April sued them, so the other party backed off, and made a public apology.

For ten months the campaign went on back and forth. April attended public events. She gave several speeches. The only problem she had with speaking events was that she could not find venues large enough to hold the number of people who came to see and hear her. The people were not fools. Too many knew her.

In the end it was no contest. She carried the state 85 percent to 15 percent.

The swearing in ceremony was a nice, but windy day. April got a little emotional as she looked at her mother, dad, and, of course, Nora.

Nora was so proud of April. "You have come so far, Dear. You handled your life with kindness for others and it shows."

All of the children were there. The media focused on the children. Tyler was so cute. Trent behaved like a soldier. And the girls kept both the young boys in line. There were no outward signs one had to be keenly focused to see the any minor problem, but kids will be kids. The media loved the children. They asked for interviews and photos, but April refused them all. She wanted her children to grow up normally, and, for the most part, they did everything a regular kid would do.

The Secret Service were the only ones to see April's children being children. They squabbled then made up with hugs. The kids included the men and women to play board games with them. Together they made paper kites to fly outside. They whooped and hollered in games and the service folks got a kick out of the children. One afternoon the girls invited several of them to their afternoon tea, and they graciously accepted. Tea and dancing, real heroes in April's eyes.

One afternoon Nora had an idea. With help they fashioned fancy homemade kites to fly and let go. On each kite was a note inviting the finder to the Governor's mansion for dinner when a head of state would be invited. The finder was screened and background checked, but no matter how old, what ancestry, or job, they were all welcome. There were children, grandmothers, moms and single fathers, fishermen, hairdressers, or retirees living on social security. They were all encouraged to have a voice and tell April what they considered to be a needed important change or if all was well. April learned a lot during these dinners, and she told Nora how much she appreciated it.

In the Governor's house her father found many things to do, like fixing things around the mansion. April did not tell him there was staff to do these jobs. He needed to feel useful. Miranda loved planning dinners and watched the cooks, giving them advice. Nora helped wherever she could. She enjoyed the children the most. She kept them away from strangers or reporters. Larry farmed much of the time, and he stayed home. When April could get away or if he could come to the Governor's mansion they were together. April reasoned he could be with her. Larry was unsure.

Being Governor was not a vacation, it was work, hard work. She balanced budgets and planned for cities and townships. There were events to be held after April was settled in. Her first agenda was to balance the budget. Sadly many jobs were lost. Some employees transferred into other positions. Most cities and townships felt the pinch.

By her first anniversary as Governor, April wanted to have a press conference to inform the people that their state was now in the black. They were on target. There were businesses interested in hiring 20,000 jobs. And she wanted to stop the questions and gossip. Yes, she was pregnant with twins due sometime later that year.

The press loved it. This was a first! The people saw pictures of April playing with her children in the yard. April still loved to mow grass. While she did, her children would push wheelbarrows and toy mowers around imitating her. The older boys learned how to prune bushes and trees. This was not a weekly event but more like monthly for them. They were in the newspaper often because of their Family Home events. When asked why April did not travel with her kids, she responded, "My children are happy when we are together and they understand my job is very important for the people, not just us."

Yes, the days in the Governor's mansion were busy, fun, and opportunistic. It was there at Ian developed the desire to become an attorney. He was young and enthusiastic, choosing that as his career.

Ben often left to go home with his Dad. Ben was quiet but he wanted to farm. He once said he wanted to go to D Farms and earn his way and April thought that was very honorable of him.

The girls kept everyone hopping. Sam loved horses and it was nothing to see her jumping over jumps on the pristine lawns with her sister cheering her on.

Rae was an expert in clothing and wanted to be a model. In time that is what she would become. April kept the photos of Rae with animals. She had an instinct for them. An attraction and the animals responded beautifully.

Trent loved to go home with his Dad and hunt. His secret service agent said at his young age he was a more accurate shooter than most of them were. Trent was the closest to Gordon and always sought out Grandpa before he would leave and when he came home.

Tyler was still in his own world. He liked to walk, go, and see things. He was thrilled when he had someone to go with him when HE wanted to go. He liked someone who could keep up with him.

Before April gave birth, Larry came with distressing news. Native Son had left them. Native Son was out eating grass, just laid down, and died. April wanted to go see him buried properly, she was insistent. April and Larry left their children in care of the secret service. Monte was there with red, swollen eyes. April knew that Native Son meant a lot to him as well.

They buried Native Son on her Dad's farm, right where he started. They contacted a craftsman who was superior in art to create a bronze statue of Native Son. It showed him standing on a small tuft of grass on a small hill. It was beautiful and befitting of this great horse that started all the successes of their lives long, long ago. April knew that Native Son knew he was loved. Not just by her, but by many. He sired many winning colts and mares. She was so glad he had a long, happy life, And she stressed really lived. Native Son loved crowds and the cheering. He loved his special times with her, his treats, and their long talks when it mattered and when it did not. April was Native Son's girl. She was always there, would always and forever be in his heart.

April gave birth to fraternal twins on the 14th of April in her second year as Governor. Austin weighed 5 pounds 9 ounces and was 17 inches. Ada weighed 5 pounds 4 ounces and was 17 inches. They were a little underweight and stayed in the neonatal unit for almost a month. It was a trying time for April. She came home and her babies did not. April worked in the early morning from 4 a.m. until 10 a.m. then she left for the hospital and stayed for three hours. She worked from that time until 5 p.m. and then went back to the hospital. April had a driver and a secret service agent who would walk with her to and from the hospital.

For those watching it was heart wrenching to see how much April loved her babies and wanted to take them home, but they were not out of danger yet. It was almost three weeks until the twins had gained enough weight to go home. The picture of them leaving with Mom and Dad was on the front page of the newspapers. The good people left small gifts for the babies. April gave a short clip on television to thank them and asked them to rejoice with her but to keep their hard earned money. The babies were too small to play and needed much care.

Later there was another photo of April at work very early in the morning. She was leaning partially over her desk with her left arm supporting a baby swaddled in a blanket and with her right hand holding a pen. Her face was serious in thought, while her right foot rocked a cradle on the floor soothing the other baby. That photo was loved by the people.

They had a volunteer who worked tirelessly for them. April tended to her children as best she could. There were many, many good days, fun days, as well as several harried, crazy ones.

It was now the third year of her term and the babies were one. April took a small leave of absence to visit Manny and Contessa who were well into their 80s now. It was so good to see them and also sad. Within eight months of that visit Manny passed away and Contessa two years later.

With only one more year to fulfill her Governorship, April felt so much more had to be done and yet there would not be enough time.

Her crowning achievement was a high-speed rail line that took commuters in half the time and less money than if they had to drive that distance. The people were happy and meanwhile the regular trains had their own rails.

When nearing the end of her term, many expressed their concern. They did not want to see April leave. She had done so much good for their state they wanted her to fulfill another term. April was undecided as there was much good to be done.

The kids were happy and Larry had turned much of his farming over to a farmer who was just starting out. He needed the work. Larry did help him often, but it sure was nice to have him with them and be with the kids more. So April had a talk with her family, her children, and her husband, Dad, Mom, and Nora. They all said they were happy here, were well taken care of, and felt useful. The younger children cried to stay and slid down in their seats. April laughed inwardly as the staff helped to console them. The staff was questioned and interviewed again and they too hoped April would agree to stay. There was an opponent but nothing her party was concerned with.

Again April won the election and continued on for another term. Her family had grown up a lot in the last six years. Ian was now twenty and enrolled in college. Ben was eighteen and working full time on D Farms. The girls were fifteen and were very mature and focused for their age. Trent was fourteen and was rarely seen. He was always wanting to go hunting with his dad or someone who would take him. Tyler was twelve. He was a home boy. He too loved his dad and Grandpa and they often left together.

Austin and Ada were four now going on five and they loved to play. They were serious old souls who were inseparable. The secret service and staff enjoyed these two probably the most. They were not crybabies they were quiet and entertained themselves very easily. They were each other's best friend and the staff always saw them walking about in the mansion. They were not afraid of anyone or to go anywhere. Nora was using a cane now and followed those two everywhere. It was exhausting work for her.

In the third year of April's second term her birth mother Nora passed away. It was a quiet, private viewing for her and her family. Her brothers and their families came. It was very emotional and healing at the same time. Nora was buried beside her sister at the Di Angelo's family burial plot.

April needed time alone. She was so grateful for a mother who loved her enough to let her go. Nora was not a selfish woman. She recognized that she could not provide for April in the way Miranda and Gordon could. Nora was so overwhelmingly grateful when the Di Angelo's offered her a refuge from her abusive home. Nora was always a quiet person who enjoyed simple things. She was always thankful and often said so.

April knew Nora's blood was in her veins and she too was sealed to April when Nora's time came. It was healing for April to know she would never lose Nora. One day she would stand in front of her again and thank her for giving her life and then helping her to live. Nora was and is an amazing woman, all that knew her loved her.

Miranda took Nora's passing very hard. She and Nora had formed a friendship when April was a little girl. Whenever Nora needed to talk to someone it was either her sister Lena, or if Lena was not about or after Lena passed away it was Miranda. To say they truly loved one another was not a lie. For two mothers to one child to get along as happily and graciously as these two did set an example for others. Miranda cried for days for her friend. Some days April walked in on Miranda and she would sit with her and cry with her. Then Miranda would say, "You know if she were here, she would scold us."

April nodded her head, "Yes, she would. I just hope after all she had been through in life that she was happy here with us. I mean I know no one forced her to come but was she truly happy here. I wonder."

"Nora told me with her own lips how happy she was, many, many times. She and I had many conversations about you as you grew up, April. And she thanked me so often that we allowed her to be part of your life which seemed crazy to us. Both Gordon and I felt that with all of us in your life you would have a greater chance to turn out well. I am going to miss her, April. I never had a sister and she was like a sister to me, a good sister. She was kind and thoughtful, a very hard worker, and very talented. She knew how to crochet and knit. She knew a lot about animals. More than I ever did. And Nora never said no to us, not ever. No matter what we asked of her, she always said yes. I am going to miss my friend," Miranda said.

April set her mind to work after that. She had to. She was not here to cry all day long.

During the fourth year of her second term, many wanted improvements were accomplished. If you were in a restaurant or hotel, and April's name came up, you could not find anyone to speak against her. They all agreed that she tried harder than anyone they knew to resolve problems and get things done. April was true to her word. She brought in many businesses, creating many jobs. Their welfare rate dropped. The schools' graduation rate was the highest it had ever been with even more going on to college. Her vision worked.

It was in the final year of her second term that there was talk of reelecting her again. April then signed legislation for "Term Limits"! No more than two terms would be allowed, not ever.

That year Miranda had a stroke. She went into the hospital, but never really recovered. Miranda's speech was slurred and her face sagged. She could not walk anymore, her legs dragged. April wanted her to come home to the mansion so she could take care of her herself.

That is when she had the biggest surprise! The girls stepped in as did the younger boys. They all had a hand in caring for their grandmother. Both girls left school and jobs to help out. The girls did most of the physical care. The boys read to her, talked with her, and took her out in the wheelchair to the lawn to see the world, to hear the birds, feel the rain, and smell the flowers.

Miranda Di Angelo, age 82, wife, mother, and grandmother passed away on December 1ˢᵗ. April's heart was broken. As bad as she felt, she had to watch over her Dad who lost his companion, his sweetheart of over 60 years.

April spoke with her Dad at long length one night and her Dad was good with it all. He said they had been sealed in the temple and would be partners for eternity. He did not want anyone else. Her Dad told her, "You know, Honey. We loved each other. We surely did, but we were not lucky enough to have children. Not until you came along and we found happiness we never knew. We used to laugh at your antics and never were prouder of you in all your pursuits. You were tenacious and often we were not sure if you would follow through. But you did, you always did. I swear I am the luckiest man alive. I have had a great life. I have witnessed many things from my own family. And my companion was right there with me the whole time."

"Dad, I will do anything you ask. I can step down and the lieutenant governor can take over for the last two years. Dad, I will do this for you," April said.

At that time, many people who had met April or her family over the years stepped forward. Old friends, singers, entertainers, political figures, all wanting to help. April expressed her gratitude and thanked them. She also told them that her father preferred a simple funeral to share with the public. They wanted April to know they cared and loved her family and were there if at any time help was needed.

"Oh, April. Come on now. We see things through don't we? We always have before. This is no different," he said. And that is what April did.

The viewing for Miranda Di Angelo was going to be public. April had her mother dressed like a queen. She was lying in state for anyone who chose to come and view her as well as walk through part of the mansion. There was extra security, of course. For April, Miranda represented the people and was a very public person. April wanted the people to see the woman who supported and encouraged her. The mom who encouraged April to do more and be more.

After the walk through at 10:00 a.m., there were services at 1:00 in the afternoon. There were over six hundred chairs set out on the lawn, and still there was a huge overflow of people. They stood along the road and hundreds more were in their cars.

There were television crews set up who were told to be respectful. This was not entertainment. And they were true to their word.

After the invocation and song "I Know that My Redeemers Lives", April stepped forth to speak which surprised many of the people. They knew this was difficult for April, yet here she was. April stepped up to the microphone.

"This is a dark day indeed for the Di Angelo family. We have said goodbye to the matriarch of our family and we will miss her. However, we have many, many good memories that outweigh the sadness." April went on to talk about some of the events and funny antics in her family, and the crowds laughed.

And then April got still and quiet. She was trying to compose herself. "You see me and you think you know me, but in reality you see my mother. At every turn of my life she reminded me who I was. I am a child of God. You are all children of God. You matter. And your relationship with Him should matter most in your daily lives. Of course we are very, very sad, but we know and believe the atonement of the Savior will reunite us all. Miranda Di Angelo was a great mother, wife, and friend. She had a way to comfort souls and bring them peace. Even in her darkest days, when I was taken, Miranda went to church. She did all she could to keep her insane life normal. Life has a way of tossing us in the roughest seas, but if you stay the course, you will come out of the problems intact and whole."

"I have a firm belief of the life and teachings of our Savior Jesus Christ. I know he died and rose again, promising that none of us would remain a slave of the grave. He broke those chains of death for all of us. Yes, we will sorely miss her," and April stopped and put her head down.

Larry stepped in behind her, leaned over, and spoke softly to her.

April lifted her head and continued. "Forgive me," she said. And then April reminded the people how short life can be, to know what was really important and those whom they loved and worked for. The job was not nearly as important as their loved ones.

"I thank each and every one of you who came today. You have truly touched our hearts. Miranda Di Angelo would have been impressed and I doubt that she would have thought her life would have made such a difference in so many lives. But it did. It truly did."

"I want to tell those here, our neighbors, our friends, and each of you across our state that we love you. This service was for you and it comes from our hearts. We hear you and understand. I thank you for giving me the opportunity to serve you. I have had a wonderful teacher who will live on in our memories for the example she set."

"As we lay Miranda Di Angelo to rest, we pray each of you find peace in your hearts as she did. Happiness is not elusive. It is a choice. I have personally seen my mother literally go through hell and still be happy. We will pray for healing for all of you in your own lives. For we know many factors influence us, such as your health, sickness, family problems, financial or job problems. Do not let these things consume you. Do not let them be forefront in your minds. Seek peace. Find yourselves lost in the service for others. That is the example the Savior set and you shall have peace and happiness." April sat down and the choir sang "God Be with You Till We Meet Again."

A dear friend gave the closing prayer and then another friend of hers stepped forward to sing her Mother's favorite hymn "Softly Tenderly".

Softly and tenderly Jesus is calling; calling for you and for me; See on the portals he is waiting and watching, watching for you and for me.

Come home, Come home, ye who are wearily come home; earnestly tenderly, Jesus is calling, calling O sinner come home!

April could no longer control her tears. She sat crying taking in the words. How often had she heard her mother sing this hymn. April knew the words, every one of them. They cut deep into her soul and she knew they were real.

Next began the task of dispersing the crowd. Several friends had the responsibility of directing the people to the exits from the property. There were shuttles available, but most walked out to their cars. Some remained behind even while the chairs were being removed.

April and her family rode in their limos to their home burial plot and watched their dear sweet wife, mother, grandmother, and friend laid to rest. April and Larry supported Gordon who was weary.

It had been a very long, exhausting day and the ride back to the mansion was needed. April rested her head on her husband's chest as they drove. He was her rock. He was steady and she was so grateful to have a good man like him as her mate. They still loved each other and with greater passion then when they started out in life. April did not want to think anymore. She just wanted to be.

After they were back at the mansion, April remembered the children had to go their separate ways in the morning. But they would have a nice lunch in the kitchen.

April did not want the staff to do a lot of extra work because of the funeral.

The staff was confused by this. Of course they wouldn't mind. That was their job. They compromised and made a light lunch. There was a delicious soup, rolls, and thin slices of roast beef to make sandwiches.

April thanked them for going above and beyond the usual. The staff was bewildered since they routinely did this and much more for others. But April was different. She was not one to complain or ask, and she never expected. She did what was needed for herself and her family but went head over heels to serve others.

Later that evening April found her dad and took him out on the veranda. They each sat in their rocking chairs. April had removed her mother's chair and put her chair in its place. The two of them rocked and said no words. April put her hand on her father's arm, but he did not look at her or say anything. April sat and wondered where Larry was. He was most likely with Austin and Ada. Larry loved his children and spent a lot of time with them. He enjoyed the different personalities they had.

As April sat and rocked with her father, she began to ponder what life would be like when they left here and went home. She was overcome with the sense of death. It was all around her. She wanted to breathe fresh air and feel alive at her farm.

She thought about what life would be like if and when she lost her beloved. Those were unbearable thoughts. April began to cry and her father tapped her arm. There was no way April wanted to have her dear sweet Larry die before her. She wanted to go first. But she had no control over any of that. This was all in God's hands, not hers. She understood how her father felt and was fearful he would give up, and not want to live. That is probably how she would feel. At times like this, it is difficult to think without sadness. There needs to be a distraction. April knew she had to find interests for her Dad and soon.

April found it in an old friend who liked to go fly fishing. She mentioned it to her dad a week or so after the funeral and her dad's eyebrows peeked.

"Fly fishing you say?" he asked.

"Yes, Dad. He wanted to take you with him up into Canadian waters. If you want to go?" April told him.

"Let me get my fishing cap and I'll be ready," Gordon said with a smile.

April laughed and hugged her father. "Hold on there. He will be here in two days and you two can make plans then. I want to keep tabs on you. You know," April said.

In two days April's friend did come. He was a business man who loved fly fishing. He felt it was the most relaxing hobby in the world. Trent asked if he could come along and the man said he was more than welcome.

That evening before dinner April asked the man to join her in her study. She asked the man candidly what was the cost for the trip. She wanted to write out a check.

The man looked at her incredulously as if in shock. "April, please. I know you mean well, but do not insult me. I am here to help a friend. I know you would be offended if you came to me and I wrote out a check. So let me do this. All right?"

April said she understood, but she knew there were expenses for travel, food, and lodging. She only wanted to pay for her family and not make a burden.

The man stood up and said, "I am going to pretend I did not hear that," and he stepped forward and embraced his friend. "You don't worry about a thing. We are going to have a great time. I am anxious to teach your dad the joy of fly fishing and we do not want you to follow, call, or check up on us. We will be fine." And that is how it was. Her dad learned to fly fish, and he sat and talked with them around the fire every night telling stories.

Later when Dad came back, he was so content. April knew the next time her friend would go fly fishing, that her Dad would not need to be asked twice.

She knew her friend would be return. He had offered Trent the job of his dreams. Trent was a big game hunter at heart. And this man hired him to take photos of big game.

When Trent was on a hunt, he was to document it in photos for readers of this magazine. Trent was ecstatic because he was living the life he loved. Hunting and taking photos and getting paid for it.

April took advantage of a quiet moment to speak to Trent. She reminded him that this did not happen by chance. "You are a rebellious soul, Trent. You always have been. But I know your heart is good. I have felt it. How I wish you would remember where good comes from and honor that."

Trent looked at his mother and said, "I will come back, and when I am out in the field I will read my scriptures. I did not fall away, Mom. I just took a little walk."

April hugged her son. She loved this wayward boy so much. Maybe it was because of all the work he was for her. She had put a lot of time into Trent as did her dad.

The last two years in service to her state went quickly. A month before their departure from the mansion, they assembled boxes of their personal things which were packed and waiting. For April was already gone, heart, mind, and soul. They lived on what they needed, nothing more. April made sure to purchase small tokens of appreciation for all the staff and secret service men and women. Everyone that she and her family had the privilege of being with during the last eight years.

A week before the swearing in of the next governor, April and her family were home. Her dad was to live with them since the older boys had finished their missions and were now at school or working. Her parent's home was rented out to produce an income for her father.

The renters were people they knew and who enjoyed companionship from church. The father was a handy man. He had five daughters that all loved to ride horses and were good girls. Their mother had passed away from cancer months before. Their father felt this move and having horses for the girls to take care would be a good distraction. That is better than being bored or running the streets, and it was. Often they were all invited to April's home for Family Home Evening and fun events.

One of the older girls told April "You make the church fun!"

April told her, "The church and its programs are a blast. It is the attitude you bring to it that makes the difference. If you are grumpy and don't want to go, I can guarantee you will be miserable. If you go and are anxious to learn and enjoy the company of the other girls there, you will like it a lot. It is in how you approach things. You need to prepare yourself to be a cook or to study. It is the same with church and meetings."

That conversation must have had a good effect on the girl because she was able to convince all her sisters to go to Young Women's group on Wednesday nights. And they found themselves laughing, happier, inviting friends over, and being active in other events as well.

The next year Ian graduated from law school and passed the bar. He wanted to represent the poor and often took cases where the people had no money. He gained a reputation of being a warrior. He knew the law inside and out, and no one wanted to oppose him in the court room. Ian was still single, but there was time for that. April was so grateful for the Heavenly Father. Certainly, he is wise and wonderful. Larry and April could not have been prouder.

Ben was home from his mission and he wanted to keep working the land farming. He settled down with a girl he had met in Idaho and the two of them were a cute couple. Before long they began a family of their own. They lived so very close to April and Larry they were so happy to have little ones running through their house and take place again.

The girls were on opposite poles. Sam was on her mission in Portugal. She would be home in a year.

Rae was in nursing school earning her bachelor's degree. In her own mind Rae was on a fast track for her education. April never questioned this. It was Rae's life not hers. April was proud of both of her girls.

Trent was happy and that statement was one April hoped she would be able to say one day when he grew up. Trent was well known for his picture perfect captions of animals. He fell in love with the camera and spent his time traipsing across continents. He truly got to see the world. Trent did not marry until he was in his 40s. He married a single mom of three children and he was the best Poppa ever. April and Larry were so proud.

Tyler was still at home preparing to go on his mission. His papers had not arrived yet and he was anxious. Tyler was the big brother to Ada. She adored him like all 11-year-old girls love their brothers. Tyler did go on his mission to Native American villages of North America. He was overwhelmed by the poverty and unsanitary conditions of the people. Tyler spent a lifetime correcting those problems. He would call his big brother Ian to help get the finances and laws passed for these people. So they could have medical clinics, doctors, stores, and jobs where they lived. Many laws were changed to help these displaced people to have dignity and respect again. Tyler and Ian often worked hand in hand and April could not have been happier.

That is where Ian found the love of his life, on the reservation. And Tyler fell in love with an aid Ian employed. It was funny and in no way a coincidence.

Austin was eleven. He was unsure what he wanted to do with his life. Dad told him not to be concerned just yet. He had a lot of time to think about it. Austin loved to hang out with Monty who was now in his mid-60s. Monty enjoyed Austin and gave him a job when he was twelve. Over the years he taught him everything he knew about horses. Later in his life Austin became a famous trainer of race horses. Austin was a faithful friend to Monty. He took him to races pushing Monty in his wheelchair.

Austin did not care what people thought. This was HIS friend and pity the fool who said anything negative to him. Austin was articulate but he did not waste his words. He found solace with the horses. He understood them. He spoke to them. They listened and obeyed him freely. April was so glad for Austin. She had hoped one of her children would love horses. And this was quite unexpected but wonderfully, blissfully exciting and welcomed.

When Austin fell in love he fell hard, but it was not to be. The family all consoled him including a friend of Rae's. That was the girl destined to be Austin's wife. She was petite, feisty, and she loved horses. Together they were an unbeatable team. April adored this girl. She reminded April of herself.

Last, but certainly not least, was #8 Ada. She was an old soul. Ada loved old things, antiques, and listening to the elderly. After high school Ada wanted to open a nursing home unlike any April or Larry had heard of. She filled out forms and paid for permits and inspections. Ada asked for a loan to buy the building and promised to pay her parents back in five years.

Ada opened a Living Center. She had permanent elderly residents. She also took in retirees for daycare. Then she made one on the other side for children. Every lunch time the little ones would come and eat with the older folks. The towns around the center kept Ada busy. Daycare was in short supply in the country and the children loved coming. April and Larry visited the Living Center often. They were impressed at how clean it was, about the caring staff, and how they all intermixed with each other.

On one occasion they played push the balloons. It was so much fun the small children squealed with delight and the old folks laughed and laughed. Every day they sang songs. Ada was a proficient piano player and enjoyed bringing happiness to both ages. She said many of the children had no grandparents and they were not afraid of the elderly. Most of the children got extra attention from the older folks and showed loving expressions of hugs and blowing kisses.

The loan was paid in less than two years, the truth is they did not want to be paid back, but Ada insisted.

Throughout April's life her children were a source of strength and joy. There were also times of loss of understanding and frustration when she looked to the Lord who had never, ever failed her. All of her children were active in church and that was a miracle. And oh, the picnics and holiday dinners they had. There was barely enough room. The relationships crossed from friends to wives. It was so amazing to April and she loved it. She and Larry were so happy with the grandchildren who came to visit. Each one rode ponies and would beg their parents tearfully, "I want to go to Grandma and Grandpa's."

Yes, life was good, it had always been good. Often, at night April and Larry would sit on their porch alone together, and sometimes neighbors or friends stopped by.

These days were good. They ate dinner at noon, went for walks, took the horses out for a buggy ride, or visited coming home at their leisure. There was usually always someone there with them, nevertheless April and Larry did what they wanted. It was their time again, just as when they first met. Larry was wonderfully romantic often teasing April. They were happy.

Their intimacy had grown. They were closer than ever in their later years. D Farms took on a persona that April could not have imagined. It had tuned into a well-oiled machine that grew bigger and stronger year by year.

When April was fifty-two she was invited to an awards banquet in her state for the accomplishments she had made in D Farms. She and Larry went. April searched for a modest gown and she chose a light blue gown that did not go to the floor. With short blue heels it looked fine and Larry was so handsome in his dark blue suit. The awards were nice, and well deserved. April had to admit that this was her idea from the beginning. Her dad and no one wanted her to start a dairy and have it blossom the way that it did. How well she remembered as she sat there at the table. She recalled her dad, gone now almost five years. April shook her head not to remember but she did anyway.

They found Gordon in his barn feeding the few remaining ponies. He had passed away straining himself to pick up a bale. He suffered a heart attack and died. April recalled how they found him with the ponies all around him sniffing him and wondering what was wrong. Her dad knew not to go out by himself, but he was determined and stubborn. That made April smile. She knew she was a lot like him too. She wondered how difficult she would be in her later years which were not too far away.

On the way home the two of them talked briefly and went to bed. That night as her husband put his arm around her as he always did, he whispered to her, "I love you sweetheart. I always will."

In the morning Larry went out to help with the tractor that the hand was having trouble with. He told the boy to call the local tractor company. They would come out and take it for repairs. The boy was stubborn and insisted he could do it himself.

Two hours later Larry came in and grabbed the telephone. The boy had flipped the tractor and was pinned underneath it. After that, April begged Larry to stay with her.

When April turned sixty she and Larry went out for her birthday dinner. A car crossed the median and hit them broadside. April did not remember much of anything. They were both taken to the hospital by ambulances. At the hospital April's condition was assessed and her only injuries were flesh wounds from the air bags. She asked about her husband, but no one seemed to know, or would not say.

April was out of emergency and walked into the hallway and there was a police officer waiting to speak to her. He regretted to tell her that Larry had succumbed to his injuries in the accident.

April was in shock. "What do you mean?" she asked. "He was right there with me."

The officer understood her questioning him and he asked for a nurse to take her to Larry. April entered the room and there he was lying on a bed. He looked as if he were sleeping. There were no marks on him. April touched his face and hair. She kissed his cheek and lips that were cold. She began to cry uncontrollably. How could this be? How could the man she loved with all her heart and soul be gone? Who would love her? She knew she should pray but she could not utter a word because they were stuck in her throat. The nurses let April stay in the room with Larry as long as she wanted.

April did not want to leave him. She laid beside him touching his body and face. She loved him more than her own life. How could God take him from her now? She needed him so desperately. He was life to her.

April was told the blunt force from the steering wheel impacted his chest and stopped his heart. "No, no, no, no, no," she said over and over. "Please, God. I am not ready, please, please, please," and she collapsed. April's doctor was a longtime friend. He ordered a room for her and admitted her with sedatives. When April awoke, she tore the IVs from her arms and walked to the room where Larry had been. He was no longer there. He had been taken to the morgue. April left the room and entered the hallway. There were no nurses at their station so she walked down the hall and down the stairs to the morgue. She pushed open the morgue doors and looked for Larry. She found her companion and wheeled him out to a small annex nearby that had a bed. She put Larry beside that bed, closed the door, and they lay together side by side.

She wanted to have a last talk with him. "Sweetheart, can you hear me?" she asked. "I hope so. I hope you know my heart is broken, and that living has no more meaning for me. We never got to say goodbye properly, no goodbye kiss, or see you later. Oh, Larry. I am broken, and I don't want to be better."

Then April found the words for a prayer. "Oh, kind, loving Father in Heaven, what am I to do now? I know you know," and her body shuddered. "You took the best one, you know. I don't know if I can breathe or if I want to live now, Father. Yes, we were sealed in the temple. I know this, but I can't let go, and I know I must. Please help me, Father. Help me accept this terrible thing," and then as if a light went off in April's head she realized this is what her father went through. This is what Larry would have gone through had it been her first and on the other table beside him. April never wanted Larry to hurt or grieve. During their life together she would often shield Larry from things.

Then as clear as a bell April heard, "He is where you will want to be, with his family and loved ones. He has come home." April's tears stopped when she heard this. She heard the voice and it was louder than a whisper.

She stopped crying, sat up, and looked at her sweet companion's face. She kissed it and returned him to the morgue covering him so he would not feel the cold room. April then went up the stairs to her room and sat on her bed.

"Where were you?" the nurse questioned April.

"I went for a walk to the bathroom and no one was here," April told her. The nurse said nothing, they wanted to re-insert the IVs, but April said she was all right and wanted to go home.

The nurse put a call into the doctor who said, "No. Keep her until morning."

He said more but April did not hear more. She had her clothing on, was walking down the hall, out the door, and going home. She hailed a cab that picked her up.

It was Joel, one of the neighbor boys. "I heard about the accident and I am real sorry Mrs. D."

"Oh, Joel, thank you so much. I need to go home but my purse is in the car. Can you trust me with paying you later?" April asked.

"This ride is on me," Joel told her.

April went home and crawled into the bed they had shared for so many years. She cradled his pajama top in her arms and went to sleep. In her sleep it was as if he were there with her. She could smell him and almost feel him there. It was a comforting sleep, no dreams, just a calm peaceful sleep.

In the morning April awoke to the telephone ringing. It was Ian, "Mom, I just heard. Are you all right?"

"I am. I was sleeping, Dear. Give me a minute to get up. Will you?" April said to him.

Ian was shocked. Mom sleeping and Dad is gone? This was not like his mom. He put his hand over the telephone receiver and asked his secretary to book him a flight home ASAP.

April came to the phone and said, "I am all right Ian. I had a good talk with Dad after you know, and God told me it was going to be all right."

"Well, I am coming home. We all will." And he did, they all did.

April acted oddly. It was as if she didn't care. And the truth was she didn't, not about herself.

If there was a short pier she would walk it. Rae recognized this right away and said she was going to stay with Mom for a few weeks.

"No you don't have to do that. Your old Mom is fine, really!"

The kids did not believe her. They began to prepare food so April left them to sit on the porch, pulling a blanket around her.

Sam came out and sat with her. "Are you cold Mom?" she asked while adjusting the blanket more securely around her.

"I am fine, Sam. Really I am. It happened. I was horrifically sad in the hospital. I had a talk with Dad, and then God made it clear that everything would be all right."

"I believe you, Mum," Sam said. There were no more words spoken. April slept on that rocker with her daughter sleeping beside her.

In the morning the funeral arrangements had to be made. Most of the kids left but two stayed behind. They sat with April having small talk, when Ada asked if her Mom was going to stay here.

"Where else would I go? This is my home, honey. I know Daddy is not here anymore, but all of our memories are," her mother told her.

The kids came home and told their mom that they would take care of every detail for her. That is when April stood up and spoke to her family.

"I know I am older, but I am not feeble. I know I was just in an accident and lost my sweetheart, but I did not lose my mind. Larry is my husband. I can and I will take care of him. What is the rush. We must wait for the others to arrive anyway. I know the funeral home has his body. I will do it all myself and you had better let me," and she walked out of the room. The kids looked at each other. They knew they had pushed their mother too far and she was right.

April went into the shower, came out dressed, got her keys, and left. She went to the funeral director who knew her well. She asked to see the caskets. The funeral director showed April the casket her children chose. It was all white and April wrinkled her nose. She looked around and found what she felt Larry would have liked best. She chose a bronze casket with off white inside.

"That's more of a man's choice," the director said.

April told him the church members would be by to dress him. She would be there as well. Then she went upstairs and chose the book and the announcements. A half hour later April was driving home.

The kids were everywhere in the house, some in their old rooms commenting on how all their stuff was still there and they laughed.

April stood at the base of the stairs and said. "If you are in your rooms keep them clean. If you make a mess in the house clean it. There will be people stopping by and I am no longer responsible for cleaning your messes."

The grandchildren were either playing in the living room or watching TV. April took them by their hands and they went outside. She switched on the sprinkler and soon the ground began to become saturated.

Soon all fourteen of the grandchildren were making mud pies and dancing in the puddles. April was laughing and having the time of her life. The Grand-kids were all smiles with mud-streaked faces, mud-caked clothing, and mud in their hair. Their backsides were soaked. In the driveway they stomped in the puddles and sat in them. April laughed and did the same.

One of the moms came out looking for her children. When she looked outside she called her husband, "Ben, come down here right now." He was followed by Ian, Trent, Austin, Trevor, and the girls. "Look how dirty they are," the wife said.

April's children looked at each other, went out on the porch, took off their shoes, the boys their shirts, and they all joined April and the kids. They all stomped through the puddles and jumped the sprinkler. They were all muddy from head to toe.

Trent's wife hollered, "Are you all crazy?"

The girls replied, "It's a Di Angelo thing."

Later they went into the pool to clean off. April laughed at their antics. She then heard the beginning of that still, small voice but wished it away. She was not ready. She prayed it would return later.

Her children teased one another and for the first time in days they all seemed to be relaxed, settled down, and no longer on edge. They did not notice their mother leave to shower, dress, and go to the barn. They were all having too much fun.

You don't need money to entertain kids and to have fun. There are many things that are free. Most of the time all you need is a little imagination. April knew when she went to her friends kid's birthday parties with her little ones many had so many gifts they could fill the back of a pick-up truck which was ridiculous. One year Ben asked for a tractor party. He had several friends, they played pin the tail on the donkey and then Larry came down with the International Harvester Tractor and gave rides.

Years later Ben talked about the time his Dad gave rides on the big tractor at his birthday party. Ask him what games he played what gifts he got? He did not remember, but he never forgot the tractor rides.

April knew that children enjoyed experiences, to do things, not having things. There are far too many children in the world who have little or nothing. April often encouraged her children to pick a gift and donate it, or to pick out a name on a wish tree. Her children had been blessed to know want, to understand what it was to be cold, to be hungry, or to not have everything. Larry and April had words once about this and April explained to him if their children grew up with the fruits that they did not earn they would never be appreciative. You cannot understand what someone is going through if you have not experienced it yourself.

Her children would be all right because of her and Larry's efforts. They would not need anything. But April wanted them to know and understand these things to keep them grounded while they were young. Now they were all grown, had careers of their own and were following their own journeys.

At the barn April greeted Dixie.

Dixie was Larry's choice. Larry did ride with April but he never liked riding. His back was ridged and straight from farming and he felt stiff riding. Larry preferred to take a buggy on the road. That's what they had in mind when they went to the auction with the trailer in tow. They looked but did not find what Larry wanted. On the way out he saw Dixie. Dixie was a large Haflinger mare that had pulled logs most of her life. She was imported from Denmark as a yearling, brought to the US, and trained to pull logs. Dixie was a large Haflinger horse, 15 hands, stout, rippling muscles, and Larry wanted her.

Dixie was fifteen years old and retired from logging. Her owner advertised Dixie in his local paper but there was no interest. So he brought her to the auction in hopes of selling her to someone as a ridable, buggy pulling, and a sweet pet. He was worried that because of her size, she might be sold to a meat buyer.

Larry asked the man what he wanted for her. The man was unsure, but said if he included all the harness equipment, collar, and leveler, would Larry be willing to pay $2,000? Larry agreed.

Dixie never went through the sale ring. She was easily loaded onto the trailer. And other than feeling her weight as Larry's truck pulled the trailer, he did not know a large animal was in it. She never swayed or moved around.

Dixie was happy. She had time off and they took her out on the buggy 3 or 4 times a week. Dixie was not shy of cars or trucks. She knew her job and did it. Often Larry and April were seen riding down a road in the buggy or taking a break on a hillside having a picnic with the cart. Dixie was good for them and they were good to her.

Dixie was spoiled and whinnied when she saw Larry who usually had carrots, apples, or treats for her. Dixie knew they had saved her and she always showed her gratitude. For the first time in his life Larry had a horse that was his and his alone. Surely April helped ready her, brush her out, and Dixie loved being fussed over. Together they harnessed her and in playful moods they got in each other's way on purpose.

As April went out, Dixie whinnied but her master was not there.

"It's just me girl," April said to Dixie. "I don't know if you will accept me the way you did him, but it's just you and me now. He is not coming back." April entered the stall and hugged the mare. Dixie stood still and felt something was very wrong. April's tears were on the mare's neck as she spoke softly to the horse.

"It's going to be all right. You'll see. I will take you out, same as before. I promise to remember your treats. This is your forever home, Dixie. You were wanted and it stays that way. Okay?" Then April rubbed the mare's head then headed back inside the house.

The following days were a blur. People coming and going, bringing food and well wishes. April received them all and asked them to sign a book, so she would remember. April was a letter writer. These days people do not take the time to write. They called, maybe picked up a card, but April was a stickler for writing notes and letters. "It matters," she would say and the receivers would agree.

At the funeral, which was small. Well, April wanted it small, but as the hour approached the funeral swelled.

It didn't matter they all knew him in one way or another. All of Larry's family was gone, and it was nice to have these kind folks come to pay their last respects. April did very well at the funeral. She did not wear black, instead April chose a deep navy blue skirt with pleats and a white top with a matching deep navy blue jacket. Her daughter put a white hankie with lace in the jacket shoulder pocket for decoration.

Throughout the service, April felt numb.

Her daughter Rae looked at her and said, "Mom."

April looked at her daughter to question her when her daughter slipped her a blue pill. April shook her head no. Her daughter insisted. April slipped the pill into her mouth and in a few minutes she could focus on what was said. It seemed surreal. The time lagged and seemed like hours. But when they went to close the casket, April stood and would not let them close it. Five of her sons stood quickly to console their mother and pull her away, but she would not move. Her daughters could not watch. This was tearing them apart inside. They could only turn their heads, look down, and cry.

They understood the deep love and devotion their parents had. It was a testament to the blessing of their marriage. April tenderly touched Larry's face, slipped her hand in his, and then she leaned forward and kissed his forehead, cheek, and lips. Only the boys heard what their mother had said.

"I will see you soon, Sweetheart. I love you, dear. Look for me. I will look for you. Please come and find me." Then she stood up, stepped back, and sat down.

The funeral director and April's Bishop had never seen anything like this before. April was lucid and understood. She just could not let go without a proper goodbye.

Her Bishop was moved beyond tears and he wanted to be sure to see her soon.

The burial was at the family plot. Larry would lie beside Gordon and April would be on Larry's left side when it was her time to go. There were chairs at the graveside but April chose to stand, so they all stood. The small grandchildren put flowers on Larry's casket and April did as well. The flower she chose was a daisy because that is what Larry brought to her when he came out of the fields. It was their signature flower. As April looked around she saw most of her family resting there: Lena, Nora, two grandchildren, Miranda, Gordon, and now her beloved Larry. How she wished her father Gordon was here to console her. She knew he would understand how she felt. But alas, no one did. No one here could because they had not suffered a loss such as this.

Her daughter suggested a bereavement class to share her feelings with others.

April wrinkled her nose but said nothing. April knew the kids would soon leave and return to their own lives. She would have to figure this out for herself. Just as April thought, soon they all left and she found herself alone. April was all alone with her thoughts and grief.

Some days April was overcome. She did not answer the telephone or cell phone. She did not shop for groceries or go out other than to church and meetings.

The farm became her refuge, her solace to grieve and pray. Anytime she felt like she was faltering she prayed. In her own privacy she had the freedom to do so without judgment.

Everyday April went out carrying carrots or apples and walked the lane to the barn.

Here she would see the markers of old friends. There lay Happy and Jet. There were other pets buried there who had belonged to her children.

Dixie greeted her and munched on her carrots until she slobbered. April brushed her down and turned her out in the cool morning weather. She cleaned the stall and then got out the smaller cart. Dixie would watch and wait for her time to go out. Once she was all harnessed, the two of them would go out for an hour or two ride. Clip clopping along always a different route. Sometimes April would take Dixie around the top fields where she and Native Son used to romp and April remembered the joy he brought her. And now Dixie brought her joy.

Dixie loved to trot along the path way, her ears up and bright for what was in front of them. Dixie never bolted or panicked, not when she saw running deer or if humans were there. Dixie was a steady mount, trustworthy, and safe. That is why Larry liked her so much.

One morning several months later, April was having her breakfast of little to nothing on the porch when she again heard that still, small voice. Surprisingly it was hers. "Well, you know Dad, I spent the last few months dying and I think it is time for living." She remembered those words from long ago and she felt the affirmation that it was time.

April went to the bedding store and bought a new mattress. It was said to be innovative for a great night's sleep. There were adjustments to increase or decrease the firmness or softness of the bed. It inclined or not as you chose and she loved the thicker pillow top. She paid for it and they delivered it later that afternoon.

Then April headed to the pound. She walked in and signed the register. They asked her what she was looking for. "I am not sure. I think I will know when I see it," she replied.

Down the hallway were big dogs and little dogs all crying for attention. Some jumped up and down barking. It was unbelievably loud in this kennel. Then as they walked they passed something. April was unsure and continued down to the end. There was nothing she felt attracted to.

"Do you want a cat?" the volunteer asked.

April declined and they began to walk out when April noticed a cage that seemed empty. She stopped and looked in the far corner. There was a medium-sized dog that faced the wall. It did not look at anyone, or bark for attention.

"What's this one's story?" April asked.

"She has had a hard life. She has been beaten, whipped, and burned. She was then abandoned and left on her own. She was found recently by someone when she was at the river getting water. She is pretty much wild having been left on her own."

April stooped down close to the wire cage and watched the dog who never noticed her. "Hey there. I see you," April said in a tender voice. "Why not come over here and see me. I think you and I are a lot alike."

The dog slowly turned her head and began to wag her tail. Then she stopped as if she knew she should not be doing that.

"I would like this one," April said standing up.

They filled out the paperwork. April learned the dog's name was Jo Jo. When they went to retrieve the dog, the volunteer almost had to drag her on the leash.

April stopped the girl and stooped down to pick up the dog. April had to steady herself before walking out.

On the seat of the car, the dog did not look at anything. This was not the "Yea you are on your freedom ride" like April saw posted on the internet. This dog was frightened out of her wits. During the drive home, she never moved, although April talked to her throughout the ride. When they stopped the dogs ears perked up. "Say you noticed," April said, and she touched the top of the dogs head gently and the dog wagged its tail. April got out and went to the passenger side to pick up the dog. Jo Jo had already stood up on the seat and was wagging her tail. April opened the door and said, "Come on then," and the two of them entered the house together.

Jo Jo and April made a life together. They had breakfast together. They went for morning walks every day, even when it rained. Often April was seen driving around with Jo Jo strapped in the passenger seat with a safety harness. April bought a motorcycle to ride around on and Jo Jo had a side car all to herself. April bought Jo Jo goggles to wear so she could see where they were going. She took Jo Jo with her when driving Dixie. Dixie didn't mind at all. Jo Jo was not a barky dog. She was quiet and when excited she quivered before she barked. Yes, April found a suitable companion and the two of them were well suited for each other. April loved to swim, so did Jo Jo. April loved long walks in the woods, so did Jo Jo. Everything April did, other than going to church, Jo Jo was with her. April's kids at first were put off, but they soon came around to understand April did not save Jo Jo it was Jo Jo who saved April.

April was out of her depression and had come full circle. She was so very grateful to know her husband and she had been sealed together in the Holy Temple that gave her great comfort.

Before long April and Jo Jo were active at town events. The year April turned seventy-seven the town committee came to her asking if she would run for Mayor again. April said she would and she won. She was at every town meeting. She and her companion Jo Jo who was lying down at her side. At one meeting someone commented about Jo Jo asking April what kind of dog was she? April said she is part Stafford, part poodle, part pointer, and part boxer. Just her kind of dog.

After her life returned to normal, or as normal as she could hope for, April went to the funeral home again. She wanted to order a stone. She took with her a picture she had found years ago and saved in her journal. It was a head stone for the burial plot. The picture was for a two-sided stone, one side was a man and the other was a woman. And they were lying in bed in an embrace. That is what April wanted. The director assured April his stone carver could do it but that was a fairly large piece and would take some time. Then there was the matter of payment could she put half down? April asked what half was and she wrote out a check for payment in full and the director signed it that way.

Later in her life April did find many more friends and companions to spend time with. She found great comfort in prayer and her children. When troubles hurt her heart, she sought the Lord first. When she turned eighty-eight she made her final will. D Farms would not go to her children. They would inherit all her personal items, jewelry, medals, and any furniture they wanted. D Farms would remain as is, to maintain itself with all profit to be disbursed to Shriner's and Saint Jude's hospitals. They cared for the children who desperately needed help. Her children did not need the money.

The home would be kept for the children to use as they wanted. The other home rentals kept up and monies disbursed to their town for future needs used at their discretion.

A huge portion of her land was donated for a park for children to play games like baseball, softball, field hockey, and soccer. There was plenty of room for all.

April Di Angelo had lived a long time, and had buried two of her own children. There was nothing left for her to do but think, think some more, and wait. She had a wonderful caretaker who was so kind to her. But for April this was a great journey and now she was ready to go home.

Every day her caretaker would wheel April out to the pasture for her to watch foals romp and play. April could sit and watch them for hours. The caretaker had an elderly dog that loved April and sat with her at the fence line as long as April was there.

One evening as April was sitting in her wheelchair, she dreamed a wonderful dream. She was somewhere that she did not know, but she saw ground, a very large pasture, and a span of woods. There, out of the woods came Native Son being led by Monty. She saw him in reality.

Her parents came, as well as the ladies, Manny and Contessa, Grandpop and Grandma, and others she loved. Then she saw Larry walking along the side of the road to greet and kiss her. Trevor and Austin were there with the grandchildren who were still so small. The boys carried one child while the other son swung the small boy out in front every other step.

They raised their arms waving to their mother and April walked up to greet and hug them. They all began to walk straight ahead on this road. It did not matter where. That was not important. What was important was that they were all together. Jet, Happy, Ruby, and Jo Jo, they all joined them and they barked leading the way. April turned to her husband and said, "I have found you. I am home."

April Di Angelo was ninety-three years young. Her body failed her but never her mind or her intentions. She had lived a happy, well lived life. No regrets. Of course she made mistakes, but she had learned from them. April lived a long life, loving and serving everyone. Honoring and obeying the commandments of the Savior Jesus Christ. Most of all she, hoped she was worthy to kneel at the Savior's feet and wash them with her tears and her hair. April was so happy to be here for this last part of her journey. Best of all April had kept her promise to never disappoint the girl in the mirror.

THE END

Printed in the United States
by Baker & Taylor Publisher Services